John Riha

The
Bounty
Huntress

RT3 Media
Ashland, OR
2017

ISBN 978-09911579-3-8

For Chris and Nick

Acknowledgements

Southern Oregon Historical Society
Chet Orloff, Director Emeritus, Oregon Historical Society
Applegate Partnership & Watershed Council
Collectors Firearms
Deb Riha
David Pederson
Kathy Scott
Jim Beaver
Nancy Beaver

Front and back cover photograph courtesy of
Eddie Daniels

Rifle sight glyph: Nick Riha

For West is where we all plan to go some day.
It is where you go when you look down at the blade in your hand and
the blood on it. It is where you go when you are told that you are a
bubble on the tide of empire.

—Robert Penn Warren

Prologue
Southern Oregon, 1932

"I'LL TELL YOU what it's like," she said, holding the old revolver dead steady. "It's like a part of you is weak and useless. But then everything else gets stronger. Your other arm. Your aim. Your heart. Your hate." The barrel pointed at his forehead. "Know what I mean?"

"A one-arm girl bounty hunter is just about the most pathetic thing I seen." He spat.

And her gun went off.

John Riha

Chapter One
Eighteen years earlier, 1914

DEXTER GREENLEE GAVE REIN and the bay leaned down and pulled at a tuft of green grass, snort from her big nostrils scattering powdery snow. The day as still and clear as glass, white dusting the limbs of firs and pines.

"Not here," said McElroy, stepping from the cabin onto its porch and hooking a thumb into a coat pocket. "Still some heat in the coals. Maybe two hours gone."

Greenlee looked to the faint trace of smoke twisting out of the stove pipe, then past the cabin to where an old skid path bled into the forest. Thirty yards away four gutted does hung from a pole nailed between two Douglas firs, pink snow beneath their outstretched forelegs.

"Probably known we was coming," said McElroy. A jay settled on the peaked roof of the cabin and began to squawk.

"All right then," said Greenlee. "We better get on after him."

McElroy clumped down the steps, startling off the bird. He swung onto his horse. Greenlee tugged the bay's head up and aimed her toward the skid path. McElroy and his chestnut mare fell in alongside.

The man's footprints were plainly visible in the thin layer of snow.

They rode in silence and Greenlee ran over in his head what he planned to say. The man would be armed; it'd be a tricky piece of business. The Smith and Wesson was a hard lump on his hip, butt forward for a cross draw. He thought to check the cartridges but he'd already done that and he didn't want the city constable here, McElroy, to think he was nervous.

After twenty minutes the horse gave a dip of her head and the man appeared on the rough-cut path before them. He had a bear skin shawl thrown over his shoulders and knee-high buckskin boots and carried a shotgun in the crook of his arm. He was bearded and burly and at the sight of the men on horseback he stopped and took the shotgun and held it across his body with both hands.

"What are you doing here?" asked the man.

The riders reined to a halt. "You Jasper Hibbard?" called out Greenlee, hands loose on the pommel.

"Who wants to know?"

The officers exchanged a look. "Well I'm Dexter Greenlee the deputized Game Warden here in Jackson County. And this here is Ennis McElroy, constable of the city of Ashland. Mr. Hibbard, I got a warrant for your arrest on a charge of illegal poaching."

"This is my land."

"There's the bullshit," murmured McElroy so only Greenlee could hear.

There was a pause. Hibbard's breath rolled white out of his nostrils.

"You gonna arrest a man for hunting on his own property? For feeding himself with what God put on the Earth?"

Greenlee took in the man's shotgun. Remington eleven, auto-loader, five shot. Probably got deer slugs. They were well within range. "First of all, Mr. Hibbard, this isn't your property. This here is federal land owned by the U.S. government."

"Federal land is owned by the people. I been here six years. I settled this place. I hunt this place. Who are you to come up here and tell me what I can or can't do?"

"We got laws about all that, Mr. Hibbard, and you can't run afoul of the laws. You gotta hunt in season, just like everybody. And you been warned before, I believe."

"I just been getting' meat. I got the right."

"Looks like you got more than enough down at your cabin," said McElroy.

"I'm a big eater. Now you two just turn around and head on back down from wherever you came and everybody gets to just go on."

McElroy looked down to his Winchester in its scabbard. He should've taken it out before this. To pull it out now might provoke a man who probably didn't have a great deal of self-restraint. The constable licked lips gone dry in the winter air.

"Mr. Hibbard," said Greenlee, keeping his hands still. "I just want you to come easy, let us take you to Jacksonville. You're under arrest. You can get a lawyer down there if you need."

"Not goin'."

"Let's talk eye to eye." Greenlee swung his leg up and over, dismounted smooth. He slipped the reins over his horse's stiff ears, held them in his right hand, turned to face Hibbard.

The shot cracked open the cold air. Hibbard had fired from the hip. The slug took the game warden square in the chest, tore through his heart, and made a hole the size of a fist when it exited the back of his duster, bursting through with a spray of pulverized flesh and bone. The warden's horse reared, backed away. The reins jerked from his hand. The sound echoed from ridge to ridge; snow startled from nearby branches floated down as sparkling dust.

Greenlee went to his backside with a hard thump but sat upright, eyes wild. He thought maybe his horse had kicked him. But the bay wasn't a kicker. Something else. He'd think of it if he could only breathe. He'd been shot. That was it. By the wooly man with the gun. He wondered if his children might have wandered out here. They would do that. Into the woods. Into this cold, this unbelievable cold.

McElroy made a belated reach for the service revolver at his hip but Hibbard had already chambered another shell and pointed the barrel of the Remington at him. McElroy lifted his hands. "I ain't doing nothing," he said.

There was a long moment that could have gone either way for McElroy but there was no second shot, just the cold dark eye of the shotgun watching him. Greenlee's saddle horse had fled at a gallop back down the cut and his own horse wanted to pivot to make after the bay but he kneed her back around best he could though he wanted with every fiber to grab his reins and bolt back down the ridge but then Hibbard would surely fire.

"I'm not drawing or anything," said McElroy to the killer, his voice low and earnest. "I got my hands way up." *Jesus Lord help me.*

Hibbard made a grunting sound, signaling his decision not to shoot the constable.

"I gotta see to him," said McElroy.

Hibbard stood unmoving and the day hung there, quiet as cold stone, save for the burbling gasps of the game warden and the nervous, unsure pacing of McElroy's mount. The poacher made assent by swinging the shotgun barrel in a slow arc toward the warden.

McElroy stepped slowly out of the saddle, one hand gripping the reins, other hand held high, and led his horse to where the warden sat upright, legs a-spraddle in front of him, as if he could not yet believe he was dead. The front of him was soaked.

"Shit damn." McElroy knelt and used his free hand to ease the warden onto his back. Blood bubbled out Greenlee's nose. His eyes stared up at nothing. It wouldn't be long. "I gotta get help," said McElroy. He tried not to see the red spray flung across the snow.

"He drew on me," said Hibbard.

"He needs help," McElroy repeated. He saw the warden's gun still in its holster, close enough to grab. But he didn't feel heroic. Not while looking into the eyes of a dying man. Not with an armed lunatic close behind. He just wanted to get beyond range of a deer slug. Hightail it back down the ridge.

"I had to shoot," said Hibbard. The shotgun pointed down but Hibbard's finger curled around the trigger.

Greenlee's eyes had turned into a substance not of the living. His breathing was pages being torn from a book. Blood crept up around his neck. McElroy's horse skittish and jerking at the reins in his hand.

"That lady down at the county road," said McElroy, not turning to look at Hibbard, trying not to look at anything, the words coming out thin and dry. "Mrs. Bodine. She's got a telephone. I'd better get down there and call for a doctor."

"I didn't want to shoot him."

McElroy stood up, measured and slow. He put his free hand up. He could feel Hibbard raise the barrel of the shotgun and point it at his back. McElroy waited. Then he said, "I'm going to get on my horse. I'm going for help. Don't shoot." He stepped to the mare, put a boot in the stirrup and waited. The horse took a sideways step and he hopped along with her. Then he swung up slow, gripping the pommel hard. For a terrible long moment his other foot searched for its stirrup and couldn't connect. His body was numb. Finally it slid in place and the heel caught and McElroy looked down at Greenlee, the first-ever game warden in Jackson County. The first-ever shot-through game warden in Jackson County.

"I'll go call for help," said the constable. There was no objection from the mountain man. McElroy reined his horse over and made off down the cut at a trot, hunching slightly to make himself smaller, praying against a slug that never came.

Chapter Two
December, 1914

McELROY PUT TOGETHER a posse that included County Sheriff Baker and two deputies and a horse-drawn wagon. The day after the shooting they rode up to the cabin with carbines in their laps and found Hibbard seated on his front porch, unarmed, with his bear skin shawl pulled about his shoulders.

"The body's still up there," said Hibbard, jacking a thumb toward the skid road. "Stiffer'n a skillet." He stood and pointed to a small, sagging pole barn. "You can grain your horses, if you need to."

They handcuffed Hibbard with his hands in front so he could ride, then had him sit back down on his porch steps. One of deputies kept watch while the other saddled Hibbard's Appaloosa.

"He drew on me," Hibbard told them. "I had to shoot him. The constable was there. He seen it. You ask him, he'll tell you the truth of it."

One of the deputies, a young man with a hint of walnut-colored whiskers, spat into the dirt. "Tell it to a judge."

McElroy and Baker took the wagon up to the body. In half an hour they got to Greenlee lying face up on the skid path in the snow, surrounded by a thin outline of melt from the heat of the body before it'd cooled. A violent corona of blood, now black, formed a scattered V out beyond the game warden's blue face.

"That's not right," said McElroy straight off. Greenlee's gun was on the ground a few feet from his hip. The dead man's right hand was bare and gray, and his glove was lying nearby, perfectly flat.

McElroy set the brake and they climbed down and Sheriff Baker began to walk around, studying the scene.

"Hibbard stood over there," said McElroy. "Shot him right here. Didn't sight down on him at all. Just shot from the hip."

"Where were you?"

"Over here. Mounted up. He shot before I could blink. He looked to shoot me, too, but he didn't. Don't know why. Minute or so Hibbard let me come down off my horse so I could check on Dexter." He looked to the body as if he expected the dead man to start at the sound of his name. The thought of Greenlee shot through but sitting there, like a puppet held up by strings, made McElroy swallow and catch himself. He'd never seen a shot man before. "Sheriff, the warden's gun was holstered. I saw it."

Baker nodded, stood, moved to the place from where the killer had fired. "Twenty yards," he said.

McElroy agreed.

"Deer slug square in the chest?" Baker shook his head. "The man was dead before his butt hit the dirt." The sheriff frowned. "Why did Greenlee get down off his horse?"

"I think he was tryin' to be, I don't know, friendly?"

"He was a friendly man all right," agreed Baker. "Looks like it didn't do him much good, though."

"Dexter never took off a glove, neither."

"You sure?"

"Pretty sure. I was right over him. He was still breathin', but just barely."

Baker looked at McElroy. "You'd swear to that? About the glove and the gun?"

"I would."

They went to the body and got down on their haunches. The glove was smoothed out. "Looks like somebody was puttin' it in the window of a damn dry goods," said McElroy.

The sheriff nodded. "I don't see no bounce marks from the pistol. You'd see it in the snow for sure."

There was a long moment of quiet, the forest hushed in crystal cold. The blood on Greenlee's vest and coat was black and stiff. His eyes were open. Baker reached out to close the eyelids but they had frozen.

"You think Hibbard fixed it up like this?"

McElroy nodded. "He's tryin' to cover his tracks. But it was nothin' but murder. I'm a witness to it."

"Let's get him loaded up," sighed the sheriff.

They brought Hibbard by automobile from Trail to the county jail in Jacksonville. The body followed a day later, departing Trail only after the coroner had finished his exam in a makeshift morgue that had been rigged up at the back of the local saloon. On the drive down Hibbard was contrite to the point of tears, sobbing as he repeated his claim of innocence to the deputies, wiping snot off his red mustache with the sleeve of his bearskin coat, his handcuffs jangling. He sounded sincere, but his bright blue eyes darted around the inside of the cab like he was looking for a way out.

At the jail the sheriff steered Hibbard into the small cell block where two young men were seated near a small pot belly stove playing checkers.

"Get back to your cells," said Sheriff Baker.

They groaned. "C'mon, sheriff," said one of the men.

"I got him cornered."

"Leave it," said Baker. "This ain't no sanatorium."

"How about I take the board and Gerald can reach through the bars?"

"I'm not in a charitable mood, so leave it."

The men got up slowly and walked into adjoining cells and clanged their doors shut. "You gonna tuck us in for the night?"

"How about I tuck you into Salem for a few years?" Baker pushed Hibbard into a fourth cell, swung the door shut, locked it with an iron key. "Hands," said Baker.

Hibbard held his hands through the small opening so the Sheriff could unlock the cuffs. Then Baker made the rounds and secured the other cells.

"What's for supper?" said one of the boys.

"Sheep shit and dog balls," said Baker as he threw a few more chunks of pine into the stove and left, closing the cell block door behind him. The big bolt slid home hard.

"Asshole." They slumped onto their hammocks. After a minute of silence one of the boys said, "Hey Red. What are you here for?"

Hibbard flexed his wrists.

"Hey Red, you deaf?"

"Maybe."

"Well?"

"Well what?"

"I asked what you did to get yourself a vacation here in Jacksonville's finest hotel."

"You first."

"But I asked first."

"You was in here first," said Hibbard, looking at his palms. "That means you say first."

The two boys exchanged a look, trying to decide if the logic stuck. "We took a barrel of heating oil from the

Grange," said one.

"We was going to pay it back."

"We was gonna give the oil to our granny. She's over at Grants Pass. Anyway, we wouldn't be in this fix if you'd had taken the oil to your uncle's place like you said instead of leaving it in the back of the truck."

"Well it wasn't no crime in the first place. We was intending to pay it all back."

"They can't say we did it to sell or anything."

"Hell, if I wasn't in here I'd be working. That's a fact. I'd be paying back for the oil. They been wanting to hire me at the automobile repair on account of I'm handy. But now I'm in here and I'm stuck. Don't seem fair."

"Okay now Red, what about you?"

Hibbard looked off to the small window at the end of the cell corridor. Bars cut the view into four stripes of tree tops and blue sky. "I killed a man," he said.

The oil-stealers looked at each other.

"Oh now that's just some bullshit there. Killed a man. What's the real deal, Red?"

"Shotgun." Hibbard sat down with his back to his cell mates. "I blew his head off with a deer slug."

"You ain't serious. I know you ain't."

"Where'd abouts this happen?"

"Up past Trail."

There was silence. The fresh pine sputtered and snapped in the stove. Hibbard turned so he could see his jail mates. "Self-defense," he said.

"You did not." The voice unsure.

"What happened? You get in a fight?"

"Something like that."

"And you killed him?"

"He was tryin' to take my land away from me. So I stopped him."

"I ain't buyin' it."

"You'll read about it in the papers," said Hibbard. He settled into his hammock and gave it a push with his foot so it swayed and the rope eyes squeaked.

The boys didn't move. At last one said, "What's that like, killing a man?"

"I don't want to talk about it any more," said Hibbard, and he put his hands behind his head.

Both of the oil thieves wanted to say something, thought better of it, swallowed the words.

(from the *Medford Meteor*,
December 16, 1914)

Game Warden Murdered
by Poacher

*Heinous crime occurs as
the Game Warden attempts to Arrest
a Notorious Poacher*

Dexter L. Greenlee, well-known and genial game warden, met death near Trail on Thursday afternoon, from a type of bullet known as a slug that is fired from a shotgun and used to shoot deer with deadly effect, at the hand of Jasper Hibbard, a game poacher and squatter of that region.

It was reported to District Sheriff Baker last week that Hibbard had been shooting deer out of season, and Baker ordered Warden Greenlee to apprehend the man. It was for reasons of prudence that Green-lee elected to have Constable Ennis McElroy of the City of Ashland, be in accompaniment, and the two men set out on horseback to bring Hibbard to justice. After searching the squatter's cabin, the officers followed Hibbard's tracks into the hills, where the deadly encounter occurred.

McElroy, a direct witness to the slaying, feared for his life but was spared for unknown reasons. He was able to return to Trail unharmed but shaken to his soul. At that point he was able to telephone the Sheriff's office and report the crime. The next day Sheriff Baker assembled a citizen's posse of able deputized men and apprehended Hibbard without further bloodshed. It is a tribute to Baker and his men that they were able to deliver the killer to the Jackson County Jail and avoid further mayhem.

The resolutions as adopted by the state fish and game commission are as follows: "Whereas, the commission has heard, with deepest regret, of the killing of Deputy Game Warden Dexter L. Greenlee in Jackson county, Oregon; and Whereas, the deceased has, since his employment in the

Service, been regarded as a
careful, honest, painstaking
and conscientious deputy;
therefore Be It Resolved, That
we sincerely deplore the un-
timely death of Deputy Game
Warden Dexter L. Greenlee,
and hereby extend the sympathy of the members of this
board to his bereaved family in
their affliction; and further,
that we lend to the proper authority of Jackson county every
available help in bringing the
slayer to a most proper justice."

Attorney Estes Everett was a man with points of view
similar to Hibbard's, especially with regards to the overreach of the federal government in the everyday affairs of
citizens. Everett had managed to build a modestly success-
ful career upon that reputation, and hoped someday to use
it as a platform to support his political aspirations at the
statewide level.

Although he had developed a taste for fine suits cus-
tom-tailored in Portland and spoke with nasally, carefully
cultivated East Coast vowels and might have been mistaken
for a man who loved cognac and the theater, in fact Estes
Everett preferred white whiskey and was an avid hunter
whose count included three cougars, eleven black bears, fifteen elk and more deer than he knew, easily one hundred,
usually with disregard for any regulations attempting to re-
strict hunting on the vast federal lands in the Cascade and
Siskiyou Mountains. He had written to the governor in op-
position to the appointment of an official game warden in

southern Oregon, quoting liberally if selectively from the U.S. Constitution to support his views (*promote the general Welfare and secure the blessings of Liberty…*) and sending laboriously re-typed copies of the letter to every major newspaper in the state. It didn't matter whether or not he won the Hibbard case. His defense would be passionate, altruistic, and much-quoted. The hard facts of the slaughter would be sure to generate interest and provide a useful frame for his ambitions.

Two days following Hibbard's arrest Estes Everett drove his Model T over to Jacksonville and presented himself to Sheriff Baker at the jailhouse.

"I'd like to have a word with my client," said Everett, an aristocratic flavor in his tone.

"What client?" said Baker, although he knew it was Hibbard.

"Mr. Jasper Hibbard," confirmed the attorney, pulling an elegant Elgin watch from a fob pocket and checking the time as if pressed on many urgent matters, although the Elgin had stopped working months ago and currently Everett lacked the resources to have it repaired.

Baker sighed. "Open your coat."

Everett pulled open his lapels.

"Any knives or weapons of any kind on your person?"

With a flourish Everett produced from an inside coat pocket a small gold pen knife that he used to trim his fingernails. He set it on the sheriff's desk with a clack.

Baker led the attorney to the cell block and unlocked the bolt and took a crude three-legged stool from a corner and set in front of Hibbard's cell. "Ten minutes," said Baker. He pointed at the other two inmates. "This ain't your affair." He left, pulled the big door behind him, locked it.

"Who the hell are you?" asked Hibbard.

"Estes Everett," said the lawyer, settling himself carefully on the stool and extending a hand through the bars. "Your attorney."

From his hammock Hibbard wrinkled his nose at the thick white hand invading his cell. "I didn't ask for no attorney."

"I've been appointed by the state," lied Everett. "If you agree."

"Where you from?"

"Medford."

"How much you charge?"

"Whatever you can afford."

"How about a mess of deer jerky?"

Hibbard was being rude but, as it happened, Estes was rather fond of deer jerky. Moreover, it was a detail that might play out very well in the papers, him trading his services for a bag of dried meat. "Done and done then. Let's say ten pounds of your best deer jerky."

Hibbard stroked his nose. "You'd do that?"

"My word is my honor," said Everett. "I think a man should be able to hunt the land as he sees fit, don't you?"

Hibbard squinted. "That what you think?"

"It is indeed. And I'm here to see justice applied to its full extent." He re-thrust his hand between the bars. "We'll shake on it. You. Boys. Bear witness to this agreement."

"We ain't supposed to be listening," said one.

"See that checkerboard yonder?" Hibbard nodded his shaggy head toward the stove and the board on top of an old keg. "Give it to those fellas. And that bag of pieces."

Everett did as told. The two boys stood and looked through the thick iron bars. "Why thanks, Red," said one.

"You two never say a word about anything you hear now, you understand?" said Hibbard.

"All right."

"I got some crazy mean friends that can find you no matter where, you understand? Now you boys set yourselves and play some checkers."

Everett re-settled himself on the stool, put his hand through the bars for a third time.

Hibbard stood, shirttails out, bottoms fringed with age and a hard life. He took Everett's hand, the silky feel of it made him wince. Then he sat down on the floorboards and turned his scuttling blue eyes toward the attorney and said, "This is what really happened up there."

"It's possible that Hibbard was waiting to ambush those men," said District Attorney Rune Davis to a reporter from the *Ashland Crier*. "He's been in trouble with the law before, is a well-known game poacher, and I'm not surprised that he committed a murderous act."

The killing had occurred on Monday afternoon. By Wednesday, the district attorney's quote was on the front page of the *Crier* along with a line drawing of an officer mounted on a horse with a caption that said, *Dexter Greenlee, Game Warden of Jackson County, dispatching his duties,* although the depiction was neither Dexter Greenlee nor a true game warden. It was a state trooper. The editors had found the facsimile in a file drawer and had decided it was close enough in spirit.

The D.A. wasn't the only one offering newsworthy opinion. From his office in Salem Chief State Game Warden Elmer Wright issued a statement to the *Oregonian* that condemned Hibbard in no uncertain terms. Officer Greenlee, asserted Wright, would not have drawn his revolver unless threatened with his own life. According to the State Warden, this was as coldblooded a killing as could be conceived. Officer Greenlee was considered outstanding at his job, a family man, a credit to his community.

The coroner's jury was convened and quickly returned the verdict that the deceased had indeed been shot to death by one Jasper Hibbard. Evidence presented by Constable McElroy and corroborated by Sheriff Baker and the coroner indicated that Greenlee had not removed his glove in preparation for a shootout and did not draw his service revolver, which he carried in a holster on his left hip. The course of the bullet through the lapels of the dead man's coat, said the coroner, indicated the coat had been at least partially buttoned at the moment of the shooting and had not been thrown open to facilitate a ready draw.

On the advice of Estes Everett, Hibbard declined to testify and waved a preliminary hearing, choosing instead to be bound over to a grand jury the following February.

Three months later the state legislature would authorize the sum of $3,000 to be paid to the widow of Dexter Greenlee for the grievous circumstances befallen the spouse of a state employee.

Chapter Three
December, 1914

HIS FACE ALL STONE AND WAX. Not her Papa. But *Yes*, Momma said, *that's him only with his soul gone floating off. I'm sorry*. Emily lifted her up and Iris reached out a finger and touched the pebbly cheek, the nose stiff as wood. The smell not her Papa at all. It was a machine smell, his bones replaced with iron pipes, his innards filled with kerosene. His hands folded like never. She made a smacking sound but did not put her lips to the hard skin. At all.

"Enough," said her mother and set her on the floor. Iris reached out and grabbed her brother's hand. Years later this would be one of her first full memories of anything. She was five. What had gone before were snatches of things. Chasing chickens in the little back yard. Henry making his awful squealing. Her daddy waxing his boots. But this is when everything started, the knowing of things in their sequence. When Henry finally said her name, at her father's funeral.

"Eye-rith."

The big coffin loomed over their heads, plain pine stained by the undertaker with coffee and turpentine to resemble a more noble wood. Atop a table draped with black fabric. Iris reached out and held the fabric in her fingers. It was smooth and pleasant. Henry batted at the cloth with a fat stubby hand.

"No, Henry," she said.

"Take him outside," said her mother, "before he has his fits."

They moved hand-in-hand through the forest of legs, Henry a heavy, draggy thing behind her, always in danger of being torn from her grasp. It was very busy and challenging; people did not see them, the little people. Then a man leaned down close, with gray whiskery cheeks. He smelled like milk gone bad.

"Sorry about yer loss, little girl," said the man.

Iris squeezed Henry's hand to make him come to a stop.

"Yer daddy was gunned down in cold blood, and there's hell to pay for that."

The words were dark to Iris but the man himself seemed sincere despite his thick, sour breath.

"All right," she said.

"There's hell to pay," repeated the man as he straightened up, nodding as if they both now knew something important. "Don't forget that."

"Yes sir," she replied.

The man winked, and she winked back without knowing what it meant, except that a man had come out of nowhere and now they shared something.

"Pee," said Henry. This was another word that Henry had mastered, and Iris knew that if Henry did not pee very soon there could be trouble.

She tugged at his hand. "Follow me."

They moved through the trousers and the dresses, the clumping shoes, the starchy smells, through the door and into a grassy place in front of the building. Away from Papa in his box. Outside was better.

"Pee," said Henry.

Iris led Henry to a small gathering of holly and helped him undo his pants which collapsed to his knees and immediately a fine stream sprung from his little thing and a dozen or so quail appeared and rippled through the air directly above and then the birds were gone and Iris knew they had passed her way for a reason.

Chapter Four
March, 1915

"YOU REMEMBER what I told you," said Emily.

Iris looked up. "Yes, Momma."

"Silver Bill hasn't done this before but we're in a pickle without Mrs. Clyburn or Jenny and he offered so here we are."

"All right."

"If Henry acts up, you know what to do. Like we talked."

Iris did not know what to do. She had forgot. She knew Momma was leaving her alone with her brother. That's about all she could figure. And that she was to be like an adult, which she supposed meant being bossy. "Yes, Momma."

"Silver Bill is gonna be here before long. He'll look after things. He just couldn't be here sooner."

Iris nodded. Henry already seemed to be acting up, swatting at something on the floor with a dirty dish rag and yelling, "Ha!" each time.

"No, Henry," said Iris.

"Henry, you be good and do what your sister says."

Henry did not look up from his swatting.

Emily Greenlee sighed. "It's supposed to be over pretty quick," she said. "I'm just over at the courthouse. When the trial's done, I won't be going off any more."

Iris nodded. The door gave its melodic squeak-bang

and then Momma was down the steps and headed off.

"Ah ant," said Henry thickly, squashing the thing with the heel of his hand.

Silver Bill showed up before long. He was not alone. He'd brought a man with him, a loud man who guffawed and coughed as he clomped up the steps like a mule. Each man held a bottle.

"Look here if it ain't the woman of the house!" exclaimed Silver Bill, pushing aside the door with his shoulder and standing and regarding his young charges.

Iris had seen Silver Bill before. He was the man who had leaned down to talk to her at her daddy's funeral. Momma said that her papa and Silver Bill had been friends. Momma had said, *They're like friends, but not really friends.* Iris remembered that very well. *Friends but not friends.*

Iris didn't like the other man. He was loud and big and scary because he had a lower lip twisted like something bad had happened to it.

"Manners!" said Silver Bill. "Children, this is Mr. Coldstone from Grants Pass. Mr. Coldstone, this is Iris and...and," he pointed to Henry, said to Iris, "What's his name?"

"Henry."

"Henry Fuckin' Ford!" bellowed Coldstone. "Inventor of the automobile! I'll be damned!"

"What's that?" Iris wanted to know, meaning the bottles in their hands.

Silver Bill held up his flask. Inside a clear liquid moved up and down. "This is medicine," he said, and Coldstone hooted.

"I'm rightfully ill," crowed Coldstone, "and I need my fixin'."

Silver Bill fished two mugs from the cupboard and the men sat at the kitchen table and commenced to banter. Iris did not care to understand what was being said. She was just glad that adults had arrived and she could go back to being Iris.

After a fashion the man Coldstone began to direct his attention to Henry. "Hey there, amigo," he said. Only the twisted part of his mouth moved. "Cat got your tongue?"

Both men laughed.

"You a little tubby, ain't you?" asked Coldstone. "You're round and soft as a glob of pig snot." They guffawed.

"Hey there, pig snot! You get any fatter and you're gonna roll out the door."

Henry kept himself occupied on the floor. Tracing a semicircle pattern in the dust, over and over, with a stray pine needle.

The man thought he was being funny, but Iris didn't think so. She expected Silver Bill to say something, to stop the man from being loud, but Silver Bill just laughed along and hit the table with his hand.

"You wouldn't stop rolling till you got to the Rogue. Then you'd just plop in and float on down all the way to the Pacific Ocean."

This was not good. Iris could tell by the way Henry's shoulders lifted up and down that he was close to a fit. She heard his little breaths coming ever faster. Like Momma would say, *It was going to be a doozy.*

But there was no Momma. There was only her. Iris. The big sister.

"And you'll float like a tub of butter until some shark comes along and gobbles you up, *rhumph!* In one big bite!"

Both men guffawed and winked. And Henry began to yowl.

"Eow eow eow," he screeched, slapping at the back of his neck with both hands. "Ya-haaah!"

"Sweet Jesus!" The horsey man looked alarmed. "What's got into him?"

"They say he's touched," said Silver Bill. "I forgot to mention."

"Well get him to shut up!"

"Hey there little fella," said Silver Bill. "How about you quiet down now?"

At this Henry began to wail even louder and scratch at the back of his neck. Iris could see fine lines of red blood.

Momma always handled these things. Sometimes Henry would wail for a good long time while Momma held him by the wrists so he couldn't hurt himself and she tried to talk to him and calm him down.

"Shut the hell up!" yelled Coldstone through his tunneled lips. "Yer hurtin' my ears!"

Iris knelt by her brother. His eyes were wide, pink, and wet. He didn't look at her—she knew he wouldn't. But just maybe he would hear her. "You don't have to look at me, Henry. I'm not lookin' at you. But watch me now. Hear? Watch me from behind so I can't see you watchin' me."

He screeched in a way that Iris knew he was hearing her, the tone of his wailing had a tinge of curiosity.

She got up, walked to the man *Coldstone*. Behind her, Henry turned his head slightly to follow.

The big man waved a finger big as a sausage. "Tell him to shut up or I'll hogtie him and throw him in a ditch for Crisssakes!"

Iris looked at the man. He had stuck one big ugly leg into the middle of their house, the boot resting on its heel, dabs of hay-flecked horse manure around the cuff. She came around sideways, squared up, and kicked that leg for all she was worth. Her hard-toed boot took Coldstone right in the calf alongside the shin bone.

"Yoww!" yelled the man through his twisted lips.

"Sweet Jesus damn! Why you little varmint!" He raised a hand to swat her aside but Silver Bill moved quick as a tomcat and grabbed the man's forearm in midair.

"Hold on there partner," said Silver Bill, loud enough to be heard over Henry's caterwauling. "I told you the boy is touched. He can't help hisself. She's just tryin' to look out for him."

"Did you see what that little skunk did? She kicked me for no damn reason." Coldstone rubbed his injured leg and glared at the girl, who stood with her hands on her hips and her legs spread wide, standing between the man and her brother.

"More hellcat than polecat," observed Silver Bill, still holding the man's arm at bay.

"She oughta be paddled with a whipsaw. And that one there, they oughta just throw him in the river. He's got the devil in him. Lemme go, for Crissakes." Coldstone shook himself free, stood, grasped his near-empty bottle by its neck, told Silver Bill, "I ain't staying here with the skunk and the devil. You can have 'em."

Silver Bill knew where Coldstone would be headed: the tavern. He remembered giving his word to Emily Greenlee that he'd watch her young ones while she was at the hearing, on account of his debt to her late husband the warden. But by the look of things the girl child could manage all right, standing there with her tiny fists on her hips, not about to back down. The temptation was too great. "I'm with ya," he said, pushing back his chair and taking his own bottle. He pointed a finger at Iris. "You be good."

Iris said nothing, watched them clomp out the door, down the steps, and away.

She went to Henry, who was still heaving, his squalls reduced to breathless pants.

"Henry, I'm sitting down and let's put our backs together." She sat down and shimmied against him and let her tall back feel his short, soft back. "You can lean on me like a chair," she said, and she felt the weight of him come close, and grow heavy against her. She felt the little cannonball of his head nestle below her shoulder.

That's how Emily found them when she returned, three hours later.

Chapter Five
March, 1915

DISTRICT ATTORNEY RUNE DAVIS was ebullient. He took a cigar from the humidor on his desk and, after a moment's hesitation, took another cigar and handed it to Constable McElroy.

"No thanks, I don't smoke," said McElroy.

"You're missing out. These are imported. A strain of African tobacco grown in the Philippines. Quite exotic." And for those very reasons Davis was pleased to return the constable's cigar to the humidor so he could enjoy it himself later. From a small tin box he took a match and fired it with a flick of his thumb, fingernail popping phosphorus into flame with practiced élan. Smoke began to drift about the room, white wraiths turning gold as they floated past windows and into the day's last sun.

"Maybe when the trial's over."

"You're unimpeachable," said the D.A., carefully removing the initial ash from the tip of his cigar by rolling it on a flat river stone that doubled as a desk paperweight.

"Well, Rune, I'm not sure there's a man alive who qualifies as completely unimpeachable," said McElroy amiably.

"Ever testified in a murder trial, Ennis?" He knew the answer.

"No. No murders."

"I've prosecuted four, three successfully." Rune Davis

smiled and smoke curled out his mouth. "The fourth beat us to it and hung himself in the county jail in Klamath Falls. Ripped his trousers into strips and made a crude rope. Inventive fellow. Probably the most guilty of the lot, wouldn't you know it. Ha!"

McElroy tapped his big gray Homburg against his thigh.

"Well," said Davis, sensing in his guest the familiar reticence of someone raised in the Oregon country, someone unfamiliar with irony. "I can assure you, a murder trial is like no other."

"I don't doubt that."

"It's a circus, of course. A grand exhibition. A man's life in the balance. The grieving widow. Newspapermen from all over the state. Perhaps even *The New York Times*. Many spectators, all come to touch the laughing face of Death."

Ennis McElroy raised his eyebrows but said nothing.

"You'll do fine on the witness stand, my friend. We have all the truth of it on our side. We have your expert eyewitness testimony. It's open and shut, as they say."

"Well, I'll be glad when it's over," replied McElroy, who was having some bad dreams lately about the shooting. He hoped the trial would be the end of all that.

"It'll be over before you know it." And as punctuation, Davis leaned back and launched a perfect smoke ring toward the ceiling.

(from the *Medford Meteor*,
March 14, 1915)

Hibbard Indicted
By Grand Jury

*Murder suspect to stand trial
for Slaying Game Warden*

Jasper Hibbard, game poacher of Trail, was indicted by the grand jury Thursday afternoon on a charge of murder, the degree being left open by the inquisitorial body, in accordance with the instructions of the court. Since the abolishment of capital punishment in this state there is no first degree murder, the highest being second degree. An indictment by the grand jury would have left a technical opening.

Hibbard is accused of slaying Game Warden Dexter Greenlee at Trail last December, while in pursuit of his duties, and the defendant has been held in the country jail awaiting trial.

His plea will be self defense, and according to jail companions he is highly hopeful of acquittal or no less than a verdict of manslaughter in one of the lesser degrees.

On the first day of jury selection the courtroom was crowded with spectators, as the District Attorney had predicted. McElroy noted the widow near the middle of the rows, wearing a plain black dress that probably was borrowed and had served more than one local woman in this capacity.

The trial had split the community into two factions. One was dead certain Jasper Hibbard was guilty of murder. Period, end of it. The other believed it was a man's God-given right to defend his property and means of sustenance, even if that man happened to be on government property *(especially* if that man was on government property), because government property belonged to the people. No restrictions nor laws nor enforcers of laws trumped that notion. The U.S. Constitution said so. The death of the game warden was unfortunate but justifiable.

Both sides were well-represented in the circuit court audience. The main rows were occupied by many of the townspeople of Medford and Ashland, while a contingent of unshaven, rowdy men occupied many of the chairs placed against the back wall, where they offered their opinions with loud voices. These were friends and supporters of Jasper Hibbard, folks from the area near Jasper's cabin and had driven down just for the trial.

"Let the common man live in peace!"

"Don't bust a man for the sake of a deer!"

"You don't own everything!"

The judge rapped his gavel and asked for quiet on several occasions.

The prospective jurors were likewise divided into the two sides, and most drew preemptive challenges from one attorney or the other and were dismissed. By the third venire on the second day everyone was weary, and the bored audience began to whisper and shuffle about in their seats.

In shifts of two or three the men at the back of the court walked out and went to the J'Ville Tavern for shots and to verbally assault anyone who disagreed with their perspectives on the overreach of governments in general and the innocent Jasper Hibbard in particular. The fellas remaining in the courtroom guarded the empty seats and wouldn't let anyone sit in them.

Attorney Rune Davis faced yet another possible juror. "Your name, sir?" asked attorney Davis.

"William T. Archer."

"And what town are you from?"

"Wolf Creek."

"Ah, Wolf Creek. A decent hamlet. Away from it all, wouldn't you say?"

"If you mean away from crazy city folk, I'd say you're right."

A few in the gallery laughed.

"Mr. Archer, are there newspapers up there in Wolf Creek?"

Archer looked puzzled. "Newspapers?"

"Yes. Daily newspapers. The *Meteor*, for example."

"Oh, sure. At the store."

"And do you read them?"

"Yup. When I get to the store. Clausen, he keeps the papers around so fellas like me that don't get into the town very often can catch up. Besides what hearsay we get in between."

"Clausen being the shopkeeper? Of the store?"

"That's right. Cap Clausen."

"Did you happen to read about this trial, and the incidents that led up to it?"

"Sure. Everybody knows about it now for months." Archer gestured toward the standing-room-only courthouse. "Lookee there."

"And in reading about the events, did you have any opinion on the matter?"

"Why, I know that Jasper Hibbard is a decent man. That sheriff drew down on Jasper. Left no choice but to defend himself."

"Your Honor..." began Davis.

"What the hell is a game warden, anyway?" Archer went on, "What the hell are they needed for? Keep a man from puttin' food on his table? What, I need to have some government man come around and tell me my business?"

Men at the back of the room cheered in agreement.

Estes Everett jumped to his feet, smacked the table in front of him and burst out, "I like this juror."

The judge rolled his eyes and shook his head. "Mr. Everett, please refrain from out-of-order proclamations. And you back there," the judge pointed at the rowdies by the wall, "like it or not, while you're in here you will respect this courtroom."

"Boo," several voices called.

"Your honor," repeated the D.A., his tenor even, "the prosecution wishes to exercise a challenge to this candidate."

The courtroom groaned.

"Mr. Archer, you are dismissed," said the judge. To the prosecutor, the judge said, "Mr. Davis, you have three challenges remaining. Please proceed."

At long last, on the morning of the third day, after two more venires had been exhausted, twelve jurors were finalized. Opening arguments began that next afternoon, and the following morning character witnesses were dutifully paraded before the eyes of the court, some saying Hibbard was nasty, mean-spirited, and cantankerous; others vouching that the accused was helpful, reliable, a good neighbor, a resourceful man with an abiding respect for the land.

The coroner took the stand on behalf of the prosecution and testified to the forensic evidence, the entry and exit wound locations (front entry one and a half inches right and one-half inch above the left nipple, breaking the third rib on impact, the slug deflected slightly downward to thoroughly demolish both ventricles, cratering flesh until it burst out the back, shattering ribs five, six, and seven as it did so), the cause of death (massive trauma to the heart, severe blood loss), and the corroborating details of clothing (entry hole through left coat lapel, vest, shirt, and blood patterns).

"Your witness," said Rune Davis to Estes Everett.

For the cross examine, Everett did not approach but stood at his court desk. For this reason it was necessary for him to project his voice, which he did with an appropriately aristocratic inflection.

"Mr. Phillips. You testified as to the condition of the deceased's clothing, correct?"

"Yes I did."

"And you examined the clothing thoroughly, I'm sure?"

"Of course. It's a matter of record now."

At the prosecutor's table Rune Davis pursed his lips. The defense attorney was setting something up.

"So you'd notice if he had boots on, for example, or was barefoot, that sort of thing?"

"Yes."

The coroner was annoyed, looked at Davis. The D.A. stood and threw in a random objection to let Phillips take a moment.

The judge rolled his eyes. "Overruled."

Everett smiled. "So Mr. Phillips, how many gloves did the deceased have on?"

"Well, one."

"Just one?"

"Yes."

"Which hand had a glove on?"

"The left."

"Now, Mr. Phillips. You've been a county coroner for how long?" Estes already knew the answer.

"Sixteen years here in Jackson County and before that seven years in Multnomah County and before that eighteen years in Coos County."

"Ah! A considerable length of time in the business, I must say. Congratulations."

"Yes. Thank you."

"Goodness, that takes you back to gunslinger days here abouts. So in your time, I presume you've seen other men who've been shot to death in various circumstances."

"Yes. Several, I'm afraid."

"Killed in gunfights?"

"That's correct."

"And you must have studied records at some point also. Other gunshot deaths."

"Correct, but I'm not sure what you're getting at, Mr. Everett."

"That's for me to ask," reproached the judge.

"Now, did you ever see any other men who had only one glove on?"

"Maybe one or two."

"I see. Now, with your professional expertise, do you happen to know why a man might take off a glove during an altercation that involved firearms?"

"Well, I can tell you what I know anecdotally."

"Please do."

Everett looked at Rune Davis, anticipating an objection, but Davis just smiled. The D.A. had wondered if Everett would be shrewd enough to pursue this little nugget, and there you go. Maybe he'd underestimated the defense attorney, but it wouldn't be enough. He decided to let Everett have at it, no need for him to stir up the bog under the weeds.

"Some men, you see, prefer to remove their gloves before handling a weapon. They feel it's more comfortable and their accuracy is better without a glove."

"And a man with a pistol would only take off one glove, correct? The glove on his shooting hand?"

"I would presume so, yes."

A citizen in the back of the room, just returned from the tavern, yelled out, "Hell I shoot buck naked!"

"Enough of that," said the judge pointing with the handle of his gavel.

"Har har."

"So it's possible, then—and I repeat, *possible*—that Game Warden Dexter Greenlee removed a glove in anticipation of gunplay?"

The coroner looked to Davis, who nodded ever so slightly.

"I suppose it's a possibility."

"That's a *yes?*"

"Sure. Yes."

"Thank you, Coroner Phillips. And we thank for your service to our county."

"Follow, Mr. Davis?" asked the judge.

"If I may, your honor."

"Have at it." The judge scratched the top of his balding head with the gavel handle.

"Mr. Phillips, as you work on the body of a deceased, how easy is it to remove an article of clothing. Say, a glove?"

"How easy is it?"

"Exactly. How easy would it be to take the glove off a

dead man?"

"Well, if there's no trauma to the hand, then very easy. You pull gently on the fingers, one at a time, until it comes off. Either that, or you can grip it by the cuff and peel it off."

"So anyone could do it?"

"Yes. Just like anyone could take a mitten off a child."

"A mitten off a child," repeated the D.A., tapping his chin with a forefinger. "So it's a possibility, then—and I repeat, *possibility*—that a no-good poacher could take the glove off a shot man and set it out to make it look…"

"Objection!" boomed Everett.

"Sustained!" The judge tried to grasp his gavel by its slim handle so he could bring it down with authority but instead sent it clattering to the floor. As he bent to pick it up all that could be seen of him was a long, black-robed arm and a pointing finger. "You, Mr. Davis, are mightily close to being contemptuous of this court," said the arm. The judge surfaced, red-faced, and said, "Mr. Court Recorder, kindly strike the District Attorney's last comment."

"Aye aye, sir," said the recorder, a former Navy man.

On the fourth day the prosecution called to the stand their prize, Constable Ennis McElroy, the only eyewitness. A few in the back of the room hissed.

In the witness chair McElroy grew instantly hot. Everyone was looking at him funny, like he was on a stage in a play but didn't know his lines. He wished he could take off his suit coat but that wouldn't be proper. His forehead was itching. What he wouldn't do for a cold one.

Rune Davis was smooth as buttermilk. He quietly asked the constable about the sequence of events, starting with the issuance of the warrant and culminating with the constable's ride down the mountain. McElroy described everything with care as best he remembered it happening. He didn't describe the bloody spray that spread out like a cape's shadow cast in red on the snow, how it came to his dreams.

"Well done, Constable McElroy," praised Davis. He smiled at Everett. "Your witness."

Estes Everett rose and without looking at McElroy, said, "Constable, at the moment of the shooting, where were you?"

"Like I said, mounted on my horse."

"And Officer Greenlee?"

"Well, on his horse. Maybe ten feet away."

"To your left or right?"

"My left."

"And then he dismounted, correct?"

"Yes, sir. That's so. Then Hibbard shot him."

Estes frowned. "So, Officer Greenlee dismounted to his own left, correct? The way most men do?"

McElroy nodded. "Right. I mean, that's right, he got off to his left."

"So his horse, the one previously described by you as 'pretty big,' was between you and the officer. At the exact moment he was shot."

Davis began to run the tip of his tongue along his upper teeth; he could feel the drift of this, and it wasn't much to his liking.

"I guess that's right."

"Objection!" said Davis. "Leading the witness."

"Sustained. Can you get to the point, Mr. Estes?"

"So at that exact moment, you couldn't see much of Greenlee, could you?"

"I saw him get shot."

"But you didn't see his hands, did you?"

McElroy furrowed up his brow and thought hard. "Maybe. Maybe not."

"You aren't sure, are you?"

"I mean, the man is dead. What more you need to know? I was there. I saw Hibbard shoot him plain as day."

Everett nodded, waited a moment, took a measured breath, said, "So you really can't say if Officer Greenlee took his gun out of its holster or not."

McElroy frowned. This had all seemed so simple at first, but now the defense attorney had managed to coax him right to the edge of a trap of words. How could he not avoid it?

"Constable?"

"He didn't take his gun out. I saw the body after. His gun was holstered. Right there by his side."

"But you can't be sure, can you?"

McElroy felt his face go hot. He looked at Rune Davis. "I'm sure about what I saw. There was no gun on the ground."

"Ah, well, that conflicts with the testimony Sheriff Baker gave earlier, doesn't it? Sheriff Baker said when you and he went up to get the body, Officer Greenlee's gun was out in plain sight. In fact, just a few minutes ago, you yourself testified that you saw the weapon near the body."

"I did, but somebody put it there," McElroy puffed.

Everett faced the jury directly, lifted his hands in front of himself, palms up, and made as if he was weighing something on a set of scales. "Conflicting testimonies," he said.

"Objection," called Davis. "Mr. Estes is playacting now."

"Sustained. A little less showmanship, if you please, Mr. Everett," said the judge. The crowd at the rear of the courtroom jeered.

Estes said, "So the truth of the matter is, the gun was on the ground when you arrived to retrieve the body, isn't that so?"

McElroy fumed. "I saw the man get shot plain as day."

Estes turned to the judge. "Move to strike?"

"The jury is instructed to ignore the last comment from the witness," the judge said wearily. "Mr. McElroy, please confine your testimony to the questions Mr. Estes is asking. Can you do that?"

"Well, the truth is the truth," muttered McElroy.

"Indeed," said the judge.

"So," Estes pursued, "the gun was on the ground when you arrived to retrieve the body, correct?"

"As I said."

"That's a yes?"

"Yes."

"No further questions."

The trial moved ahead, but there was little that Prosecutor Davis could do to uproot the seeds of doubt that had been planted in the jury's mind. The vote was eight to four for conviction and Jasper Hibbard was a free man.

(from the *Medford Meteor*,
May 28, 1915)

A TRAVESTY OF JUSTICE!

*Jury Finds Poacher Not Guilty
in a Stunning Vote of 8 to 4*

Jasper Hibbard, game poacher of Trail, was found Not Guilty by a jury of his peers in the district court of Jackson County. Despite the most damaging testimony of the prosecution's eye witness, Constable Ennis McElroy, the jury was presented with conflicting testimonies that made the outcome a matter of conjecture until the final deliberations were handed to the bailiff.

The courtroom audience was divided on the outcome of the verdict, with several members protesting the decision and another faction very vocally letting their approval be known. The outcome is not without its positive effects in the community, as a brand new gallows has been constructed behind the jailhouse and now awaits, like a lonely sentinel, to dispense the sure, swift justice it was designed to mete.

Chapter Six
September, 1917

"SOME PEOPLE ARE JUST MISSING that something that makes them regular folks," Doctor Lloyd Finister said, clicking his bag shut. "It's because the brain doesn't get fully developed during gestation. But there's no cure for insanity. The only thing you can give him is kindness and patience, which I guarantee will be tested to your limits. I've seen others like this, some worse. But most end up in an institution, sooner or later. Families just can't manage it all."

"He ain't insane," said Emily.

"Yes well, that's not a term I'm particularly fond of. There are many variations of mental disturbance. I know other young people like Henry here that have the same sort of thing, drifts off, hard to get him back sometimes, tends to get real interested in some little thing and will stare at it or play with it for hours."

"He knows everything that's going on. He's got feelings like anybody. He's just particular, and he gets out of sorts when things don't go his way. He sure as hell ain't going to end up in some loony bin. I'll see to that."

"The Oregon State Hospital in Salem is doing wonderful things with the in..., ah, with people who have these kinds of problems." The doctor put on his hat. "Most of the patients are employed at useful work. There's a bakery, for example, and an immense garden. Did you know they produced some seventy thousand cabbages last year? Good grief, seventy thousand! And an equal amount of carrots and potatoes, and that the patients do most of the tending and harvesting and such. They're quite active and quite well cared for."

"The patients or the cabbages?"

"What? Oh, ha. Yes, the patients of course."

"We got a garden right here, thank you very much," said Emily.

"Things could get scarce," advised Finister, "because of the war. Shortages. Rationing. That sort of thing. You should know that the costs at the state facility are quite low, thanks to all the produce they sell, along with bread and even some hogs I believe. It's very well-managed which keeps the cost of care—and that includes clothing, food, and medical attention—to only about fifteen dollars a month."

Emily said nothing.

"And it would be one less mouth for you to feed."

"We'll manage." Hands on hips.

Finister nodded, looked at the front door. "Well, Mrs. Greenlee, the boy is only seven, and children that young aren't prime candidates for the State Hospital anyway. Although they have a ward for children. So if you change your mind, I'd be pleased to write up a formal examination that would allow Henry to be admitted. Meanwhile, just don't expect to make much headway with him."

"I was thinking that maybe he could get to school, you know for some basics."

"I certainly wouldn't recommend school. He won't fit in."

"Well we'll see about that."

The doctor said good day and left.

"You're growing up Henry," said Emily, trying to tuck his shirttail inside his pants while Henry was dedicated to pulling it out. "It's time you got some schooling." Emily hadn't talked much to Henry about school except to say he would now be going to a classroom like every youngster in the county and that it was the most natural thing in the world.

She stood up. "You're his guardian angel," Emily said to Iris. "You look after him."

Iris took her brother's soft hand in hers and led him down the steps and toward the big schoolhouse sitting atop Bigham's Knoll. As they walked Henry was quiet, his over-size cuffs swish-swishing, lunch box squeaking in whispers, lagging his customary pace behind so Iris had to lean forward to keep them going.

At school the primary teacher, Mrs. Cunningham, stood by the front door to greet the children and to keep an eye out for Iris and Henry Greenlee, hoping against hope they would be truant. If they were, she could write a report and send it to the school board as rebuttal for their decision to let the boy attend. After all, she had witnessed Henry having one of his fits, right there on 4th Street in broad daylight, and it was a thing to behold. She did not want that kind of disturbance in her Jacksonville School.

Months before, Emily Greenlee had come by the schoolhouse when it was not in session and met with Mrs. Cunningham in her classroom. Emily had said that she wanted Henry to attend school this coming school year.

Mrs. Cunningham had given a bemused smile and said, "Do you really think school is the best for Henry? I wouldn't want him disrupting the class."

"He's particular about some things. He doesn't like to

be looked at directly, for one. But mostly he'll just sit there and be quiet and take it all in."

"I expect my students to actively participate, Mrs. Greenlee, and to answer when called upon," said Cunningham.

"He might answer all right," Emily had said, "he just might not say what you'd expect.."

In the end Mrs. Cunningham had to agree to let Henry attend—state law said so. But only moments after Emily Greenlee had left the school Mrs. Cunningham was at her desk writing the school board urgently requesting that they deny Henry Greenlee the normal channels of education due to "severe mental insanity," a request that eventually was rejected with a disquieting lack of explanation.

Now, as she scanned the streets below, she sighed. Truth be told? That Greenlee boy would be a whole lot better behaved if the parenting abilities of the widow Greenlee didn't leave so much to be desired.

Her heart sank as she saw the Greenlee children walking up the roadway leading to the school. Perhaps fortune would intervene; perhaps the big brick façade would intimidate him as he came near, facilitating one of his fits and allowing her the de facto authority to prevent him from entering. But they came up without incident, holding hands, the boy watching the ground in front of his feet, the mischievous girl—a handful in her own right—looking up defiant and scrappy as her mother.

Mrs. Cunningham put on a generous smile. "Why hello, Iris," she said.

"Hello Mrs. Cunningham. This here is my brother, Henry. I suppose you know he was coming today."

"Hello Henry."

"He's not a real talker right off," assured Iris. "But he can get going sometimes. He's just shy."

"Well, let's hope he can find his tongue in class."

The schoolmarm ushered them inside to a side row away from the windows. Iris showed Henry how to sit in the desk seat, then she took the seat right in front of him so he could see her plain.

The other children were abuzz with the news that the insane Greenlee kid was right over there. No one wanted to sit near Henry or Iris, for that matter. One of the girls, Loretta, was overcome with curiosity and walked up and said, "Who's that?"

"That's my brother, Henry."

"Is he…?" Loretta circled her ear with a forefinger.

"No, he's just temperamental." This was an impressive word Iris had learned from her Momma. It was a big enough word that sidetracked folks from saying out loud that Henry was insane. People generally didn't have a comeback for *temperamental.*

Loretta squinted at Henry. "Doesn't he say anything?"

"Not much, no."

"How's he supposed to answer in class?"

"I'll help him."

"You can't answer for him. That wouldn't be fair, would it?"

"We'll figure something out."

As it turned out, Henry's time as a student didn't last long at all. Silent and still as a mouse, Henry stared at his desk surface and lost himself in the squiggles and letters carved over three decades by restless children with pocket knives. They were fascinating marks, black with age, and they told stories. He rubbed a finger against the biggest gouge, felt its touched-smooth edges. The woman at the front of the room began to talk and occasionally one of the other youngsters said something but to Henry it wasn't as interesting as the hieroglyphics on his desktop. He was only here because Iris had taken him and told him that this is what they were to do.

At recess he allowed himself to be led outside by Iris and they stood together a ways off while most of the others crowded into a well-worn circle at one end of the playground to play Fox and Geese. "We'll just watch, Henry," said Iris, although she was itching to do Fox and Geese because she was quick and elusive and hard to catch.

A few of the older boys had gathered apart, and now one of them came skipping across the lawn, arms outstretched, squawking like a raven. He dipped around in a circle while the other boys laughed, then he came up to Henry and Iris and swerved around them and said in a screechy raven voice, "Hey Cuckoo! Cuckoo!" Before long all the older boys begun to make sport, running past with their arms outstretched like they were birds of prey, swooping past Henry and saying, *Hey crazy boy!* and *Nut job!* and *Where's your loony bin?* The game was to see who could come closest to the idiot and provoke him without getting swatted in return.

Mrs. Cunningham stood in the shadow of an eave and watched through narrowed eyes.

Iris stood in front of Henry and tried to defend her brother but the boys came from all directions and she became part of the game, the boys flying past trying to cuff her or Henry on a shoulder and one landed a good blow to the back of her head. Boys who were not normally given to bullying joined in and even a few of the bigger girls, delighted by the newness and naughtiness of the game.

Henry began to heave, his breathing coming fast. He didn't know why everything was directed at him, all this noise and taunts and flying children. He wanted to be on his kitchen floor in a warm spot of sun. This was not a good place. He began to hiss.

Iris grabbed a plum-size rock and heaved it at one of the boys. It clipped him on the heel as he skipped past and made him stumble for a few steps before falling hard to his hands and knees. He got up limping and red-faced, said to Iris, "That didn't hurt."

The throw brought Mrs. Cunningham marching down the slope from the shadow of the school. She grabbed Iris by the arm. "That's quite enough!" she commanded.

"They're trying to hurt him," Iris protested. "They're being mean."

"They're just having fun," scolded the school teacher. "That's no reason for throwing rocks."

Henry turned, wide-eyed. He hissed at Mrs. Cunningham with such vehemence that spittle flew from his lips. The schoolmarm took a step back.

"You," she said to Iris, squeezing her arm so tight it hurt, "take this devil child home and don't bring him back here."

"He's not hurtin' anybody. *They're* the ones making fun of him!"

"That's not what I've seen," Mrs. Cunningham declared, already formulating a follow-up letter to the school board outlining the many transgressions and disruptions she'd witnessed.

Iris smoldered. "Well then you're blind as a bat!"

Mrs. Cunningham drew herself up. "Life is unfair, child. You should know better than most." With that she released Iris' arm and pointed down the hill toward town. "Now take your brother home where he can't cause such a stir."

Chapter Seven
May, 1919

AFTER BEING A WIDOW for five years and then court-
ing for four months Emily Greenlee married the town
blacksmith John Rink and in the spring they all packed up
and moved out to where Rink had bought one-hundred and
sixty acres along the Applegate River. A broad river floodplain with oaks and alders and thistle-laced meadows, ter-
racing up to a shelf of pines and madrone and at last the
land steepened and climbed and big bald knobs of gray
granite poked from the earth waiting centuries now for the
liberating tremor that would send them down the mountain
flanks toward the river. Up toward the top of the ridge
were the big hairy-barked cedars and dark Douglas-firs with
their sweet woody smell, humus thick and shadowed beneath outstretched branches, this side of the river still un-
cut, too steep, the virgin giants of the valley majestic, serene. The river in its clean, clear trembling, the air above it
charged with shimmering mayflies and eye-blink swallows
that cut around the hanging willow fronds and were gone.
John Rink had ideas to put in pear trees on the floodplain
which he said would start producing in three or four years.
Pears were the future. Some folks said the river would
sooner or later flood out his crop but Rink said that was a
chance he'd take.

   Emily agreed. It sounded like a sensible plan and it was
tinged with adventure, this bull-stout man coming into their

lives and taking them all out to a new place in the country. Away from the eyes and the tongues. By a cool river where you could swim in the summer. They'd have animals. A draft horse for sure, but also chickens and maybe goats. A dog. Henry liked animals. Being around animals probably made a whole lot more sense than being around most people anyway.

She had the proceeds of her cottage sale and another $2,300 still remaining from the state's compensation for the death of her first husband. They figured to use that money to build a house, barn, chicken coop, get a horse, and start up the orchard.

Up off the flood plain where a big oak gave shade from the western sun the blacksmith began to build a two-room rough-board cabin. There was to be a bedroom for the couple and a kitchen room with an iron wood-fired stove and a sleeping porch across the back facing the river and across the front toward the road would be another porch for sitting. Rink got a big ten-man tent and cots from the Army Surplus store in Grant Pass and a tin stove and that's where they stayed while the house went up.

At seven in the morning their neighbor Mr. Cale came along in his covered Ford hack and he'd pick up Iris and four or five other kids from families along the upper river and deliver them to the one-room Applegate School in Ruch. There were canvas shades hung under the edges of the roof and if it was cold or rainy they'd roll those down to block the wind and wet.

Emily bought an eighteen-hand Percheron from a neighbor that was an oddly mottled gray and white in a way that the farmer said "wasn't right" and made him willing to part with the animal. She named him Parker.

"That's a peculiar name for a horse," said John Rink, stroking his wide chin. "You know any named Parker?"

"No I certainly don't," said Emily. "Maybe that's why it appeals."

Emily hitched Parker to a wood sled and spent large parts of her day down at the river gathering round river rocks for the foundation and chimney. Henry rode in the sled on top of the loads and amused himself by hefting rocks overboard while Emily was busy driving the big Percheron. When they returned to the river the path would be littered with strays that Emily dutifully reloaded while Henry grinned as he stared up at the sky.

Rink built a pole shed and set up his anvils and rigged a coal forge with a brake drum for a blower. He made a stool out of half a keg and sat Henry on it and Rink taught him to crank the blower and after a while Henry got the knack of it and the only trouble was getting him to stop. Rink pounded out gussets and hinges as the sparks arced and danced and steam billowed out of the slack tub. He showed Iris how to hold quarter-bolts of cedar upright between her knees so she could set the froe and crack off tapered shingles two feet long. Iris sat in the shade of the big oak and split shingles and stacked them, butt-to-taper, in piles two feet high. She decided few things were as satisfying as a new-cleft shingle popping off a bolt and the burst of cedary aroma that followed.

When the walls were up and the roof weathered in, Rink made an iron firebox with a plate flue and set it to the north wall and veneered it over with river rock. A last detail was a sturdy table and four chairs made from rip-sawed, hand-planed sugar pine, tight-grained and arrow-straight. Into the back of each chair he carved a symbol for each member of the family. An elk with a ten-point rack for himself. A cougar for Iris. Henry's chair got a salmon. For Emily he carved a horse in the likeness of a Percheron.

When the cabin was finished Henry and Iris slept on

the open air porch facing east to the river and in the summer they heard the cottonwoods shuffling in the air and the trilling frogs and the hurrying river. In the winter they buried themselves under blankets and listened to the coyotes cry like wailing infants and always the river, the noise constant but for the careful listener never repeating a chorus or even a single note in its restless urge to join the sea. In winter she'd wake to see icicles hanging from the eaves, glowing in the moonlight, and sometimes she'd get up and walk the cold hard floor and break one off and eat it like candy. Once while she was crunching an icicle she saw a tawny mountain lion come slinking along not thirty yards away and it stopped and looked at her with twin disks of reflected moonlight before moving silently into the shadows.

The next morning John Rink nodded as Iris told him of the cougar. "We're gonna have to teach you to shoot," he said.

Water came from a spring some two hundred yards from the house. Rink made a rough aqueduct out of old barrels and some steel pipe he welded together that channeled clear spring water into a cistern by the porch. Even in summer when the sun made the pipes too hot to touch the water came out of the cistern sweet and cool.

Rink built a chicken coop with stout wire underneath so raccoons couldn't burrow in and Emily traded sewing for Dominiques and Rhode Island whites and they had eggs enough to sell on the side. They had a sign out on the road that said *Good Brown Eggs* and on Saturdays Emily and Iris took the flatbed Packard into Jacksonville and sold what they could to the townies. Momma would say that all in all it wasn't much of a living but it was better than nothing.

At a crook in the river where the floodplain leveled out for a good twenty acres John Rink hitched Parker to a short-blade plow and ran irrigation ditches across the flats.

He pried out five dozen two-hundred pound stones and skidded them upriver and set them in a semicircle so the water would pool up behind. Nearby he dug a pond 30 feet across and cut a channel from his river dam to the pond and set an iron gate like a guillotine in the channel to regulate the flow. From the pond he added three more channels to reach the irrigation ditches he's already built. It took him fifteen days and when he was done he brought the family out and straddled the iron gate and lifted up the iron doorway to let the water course into the ditches. They all clapped as blades of silver cut across the fields.

"Damn it works," said John Rink.

"It sure as hell does," said Emily.

Three days later Rink returned from town in the flatbed truck and Iris felt something special in the sound of the Packard when it was still two miles away. When the gravel crunched under the tires she went out on the front porch. Her stepfather climbed out of the cab with an odd shape in the crook of one arm.

A dog.

Iris skipped down the steps. "A dog!" she yelled.

Rink smiled, put the coppery puppy on the ground and it flopped around, glad to be out of the rumbling truck cab. "That's a Chesapeake retriever. He's a good water dog."

Iris knelt down and the puppy bounced into her waiting hands. It had soft brown nappy fur and green eyes.

"Chessies are tough dogs," said Rink. "He'll keep the bears and cougars away, hopefully. But he'll need a lot of work, teachin' him how to behave. They're headstrong. Can you help me do that?"

"Yup," said Iris, twining her fingers in the softness at the back of the dog's neck.

"He's got to come when we call, even if he's hot on some rabbit or squirrel."

"He'll come."

"I won't abide a dog that don't listen."

"What'll we name him?"

"You think on that. Tell me when you figure it out."

But she already had it figured. She wanted to call him Ajax. A name she remembered from a school lesson. Ajax was one of those old Greek heroes. He got double-crossed somehow. She forgot why exactly. But she remembered Ajax was fierce and loyal. And she liked that. A lot.

Chapter Eight
October, 1919

"I'M GOIN' HUNTING," said John Rink, pulling on his dark leather boots. He straightened, addressed the wall, "I'm takin' the girl."

Emily put a cup down on the table; the sound came hard.

"Not the boy," said Rink, turning to look at Henry sitting cross-legged on the pine floorboards, his head bent to some attraction only he could see. "Guess that goes without sayin'."

Emily nodded. Sometimes the days went on with Henry being just part of everything; sometimes she was reminded what Henry was not.

The girl was a different matter. Emily could hear her out on the porch as she sorted through her things, all a-flutter for her first hunt. Then Iris came clomping out in deerskin pants and an old pair of John Rink's boots, cotton shirt loose and covered with a wool vest. Emily thought, *this is another child of mine who didn't come out fully right, buckskinned and wearing trousers and man boots.*

"How you gonna walk in them boots?" said Emily with a twinge of guilt that the girl had started to outgrow just about all her clothing and they hadn't got to town yet to find some replacements.

"I put some rags around my feet so they'd fit."

"Them pants make you look like an Indian hellion,"

said Emily without a whole lot of approval.

John Rink considered his stepdaughter through squinted eyes, as if he was trying to conjure a ten-year-old boy instead of this braided, rough-worn, ten-year-old girl. At last he nodded. "Looks like a Takelma chief."

"That's me," Iris said firmly.

"John," said Emily, knowing everything here was foregone, "you sure?"

"We've been practicing," said Rink. "She knows how to handle the rifle. And we're gonna need another hunter in this family besides me." Taking the Winchester off its pegs and checking the breech. "Suppose something happened. Maybe I get real sick. Suppose I chop off my own arm splittin' wood." He winked at Iris.

"I can hunt," Iris declared. "I can hunt deer."

Emily sighed. "There it is."

"Get me a box of them thirty-two forties," said Rink.

Iris dragged a chair to the wall where the ammunition was stashed in a small wood cupboard they'd put up high enough where Henry couldn't fool with it. She lifted the latch pin and swung open the rough board door and took a box of one-hundred-fifty-grain cartridges that John Rink had reloaded himself with what he called a *deer load*. She was glad to leave the big 180s behind. John Rink had let her fire one last year and it about knocked her on her backside. They were for bear and elk, he said. Her shoulder was purple for two weeks after.

They walked up the road a ways, John Rink carrying the rifle with both arms like he's nursing a baby. At a madrone with five massive trunks a light track took off through the scrub and the hunters followed it up through a twisted fantasia of manzanita, thimbleberry, pines, and more rust-red madrone, their trunks carpeted with little curlicues of bark and where the bark had fallen off were smooth and green, surfaces so silky that Iris brushed each one with her fingertips as she passed.

Iris in her oversize boots followed as best she could. As they trudged up the deer trail the rags had started to bunch in places and make hot spots on her soles and heels. She didn't say anything to John Rink about it. She wouldn't complain and she sure as hell wasn't going to stop. Nothing was going to stop her first deer hunt. She would follow him no matter what.

As they climbed the big pines began to take over and the understory thinned out. Halfway up John Rink left the track and headed off into the trees, Iris staying within reach of his shadow. At a big fir blow-down Rink climbed over and settled himself on the uphill side and Iris followed and sat on her knees. Rink handed her the Winchester.

"Rest the rifle," he said, patting the upper curve of bark.

She did as told.

"They start coming down now, looking for more green to eat."

"Uh huh."

"How far to the deer trail we was just on?"

"Thirty yards."

"Forty-five." He reached over and flipped up the tang sight and twisted the knurled knobs a quarter turn. "Kill shot is here,"—pointing to his own ribs—"right behind the shoulder, right in the middle."

Iris sighted down, brought the bead into the curved V-notch. "I know that," she said.

Rink grunted. "Don't dally. Line it up, then breathe out, hold, shoot. One, two, three."

They waited. The forest snapped and crackled as the heat of morning brought it alive. Warbler notes fell from the branches. A wind came up and made the trees heave and sough.

"Lord, I like that," said Rink.

"What?"

"Wind in the trees. The sound. Reminds me of something, I'm not sure what though. Maybe from when I was a boy."

Iris knew the sound. Out on the porch at night, the breeze moving through branches and needles, loud then soft, whisper then chorus.

"I was raised in Canada," he said. "Saskatchewan. You know where that is?"

Iris shook her head.

"Middle of the country. It's like a state. Like Oregon. Only up there they call it a province. Don't know why. We were outside of Regina. That's the capital of Saskatchewan. Lots of spruce, poplar, birch. Different kind of forest cover. My daddy took me hunting when I was eight. We had an old Colt carbine thirty-six. Six-shot with a revolving cylinder. Not that accurate but reliable. Had to get close with the old Colt, that's a fact."

Iris waited for more but Rink went silent.

"Did you get one?" she asked.

"I did. It was a good day." He looked up into a sky torn with thin high clouds. "Like today, as a matter of fact."

Iris shifted to sit on her hip and she put the butt of the rifle on the ground and rested the stock on the log.

"How come you didn't go to the war?"

"Too old. Enough on that. Just stay ready. And hush up now. This is gonna be your day. No jabbering."

"You're the one doing all the jabberin'."

They waited an hour. The forest crackled and madrone leaves drifted down. Every squirrel in the brush got Iris' heart to thumping. Silent as a ghost, a six-pointer stepped into a stripe of sunlight along the path and came to a stop, its one visible eye looking right at them.

"Slow," said Rink in the smallest whisper. "Head still."

The barrel came up, sliding quiet over the top of the log like a thing alive. Iris brought the bead into view and set it in the V-notch sight and directed the sights to the middle of the animal, right behind where the foreleg met the chest. But every time it was all lined up the barrel would twitch of its own accord and fall off and she'd bring it back knowing the deer was going to bolt before she could come on it clean. Her eyes went dry and she blinked hard to center the bead. Inhaled, exhaled, held, squeezed the trigger.

She'd been so intent on her target that the blast and the recoil took her by surprise and the butt of the rifle bit hard at her shoulder and the barrel kicked upward to point at the sky. Rink caught the weapon by the stock. Ravens squawked and took to the air on heavy wings. Burnt powder smell drifted.

"Damn!" Iris pushed herself back upright. "I missed him."

"You hit him. He jumped a mile."

"I did?"

"Wasn't clean, though. He took off. We'll have to track him down."

Iris got to her feet. "I got him?" She looked toward where the deer had appeared in the forest.

"If we find him down then you got him. Elsewise you didn't get him at all."

They set out along the blood trail. It was generous in places, splashed along the dried madrone leaves. "He's bleedin' himself out," said Rink.

Iris was floating. She didn't feel her blistered feet; she was light as air. Here, in blood markings, was a story of something she'd done. Everything around her—leaves, branches, clouds—was bright and etched cleanly into the world. The forest smelled of baking pine. Twigs and cones crunched under her oversized boots.

The dead deer lay in a shadowed alcove formed by three big Ponderosas. Rink made sure he had a chambered round and walked up slowly and toed it in the back, then relaxed the rifle. "He's dead. You did good."

Iris was radiant.

He knelt by the carcass and pulled the head up by the antlers. "Six pointer all right." A dribble of blood came out the deer's mouth and nostrils. He let the head down. "What now?"

Iris thought. "We gut him."

"That's right. So watch, I'll show you." Rink put his rifle aside and pulled his boned-handled hunting knife from its sheath. The blade flashed in the dappled shadows. Every deer she had seen had already been dressed out by John Rink before he brought it home. Now, she'd see it all for herself.

John Rink looked her in the eyes. "You know your ABCs?"

She shook her head, then nodded. "You mean the alphabet?"

"I mean the ABCs of deer cleaning. A to B. Anus to brisket, then cut. It's that simple. Anus, brisket, cut. A, B, C. You know what the anus is?"

"The butt hole." She pointed.

John Rink pulled the tail away from the haunches and placed the point of the knife on the deer's rectum. "That's right. The old butt hole." He gave a rare grin and took the tip of the blade and sawed a quick triangle around the deer's anus. "We start freein' up the guts right here." He grabbed the triangular flap of skin and its attached butt hole and jiggled it like shaking somebody's hand. "Get the butthole loose, you'll be needin' that later. Now where's the brisket?"

She shrugged.

"Here." He touched the blade, now slick with wet, against the deer's midsection. "Bottom of the breastbone. Now you grab his legs." Rink nodded in the direction of the forelegs.

Iris took up the deer's legs right behind the hooves. The animal smelled damp and musky, like a dog.

"Stretch him on out and keep his belly up."

Iris moved back a step and put her weight into the hold and the deer arched slightly, it's head loose and crooked back on its antlers, one half-closed eye staring up at her.

Rink kneed apart the back legs, pinned them under his weight, returned the blade to the anal incision, slid the steel inside, rolled it a quarter turn to bring the cutting edge under the skin, lifted.

"Don't cut the paunch; just the hide." The fur began to part and reveal the gut sack, whitish and translucent as ghost skin, with the shining purple viscera underneath quivering as if yet alive. Rink scraped side-to-side as he went, loosening the hide from the membrane.

"Don't want to cut the bladder or the stomach or the gut," he cautioned, "or you'll ruin the meat."

The knife made a sluicing sound as it slid through the hide. The scent of flesh and blood came clear then settled back into the smells of the forest.

She watched, rapt, as Rink brought his knife hand sideways to cut away at whatever was underneath the breastbone. When he was done he set the knife aside and reached in and balled up the jiggling mass of guts and rolled them out onto the ground. The gut smell swelled. "Liver," he said. "Stomach. Lungs. Intestine." Pointing to each with a bloody forefinger. He wiped at an itch on his nose and left a streak of red across his upper lip.

63

She'd seen guts before. They gutted every salmon and trout they caught, and she got to be good at that, flicking open the stomachs with the puka, washing the limp bodies in the clear cold water until they shone like new nickels. But she had never seen such a mass of bloody inside stuff as that of a deer. Pieces big as melons. Was this what the inside of a person looked like?

"Come over here."

She dropped the deer's legs and walked to his side.

"Reach in there."

"In there?" She pointed at the shadowed chest cavity.

"Up in there," said Rink, "is the heart. You reach in there and get it. It's partial cut already. You'll feel it."

Iris got to her knees, leaned over the body, ran her hands up inside. It was wet, warm. Up to the elbows. The carcass was inches away from her nose, smelling of vitals. She found a viscous lump, put both hands around it, pulled. At first it wouldn't yield but she knew John Rink expected this of her and she closed her eyes and willed all her strength and it came away with a sucking sound, and then she held it in her bloodied hands, the rich red prize.

"Throw it over there."

But for a long moment Iris held it in front of herself, marveling at the jelly feel of it on her palms, the slippery pliable mass with its web of veins.

"Is this what a man's heart looks like?"

John Rink nodded. "Just about like that."

"How do you know?"

"I seen it."

"A man's heart? A real man?"

"Is there another kind?"

"How did you see it?"

Rink looked off. "Years ago, logging the Big Berny. A choke cable snapped and whipped up and sawed this man about clean in half. Laid him open from here to here." Rink pointed from his neck to his waist. "Wasn't that dead yet. The heart was still beatin'." Rink opened and closed his fist several times. "So there it was." He reached down and began to scrape at the insides of the hide with his skinning knife. "That's why I quit setting chokers and took to blacksmithing. And now farming and fishing. And a little hunting." He glanced sideways. "Now throw it over there."

John Rink carried the deer across his shoulders, the legs gripped in his big hands. Ninety pounds. Iris held the carbine as Rink would, cradled in crossed arms. She pressed the heft to her chest and against the hardness of steel and wood felt the measure of her own heartbeat, her own bloody, shapeless clock inside.

At the road they turned for home and after a piece they heard the rattle of a vehicle behind and were soon overtaken by the game warden and his spindly Ford coup. He pulled up alongside, stopped, and got out. On his hip was a big .45 automatic in a leather holster. Dust rolled along the roadbed.

"Hello there John."

"Hello yourself, Derek."

"Looks like you been deer huntin'."

"You don't miss much, do you warden?"

The warden smiled but did not look amused. "Look here, John, you're out of season."

"Go on, Derek," said Rink, head bowed forward on account of the weight around his neck. "Deer season started couple weeks ago. That fella Kirkland told me."

"Well, you was both misinformed. Season starts this coming Wednesday."

Rink frowned.

The warden looked at Iris and her cradled weapon. "You shoot this deer, little missy?"

She nodded. "Yup, I did."

The warden raised his eyebrows in surprise. "That so?"

Rink cut in: "There a law says a youngster can't go huntin'?"

"Can't nobody hunt out of season," the warden replied. He considered them both, the man and his rifle toting stepchild. To Iris he said, "I knew your daddy."

She said nothing.

"He was a good man. I guess I'm now doing what he used to do. Being the game warden." There was a pause as the warden nodded to himself several times. "All right," he said. "Get on with it."

The warden's Ford left a spiraling cone of dust on the road.

They walked quiet for a while, then Iris said, "My daddy was a game warden."

"That's so."

"Did you know him?"

"Not at all."

"Do you know the name of the man who shot my daddy?"

"I heard the name. I don't know the man myself. Do you know it?"

"Jasper Hibbard."

"That's him."

"Did my daddy have a gun like that man just now?"

"I'm not sure what your daddy had. Probably a thirty-eight. That was pretty much the standard."

"What did that man have?"

"Looked like a Colt forty-five."

"Which is better?"

"Depends on what you want to do with it."

"For killing a man."

Rink looked at her, carbine hugged to her chest, hair tangled with twigs and flecks of dried moss, buckskins bloody at the knees, bloodied to the elbows, smear of red on one cheek.

"We got to look for ticks when we get back," was all he said.

After dinner John Rink sat with Emily on the front steps. The night was cool and the air sweet. Rink lit a thin Mexican cigar, watched smoke curl out to the stars.

"You can't turn that girl into a boy, John."

"Not aiming to."

"You know what I'm sayin'. There's work enough around here, and with Henry, well, I can't have her off in the woods for days tracking down deer."

"She's a natural hunter," said John Rink, not so much as argument as just stating the words out loud. "That is a fact."

Emily pressed out her apron with the flat of her hands. "You're gonna have to be on my side with this, John Rink."

He knew that was so. He stretched out his legs and the board steps creaked.

"There's one thing missing in that girl of yours," he said.

"What's that now?"

John Rink blew smoke. "Fear. That girl hasn't got a gnat's ass worth of fear."

Chapter Nine
August, 1922

JOHN RINK GAVE HENRY AN OLD PAN with hand-beaten riffles and took him down to the river and showed him how to wash for gold. Rink figured it was as good a job as any for a boy who would settle into a task for hours on end. And who knows? Maybe little Henry would come up with a nugget or two and they all go into Medford and whoop it up.

Rink showed Henry how to shake and swirl the grit, how to dip it just so that you could send little waves over the sand to wash it out, and how to stop when you got down to the black sand so you could hunt any good-size pellets out of the slurry.

It didn't seem likely Henry might get all those steps in the process but as it turned out he was a pretty good pro-spector, his fondness for repetition and the comforting scratch of the sand against the pan being handy characteristics to have. He'd crouch down at the slurping edge of the Applegate and shake and swirl from noon till dinner, and at the end of the day he'd have half a thimble of mica flakes mixed with black sand. The sound of his pan became to the day as crickets were to the night.

"You get any nuggets you'll have to hide them from the ravens," said Rink.

"Yes," said Henry. "I'll hide them until they're ready."

"Don't fret on that," said Iris. "We got Ajax. He scares away those darn ravens."

The big puppy was lying on his side in the shade and his tail thumped on the dry grass at the sound of his name.

One Sunday everybody'd had enough of chores and schooling and John Rink went upstream with the dog to fish for trout and Emily sat in a newly made rocking chair on the front porch to read *Argosy* while Iris and Henry went down to a spit of sand by the river that was a good place to let a day drift past. Henry brought his pan.

Iris lay on her back in the sun-hot grit with her bare feet near the current. She could feel the coolness along the soles of her feet. The water still had a good flow and shouldered its way around rocks and shimmied over shallow gravel beds and boiled through deep rifts and the sound of the river filled everything up—the earth, the sky, her skin.

Henry hunkered down barefooted with his toes just touching the undulating river's edge, the slivery thin shelf of water that pulsed with currents and surges and made the shallow sand alive with color and movement. Before long the rasp of his pan had found its way inside the chorus of the water and the stir of the cottonwoods and the random notes from the robins.

She was lucky she had sway with Henry. Except for when he was really having a doozy, he pretty much did what Iris asked him to do. Not even Momma held as much sway. When Momma told Henry to come to supper he might come or he might shake his head no no no or he might plop right down on the floor and fake going to sleep. You never knew. But if Iris told him to sit on down for supper he'd come right over. *Why do you think that is?* asked Iris. Momma would say, *Sometimes life asks a question and nobody's got an answer.*

Iris knew you couldn't budge Henry from prospecting

if you stuck a lit stick of dynamite under his butt—
especially if she told him to stay put—and occasionally
she'd take advantage and slip away, maybe a run through
the nearby wood lot and its reaching limbs of pine, dodging
outstretched branches. Or she might walk along the river's
edge, balancing stone to stone along the high granite banks
above white water riffles and clear, mineral-green pools,
chasing trout with her shadow arms.

And on this day, hot to sweating, Iris got up and said,
"Henry, you stay right there and don't go in the water for
nothing."

"All right."

"You happy?

"Yes."

"Good. I'm going to take a short exploration, and I'll
be right back."

"I'm panning for gold."

"Thank you, Henry. You keep that straw hat on."

"Yes."

Iris went off fifty yards or so to where there was a nice
deep pool and she wriggled out of her dress and plunged in,
cleaving into the coolness. As the streaming bubbles cleared
from her eyes she could see the darting shadows of fright-
ened trout and the pebbled carpet of the river bottom. She
rolled over on her back and followed the bubbles up to
where the surface of the river melted into blue sky and
there wasn't a difference between them that could be seen,
just open space that went on forever and a place where the
bubbles wavered and quivered and then disappeared.

She was thirteen and coming on, five-foot-six, sturdy-
boned, brown hair straight and long and streaked by the
sun with flashes of gold. Filling out in places just like
Momma said she would, with actual breasts and hair down
below and hair under her arms and ridges of hips and feet

too big but good for swimming. All these places on her body were promises made and promises kept. In the river the stroke of the water danced on her skin.

She came up, grabbed air, then dove for the bottom. Her fingers rummaged through bits of rock until she found a good piece of serpentine to give to Henry. When she raised up for breath, hair streaming back like an otter, there on the other bank stood one of the McClellan boys.

He was in his overalls and a white undershirt and miner's boots and he carried a fishing pole. He was staring at her with his eyebrows raised and a stupid smile on his face. After a long moment he said, "I seen you naked."

This was the first time anybody outside the family had seen her without clothes, and if anybody was to see her buck naked the last person she'd pick out of the entire world would be Rufus McClellan and his stupid face.

"Okay," said Iris, huddling herself up under the shield of the water's surface, treading with legs and feet. "Now you seen what you can see, so get on."

"I ain't moving," said Rufus slowly, realizing he had her in a fix. "I wanna see your butt, and your front."

"I'm gonna get my daddy down here."

Rufus looked up across the meadow to the house. "Your daddy's upriver. I seen him. You can holler but he ain't gonna hear it from here." He grinned through his big horsy teeth. "Anyways, he ain't your daddy, is he?"

"Get out of here, Rufus! What are you doing down here, anyways?"

"Fishin'. Me and Doren is fishin'. What you own this river?"

Shit on a stick. If there was a stupider boy in Jackson County than Rufus McClellan, it was his brother Doren. The McClellan's were three grades older than she was, and Doren even older than that because he couldn't get past the fifth grade on account of being slow with reading and math. Rufus seeing her was bad enough; Doren would be worse.

"So where's he at?"

"Helpin' your dumb fuck brother pan for gold."

There was no good being shy now. Iris stroked hard for the bank and hauled herself out. Rufus could help himself all he wanted to a view of her backside, but she wasn't about to let Doren McClellan fool with Henry. Rufus gave a low whistle as she shimmered wet into her dress and hopped barefoot over the rocks to the sand spit.

It wasn't good. Doren McClellan, big dumb mule, was crouched down next to Henry while her brother rocked back and forth.

"Get away from him!" Iris shouted.

Doren eased himself full upright, put on an off-kilter grin full of mismatched teeth. His pants were wet to the knees from crossing the river at the riffles.

"We's just doin' some prospecting here, Henry and me. Ain't that right, Henry?"

Henry began to pant.

The older McClellan held up his hand. Between his thumb and forefinger was a small gold nugget. "Lookit what Henry gave me."

"That's his," hissed Iris. "Give it back."

"Why'd I give it back? He gave it to me."

Iris came up and put her hand on Henry's shoulder, stared straight into Doren McClellan's face. "Henry, did you give this fella your gold?"

Henry shook his head, breaths in short gasps.

"See there? He didn't give it to you. So give it back. It's nothin' to you."

Doren McClellan took a step. He held the nugget in his closed fist. "I don't take kindly to Indian givers. You an Indian giver, Henry?"

"Give it back," Iris said, low.

"Or what?"

Rufus appeared on the opposite bank. "I seen her bare butt!" he crowed.

Doren took in his brother. "What?"

"Her bare butt!" yelled the younger boy, hopping up and down with triumph. "I seen it!"

Doren's eyes narrowed and his grin got hard-jawed. "That right?"

"She showed it to me. Naked as a jaybird."

Doren McClellan nodded slow and his eyes went up and down over Iris, top to bottom and back again, every part of her scrutinized. "You showed him…" jerking a thumb at his brother, "…show me."

"I ain't showin' you nothin'."

The older boy knelt down. He put his big mule face close to Henry, who was shaking his head no, no, no. "You don't, and old Henry here might just take a bath."

"Don't touch him."

"Can you swim, Henry? Regular fish, are ya?" He looked at Iris with bright, expectant eyes.

She stopped. Everything became calm and clear. "Just don't touch him," she said in a way that the bargain was struck. She stared at his broad white forehead and put a crosshairs there and thought: breathe, hold, squeeze the trigger. "Put that little nugget down," she pointed to a spot beside her brother.

McClellan hesitated.

"You wanna see or not?"

The large boy licked his lips, knew the girl was giving up and that what he really wanted, what he wanted with every piece of himself, was about to happen. He let the little piece of gold rattle onto the rock.

"Get away from him. You're scaring him."

He stood up, transfixed.

"I do this, and you and your brother get gone outa here."

"You better do it. Or Henry here is going for a swim."

"Swear you'll get off our property. If you wanna see."

He looked across the river to where Rufus stood, unable to hear the gist of the conversation for the sound of the river. Doren McClellan had this moment to himself. His brother would have to watch from across the way, watch the amazing event that he was about to command. "All right. I swear."

Iris grabbed her shirt bottom and flipped it over her head and stood naked to the waist, her slim body pale and bright in the day. The air warm against her river-cooled skin. She did not take her eyes off Doren McClellan. She did not know what the older boy felt, whether he was about to do something wicked, but she was fully calm. Exposing herself was only a thumbing back of the hammer. Next was she'd grab a chunk of granite and bash his head. There was a round rock three feet away that would fit her hand. Grab it but don't throw it; hold onto it. Keep hittin' at him. Go for that big horsey head.

McClellan stared at the nakedness in front of him. The ripening breasts and their tips of pink. He took a step forward.

"Lordy lordy!" cried Rufus from across the river.

"My daddy is comin'," said Iris quietly.

Doren McClellan looked up to the tree line that separated the house from where they stood near the green, rushing river. Looked up river where he'd last seen John Rink. Looked at Iris. Then he was at her, his coarse hands rasping across her small breasts. She'd missed the chance to grab the rock. She didn't flinch, wouldn't let him know that she felt anything at all. His face loomed above her, breath like carrots. A big dumb horse that's just been eating a treat. His hands were clumsy crabs scrabbling after something they couldn't quite grasp. Dumb, stupid hands. Hands easily hated.

Rufus shrieked, "Wait, oh God! Wait for me!" He flung down his gear and almost leapt right into where the river ran deep, but caught himself and scampered toward the upstream riffles and as he stepped across he slipped and went down with a splash.

She looked into Doren McClellan's face, his self-absorption, lips slightly parted. "My daddy's gonna kill you when he finds out," she whispered.

The glassy-eyed trance flickered. His hands stopped. He began to massage again then stopped once more, frowned.

"He'll kill you," she said again, softly.

He took his hands away, slowly, narrowed his eyes. "Well, you're a whore. A titless little whore. If you tell your daddy then I'll tell everyone you took off your clothes for me. I'll say you wanted me to touch you. Whore."

"I'll tell my daddy all right. And then he'll kill you and your stink-ass brother too." She thought about getting her blouse back on but decided against it, wouldn't give him the satisfaction of diving for cover. Stood there defiant in her nakedness, unafraid.

Doren McClellan worked his jaw. Then he turned and reached down and plucked the gold nugget from the rock and held it up. "I'm keepin' this." He turned and Iris knew in the way sometimes you know things before they really happen that Doren McClellan was about to touch Henry on his head.

"Don't…" she began, but too late. As McClellan passed the boy he reached out and swatted Henry's brown mop of hair and all the built-up tension busted out of Henry and he began screeching and swatting at his face like he was being attacked by hornets.

"Henry," said Iris, softly.

McClellan snarled, "Stop that noise, you freak." Which sent Henry into a fresh frenzy.

"Shut up!" yelled the big boy, and he picked Henry up and held the squirming, thrashing mass out at arm's length, as if he'd picked up a live bobcat. The McClellan boy took a step and heaved Henry into the river.

"He can't swim!" screamed Iris.

Doren McClellan stalked off.

Henry was already sinking, only his hands visible as they churned the water. Iris sprinted over the rocks and dove straight into the pool. She came up underneath her brother and grabbed him around the chest and her momentum took them both back to the surface, Henry choking and flailing about.

"I got you. I got you."

Henry might not have been strong for his age, but in the grip of panic he was a human cyclone. Iris struggled for the bank with her free hand, frog stroking with her legs, fighting her squirming brother and the current that had swirled them out of the pool. Her fingers found rock but they were swept past. She could hear Henry gagging with the water going into his mouth, down his throat. His flailing elbows struck the side of her head. She stretched for all she was worth and grabbed an exposed root that held firm and her feet gained the rock bottom and she pulled them both toward the bank and she held her brother against the flow and the ghosted rasp of Doren McClellan's fingers against her body made her strong with cold fury and she dragged Henry, sputtering and coughing, out of the river.

Henry shook and hacked clear his lungs and began to cry.

"It's all right," she panted. "I got you. You're safe."

"Iris…"

"It's okay." Iris looked around for a weapon. There was a good-size stick a few feet away. She scrambled over and got the branch and came back and sat next to Henry and put her arms around him and held him, his salty face hot on her shoulder, the rest of him trembling. Thank Jesus the sun was out, they'd soon be warm. She was listening hard, trying to decide if the McClellan boys were coming after them and after a long while she decided they'd ske-daddled for home. She stood up with her club in hand and scanned for their tormentors but they had left.

"I don't like the river," said Henry.

"I don't like it much either today, that's for sure."

They were quiet for a spell, then Iris said, "It ain't the river's fault. It's the fault of them dumb-ass McClellans."

Henry said, "He took my gold."

She nodded. "You'll get more."

He lifted his head, began to blink; he was on the verge.

"You're the best gold panner ever."

"I have gold."

"And you'll get more.

Henry stared straight ahead, breathing in bursts.

"It's all right, Henry."

His breathing slowed. He lowered his head.

"It's all right now. I'm here." She put a hand on his shoulder. "I'm not looking at you."

He gathered himself, stood.

"All right, follow me."

She began to walk through the deer grass and golden-rod and scrub willow along the river bank. The club-like branch in her right hand and Henry's hand in her left.

He followed her, fascinated by the flash and shadow of his sister's bare back.

They came to the spot. It had been their spot. Now it was tainted. She got her blouse on and picked up Henry's gold pan and handed it to him. "From now on, we'll bring old Ajax," she said. "He won't let anything happen to us ever."

Henry sighed.

"But we're okay now. So let's sit."

They sat on rocks in the sun until their clothes were dry, then Iris said, "Come with me."

She walked up the path that led through the wide meadow through a stand of big alders and beyond to the house. "Don't tell Momma or John about today, all right? About what happened. It's just gonna be between you and me. Our secret. Can you keep that secret, Henry? For me? For Iris?"

"All right."

"Good."

"Iris?"

"Yeah?"

"Thank you."

"I know."

"Thank you, Iris."

"You're my brother. We look out for each other."

"Yes."

"Yes indeed."

✥

One Sunday that fall Iris wandered over to John Rink's smithy shed and took up an old ax handle. It was a broken one, split along half its length, and Rink had intended to mend it but never did and so stuck it in a corner where it gathered dust and spider webs. Iris cleaned it off and bound up the split with hide glue and twine, tight as she could muster, then took the handle out to the road and covered it with dirt and needles. The next day when Mr. Cale came to pick her up for school she grabbed up the handle from its hiding place and climbed up onto the truck bed.

"What's that?" one of the Cale kids wanted to know.

"In case we break a baseball bat I thought we could use this," Iris explained.

"That's dumb," said the Cale boy. "It don't even look like a bat."

"It does," Iris insisted. "We use it for playing baseball sometimes at home and it works just fine."

When they got to the school Iris went off to the privy and hid the ax handle behind the shed. That morning she was fidgety and distracted and when Mrs. Dunham called on her for math she didn't even know what page everyone was on and they laughed at her. She looked over to where the two McClellan boys were sitting in their red flannel shirts and they weren't even paying attention to her being a fool in front of the whole class. Good.

At recess Iris went off to the back of the privy and took up the ax handle. The certainty of what she was going to do took away any fear, any second thoughts. The air rang clear.

She walked back to her schoolmates, sorted into their chattering play groups, the ax handle held behind her with her right hand. She made like she was wandering aimlessly, looking for things in the grass, as she moved ever-closer to where Doren McClellan and his boys sat in their usual spot underneath a big oak, holding themselves apart from the squeals and games played by the younger children. Slowly, she made her way up behind the older McClellan.

Rufus McClellan, who had a clear view of her approach, stood and squinted at Iris. He looked perplexed. "What're you lookin' for?" Rufus called out.

Doren McClellan caught his brother's puzzlement and turned slowly and as he did Iris raised the ax handle and charged across the last fifteen feet and brought the weapon down hard as she could.

Henry was asleep. In the night the river ran soft with autumn flow. Emily sat on the end of Iris' bed, her hand on her daughter's knee. Looked off into the dark.

They'd taken the McClellan boy to Doctor Finister's house in Jacksonville where eighteen stiches sewed up a gash running from above his ear almost to his neck. He had managed to lean away from the blow just enough that he didn't get the top of his skull cracked open. Too bad, thought Iris when she heard the report. After all that good planning. She hoped getting those stitches hurt like crazy.

Iris was suspended from the Jackson County school district indefinitely, which to Iris wasn't much of a punishment on account of she didn't care that much for school anyway. She could tell her Momma wasn't entirely displeased, either, because now there was someone to help her do chores and watch Henry. Maybe she could go hunting more often with John Rink. Thank Jesus for that. The district attorney put the matter down as a schoolyard scrap and didn't see the need to prosecute, especially in light of a girl beating up on a much bigger, older boy.

"You gonna tell me why you hit that boy?" said Emily.

Iris debated. The thing that Doren McClellan had done, those awful crabbing hands, and what he had done to Henry. She didn't want to say. She wanted to hold onto her anger, let it fester. She wasn't sure why. But she wanted her anger to get hot and blistered inside. Let it hurt. She wanted the pain; didn't want to let it go. Didn't want her Momma to soothe her. Not yet. Maybe not ever.

"I told you, he was a mean son of a bitch."

"Did he go around hittin' folks over the head with an ax handle?"

"I've seen him hit kids at school when the teacher wasn't looking."

"Like who? Who'd he hit?"

"Some kids. The Whirly kids." That was a lie. The Whirly kids were from one of the swankiest homes in Jacksonville and Iris knew her momma wouldn't be likely to check that one out.

"He ever do anything to you?"

Iris hesitated. She felt the scaly hands on her breasts; smelled the horsey breath. "He's just one of the meanest boys I know. One of the meanest I've ever known. He called Henry names."

"What kind of names?"

"I'd rather not say."

"You can't tell your Momma?"

"It was mean things."

Emily sighed. "There's no shortage of meanness in this world, that's for sure. But you can't return meanness for meanness."

"Why not?"

"'Cause then you're no better than that McClellan boy."

"I don't want to be better than Doren McClellan. I want to be worse. I want him to know what bein' mean and hurtful is all about."

"Good Lord, Iris, you coulda killed him."

"I was tryin'."

"You don't mean that."

Iris folded her arms, said nothing.

Emily folded her arms, too. "I didn't raise my offspring to be un-Christian."

"Eye for an eye."

"You would remember that one particular scripture." She sighed. "Revenge is mine, sayeth the Lord."

"The Lord's gotta make up His mind one way or the other."

Emily sighed. "Daughter, daughter, we all gotta figure out which way we tilt. We surely do. The good or the bad."

"Well, I'm workin' on that."

Chapter Ten
October, 1922

THAT AUTUMN JOHN RINK ORDERED one-hundred and sixty Bosc and one-hundred and seventy-eight Comice pear saplings from a supplier up near Portland, and when the train rolled into Medford he'd been at the station two hours already with a cold pipe stuck in his mouth, leaned up against the nose of the flatbed. He helped the dock men unload, the men handing down the whips, their skinny root balls wrapped in coarse brown burlap, and Rink setting eight in a wheelbarrow and carting them out to the truck and hefting them up onto the bed. He could only load four dozen at a time on the flatbed so they set out the rest of the trees alongside the stationhouse. It was full sun and Rink wasn't all that happy with the condition of the trees to begin with, some had dried out and the wrappings were loose and bunched, so he borrowed a bucket from the stationmaster and had Iris wet down the root balls with water from a hand pump behind the station. Then he drove the first load of trees out to the farm.

The work unfolded, it's rhythm of squeaking pump and sloshing bucket and the spread of wet across the rough-hewn cloth under the breezeless sun. She immersed herself in the cadence, the going and coming, squeak of pump, the haze-softened rooftops of town in the near distance, her own shadow just underfoot. She liked the work, the purpose, blouse sweat-stuck to her back. By Rink's fourth run Iris had soaked all the trees so he brought her home as the last hot gob of sun melted down into the horizon. He made one last run by himself, and when he finally walked into the house at midnight the family was waiting for him.

"Well I guess we're all in now," said Emily.

Rink jerked a thumb over his shoulder. "I got two Mexicans in the truck."

"What do you mean, Mexicans?"

"I mean Mexicans. From Mexico. Migrant workers."

"What are they doing here?"

"For the planting. Got 'em from that big pear outfit in Medford. Talked to the foreman. Their work is slow right now, so I got these two Mex fellas for a few days. Help me dig holes."

"I can dig holes," said Henry.

"There's plenty of holes to dig. I want to get all the trees in by next week."

"Are they…?"

"They're fine. They're harmless little cusses. You could beat 'em down with a feather pillow. They'll sleep in the barn. We'll need to get 'em grub, though."

"Well, they eat what we eat. I don't know how to fix Mex food."

"Throw some of your red chili pepper on it. That's all it takes." He winked at Iris. "Anyway, I'll need some blankets and a canteen."

Iris followed Rink and his lantern out into the night where the Packard sat cooling and ticking. He gave her the blankets to carry. She held them tight to her chest and the folds of wool were itchy under her chin. The two migrants sat hunched on the bed with their backs against the last remaining whips. Rink motioned for them to get out, and they climbed down slowly, unsure and shy.

"Sleep in the barn," said Rink, and he set his head sideways on his upturned palm, pantomiming sleeping. He pointed at the shadow of the barn. "We'll unload in the morning."

The two men exchanged glances, then nodded. "Si."

Iris had never really seen Mexicans up close, although she'd seen them in the fields and driving the wagons and sometimes nearby on the streets in town. They were small men, not that much taller than her, with dark eyes and hair and dark everything. They seemed ill-fitted to the rigors of digging holes. One with a thin, wispy moustache. The other with thick glossy hair cut in a bowl shape. Skin so coppery they glowed even in the night. They walked to the barn, Rink's light a swinging orb on the ground around them. He showed them pallets of straw and gave them the canteen and Iris handed them each a blanket.

"Gracias," they said several times, with small bows.

Impulsively, Iris stepped forward and stuck out her hand. "Iris," she said. "Howdy."

Again the migrants exchanged looks. The one with the moustache looked at Rink, who stood by impassively. The Mexican carefully took Iris' hand and bowed.

She pointed to herself. "Iris," she emphasized.

"Eduardo," he said, pointing to himself. Then to his partner. "Ernesto."

"Ernesto and Eduardo." She shook her head. "That's a set-up for a mix-up, if ever."

"John Rink's my daddy." She pointed at her stepfather.

"Si. Senor Rink."

The next morning Ernesto and Eduardo were sitting in the grass in a patch of sunlight outside the barn when Iris came down with plates of fried potatoes and eggs. The migrants ate carefully, as if the next bite might reveal something foreign and perhaps unpleasant. Iris sat on a round of fir that had always occupied a spot by the barn door. She figured she'd have to retrieve the plates anyway, so why not just wait? She sat by the doorway and watched the men fork food into their mouths as they squatted on the dirt in the sun. They watched her also.

Iris stood and put her hand on one of the beams that framed the doorway and with her other hand she waved in the general direction of the structure's insides. "Barn."

Ernesto and Eduardo stopped eating, forks poised halfway to their mouths.

"Barn," she repeated, with more emphasis, slapping at the doorframe, pointing around.

Eduardo nodded. Looked up. "Si. Barn. Granero."

"Granero?" She tried the word. It seemed to come out right.

"Si." Ernesto pointed to the ceiling with his fork. "Granero."

"Granero. Like where you keep the grain."

The men nodded and smiled and resumed eating.

Iris brought the dishes back up to the house, then she and John Rink and Henry got into work duds and went down to the barn and hitched Parker to the wagon and loaded up trees and shovels. Rink took off the back gate of the truck so Henry could sit on the bed with the trees and let his legs dangle. They headed off for the meadow with Eduardo and Ernesto walking a few paces behind. Henry pointed at the pair and said, "Tree men."

Rink had set out the orchard, driving cedar stakes every twenty feet along lines he'd dead reckoned and that came out unerringly straight and true. As they set out the first batch of trees Iris took one of the saplings round its slender trunk and pointed to it and said, "Pear tree," to Ernesto, who nodded and said, *perro tre,* rolling the R's.

Iris shook the whip sapling. "Pear tree. What's the Mex

for pear tree?" Looking at Ernesto.

Eduardo, who was standing nearby, said, "Peral."

"Peral?"

Ernesto frowned at Eduardo. "Ella estaba hablando a mí."

Eduardo shrugged. "Luego responder a ella, maniquí." Then he turned to Iris and said, "Peral. Si."

They set out canvas tarps alongside and threw the dirt on top of the canvas and when a three-foot-by-three-foot hole was dug they cut the burlap off a sapling and set in the hole and back filled with the loose dirt and a few shovelfuls of chicken manure that Rink had been stashing in a pile at the edge of the meadow. Leftover dirt was hauled out to the river and dumped in a pile that Rink planned to shape into a dike to help keep floodwaters from reaching the orchard. They'd return dragging the canvas and carrying buckets of water for the trees just planted.

Rink assigned Iris and Henry their own holes and Iris began to cut into the heavy clay, pounding the blade in with the heel of her boot, while Henry sat nearby and held his shovel by the handle and swung the blade back and forth, scratching an arc into the ground in front of him. Iris was amazed at how quickly the wiry Eduardo and Ernesto carved the ground, sprays of tan dirt thumped onto the canvas with a steady rhythm. Each had several holes dug before Iris had finished her first.

By evening they'd put thirty-five trees in the ground, sixteen Comice and the rest Boscs. Rink planned to alternate varieties, row by row, so they could cross-pollinate easily. John Rink said they'd just planted juicy gold. He and Eduardo and Ernesto were out until the very last light, working on the irrigation system and cleaning out channels.

The Mexicans stayed on another six days and on the evening of the last day they worked until after dark by the light of lanterns. In the morning Iris told them to come up to the house and they all ate sausage and flapjacks with jam while sitting on the porch steps and nobody said much and it felt like the Mexicans had been on the farm forever. John Rink paid them and they climbed up on the bed of the Packard and John Rink drove them back down to the migrant village outside of Medford. As Eduardo and Ernesto rode away on the bed of the truck they waved to Emily and Iris and Henry.

The next day Emily and Iris and Henry and John Rink stood at the edge of the meadow and looked at the new orchard and the rows of spindly whips with their juvenile canopies and the brown earth upturned and the smell of it strong and wet and the river beyond.

"It's good," said Rink.

Two weeks later Emily took the Packard into town saying she needed to do a few errands. When she returned she had Iris come out to the truck to help unload. On the bed of the truck were four pear boxes filled with books that all had the same dark green color.

"It's the *Encyclopedia Britannica,*" Emily announced. "The entire set, eleventh edition, except it's missing Volume Ten and Eleven. I'm thinking there's not too much to be had in those categories. Anyway, I got it all for a bargain."

Iris wrinkled her nose. "What are we gonna do with all these, Momma? Why'd you buy them?"

"Well, learning of course. We're going to read 'em."

"All of them?"

"We're gonna try. Help me heft them into the house."

That night they had a fire in the fireplace and John

Rink and Iris sat on the floor and Henry sat on a pillow off by himself but within earshot. Emily got with her back to the flames so she could get the light. She opened the first book at random and began to read out loud:

Anaconda. An anaconda is an immense snake native to the steamy jungles of South America. By weight it is the largest snake in the world, often exceeding 500 pounds with a girth more than 12 inches in diameter. It's got an italic here that says, *You-neck-tees mure-eye-nus.*

"That's the real name. The science name," put in Rink. "The scientists, they gave every living thing a different name."

"Why's that?" asked Iris.

"Something to do with not wanting to call two different things by the same name," said Rink. "Like, you could say horse and mean either a pinto or an appaloosa. It's a fancy way of saying pinto."

"Good Lord!" said Emily. "It says here this snake can kill a cow and eat the whole thing all at once. And they've been known to kill a man!"

Over on his pillow Henry giggled.

"Read more, Emily," said John Rink.

So she did.

Chapter Eleven
October, 1924

THE PEARS WERE YEARS from coming in so John Rink took on some blacksmithing for people out in the country but it didn't add up to much. Then a fellow down at one of the mills in Medford let Rink know of a job, and Rink got a part-timer ripping fir and pine logs into lumber, everything from twelve-by-twenty beams to one-by skip sheathing. He put in three days a week and it kept the wolf from the door and there was time left over for keeping up the farm and doing a little hunting.

One day down at the mill they were making the first flat cut on a big Ponderosa, shearing off the outside slab, when part of the fall-off cracked and caught on the big blade and a six-foot-long, twenty-inch-wide splinter went shooting out, catching Rink in the right shoulder and nearly taking off his arm. The force of the blow flung him backwards six feet into one of the iron posts that supported the mill roof, cracking his skull. Being tough, John Rink lasted four days before he died. He never woke up. The undertaker made him look peaceful and gave him a nice clean shirt and vest and folded the short, hard-working hands over his chest so you could see the plain steel ring that was his wedding vow.

Late that month, Iris moving toward a hump of a ridge that saddled over to Old Baldy Mountain. Along the saddle was a wheatgrass meadow and a stand of gnarly oak trees where a buck was likely to come and set up a scrape. They'd taken two eight-pointers there the last two seasons. Her and John Rink.

She followed the narrow deer path up through twisty manzanita and pine almost to where the firs took over, then back down the other side until the land flattened and the meadow rang out in a wide swath of open gone yellow and brittle with fall. The snows would come any day now. When they did, the tracking would be easy.

She made for the northeast side where there was a shadowed background to help keep her hidden but there would be patches of sunlight in which to set and keep her warm. There was an old blowdown half melted into the duff where they'd been before and she knew it and sat on her haunches behind it and put the Winchester alongside. She had an old Army canteen and she took a drink of spring water and then breathed in October's sharp scents, the hard-baked forest and the tang of sun-warmed granite and the cool blue undersides of clouds. She set the sights for fifty yards and the edge of the meadow. And waited. She was good at that.

The sun had just touched the far ridges when the buck stepped out of the unsure light along the edge of the meadow. Broad chest and thick neck and eight-point rack. Maybe ten. Legs skinny under the big body. He was headed to set up a scrape under one of the oaks, making halting progress, wary, stopping every few feet to survey the meadow with its edges of shadow.

He knows I'm here, thought Iris. He just doesn't know where, or why.

She slid the rifle up slow and steady, upper body rock

still, lined up the bead. Fifty yards. She exhaled low and as the air left her lungs so did whatever demon it was that chased her up here in the first place, chased her with the need to escape, climb the ridges till the sweat ran down her spine, smell the dirt, hear the wind sweep through the pines. The big buck coming out of the forest was a thing dreamed more than real. The animal moved under the tree and began to rub its antlers on the lowest branches, raising its head in the ecstasy of its ritual.

Breathe. Hold. Squeeze.

It was big. Ten-pointer all right. Maybe a hundred fifty pounds. Too big to pack out; she'd have to cut off the haunches and the shoulders and hope the rest would be there the next day, not eaten in the night by some cougar or bear. She wondered if John Rink would have walked out with the whole animal slung over his shoulders. He woulda tried, that's for sure. She got out Rink's old skinning knife and gutted the animal and rolled the viscera into a loose ball and pushed every-thing under a pine and covered it with needles. The haunches took awhile, sawing through the hip joints, then through the knees to get rid of the forelegs, then she carved out the shoulders, right in front of where the bullet had gone through.

When she was done she had a good sixty pounds of meat. She took the carcass and dragged it fifty yards from the guts, wiped her hands on the hide. Then she cut some poles and rigged a small travois with the rawhide twine she carried and set the meat on it. Cradling the Winchester in the crook of her right arm, she dragged the venison through the forest. Going up the lip of the saddle was hard and it took time to get around some of the brushier patches but on the downside of the ridge the going was easy. In-sects hummed in the last light, curious at the scent of blood in the evening air. The full moon came up just as the sun slipped away and the pale light brought her home.

⬥

Emily awoke at first light feeling Iris hadn't come home from hunting. In the blush of dawn she walked out and down the front stairs and around the house to find Iris sitting on the steps to the sleeping porch. Six in the morning, and the red was just beginning to cap the far ridges. Iris held the Winchester in arms streaked with dried blood.

"I'm gonna get you some water and a cloth," said Emily. She brought back a white ironstone bowl filled with water and a square of cotton cloth and began to wash Iris' arms.

"What'd you get?"

"Ten pointer," said Iris. "A hundred and fifty pounds, I'd say."

"Well, you did good." said Emily.

"I couldn't bring it all. Had to leave about half. It was too heavy."

"Sure."

"He would have brought it all back."

"He would have tried."

"I put the haunches in the root cellar. Guess we'll have some steaks tomorrow and maybe do some jerking. I'll have to go back up and get the rest, though."

"Did you just get home?"

Iris shrugged. "Been out here a while. Just sittin' here."

The sun struck through the crowns of the nearby trees. In half an hour they'd be in full light.

"The jerking can wait. You should get some sleep. Later on I need you to watch over Henry," said Emily. "I'm goin' to old Miss Jean's today. And I can't miss it."

"Really Momma? Miss Jean? That woman's ideas ain't

worth a lick of salt. She doesn't know the future more than you or me."

"That's not true, Iris. She knew the month that the war was supposed to end, and that Elena Pardwick would have triplets. She also said President Harding would die in office. She didn't say that publically out loud, but she said it to me. If she'd said it to everybody, they would have thought she was a traitor. Or a spy."

"She didn't know about John Rink."

Emily drew in a breath—the face of her first husband, Dexter Greenlee, flashed in her daughter's velvety brown eyes. She gathered herself. "You may be right, Iris. She doesn't know everything. Nobody does. But it makes me feel good to go, to walk away from myself a bit. Besides, she's not all gloom and doom. She mostly tells me everything is going to work out all right. I need to hear that sometimes. It's kinda like going to church and hearing a few kind words."

"That'd be a crazy kind of church."

"Maybe it's a good crazy."

"Can somebody be plumb crazy and good too?"

"Of course. Just look at you."

Iris rested her head on her mother's shoulder. "I'm sorry we lost John Rink. I loved him for real."

"I know you did. He loved you, too."

They stayed that way, head upon head upon shoulder, letting the edge of sunlight creep down the side of the porch until the daylight rang in their eyes.

"Are we going to be all right, Momma?"

"That's a question nobody knows the answer. But to tell the truth, I've been thinking about selling the farm."

Iris frowned. "What do you mean, *sell the farm?*"

"I'm not sure. Get us a little place in town again. Like where you were born."

"And what about the chickens? And Parker? What about the pears? They're gonna come in next year, I know it."

"I know you love it here. I love it here too, mostly. But there's more to than that. We sell this farm we could buy a little place and have some money left over. It's a lot of work here, you know that, and it's not gettin' easier with Henry."

"We watch over him good. He's okay. He does fine."

"Iris, there's some folks in town that can help Henry with talking and maybe some schooling. I could find some work. Maybe you could find a job, too. We'd be a sight better off."

Iris was suddenly too tired to talk. It was all crazy talk. Move from the river, from the farm. "We got fish here, too," Iris said, but it was mumbles.

"Get some sleep. I'm going to town later on, so there's time for you to rest up so you can watch your brother."

Chapter Twelve
February, 1926

IN THE LATE WINTER OF 1926 it rained off and on for two weeks, then for three days without pause. The sky was dead gray clouds and every piece of open air was filled with deluge and the rains came and came and the dirt around the house was filigreed with coffee-colored runoff and the rivers churned brown and dirty white.

In the middle of the third night of ceaseless rain Iris awoke. Beyond the sound of the water hammering the roof and the ground and the boughs of the trees was a heavy, relentless presence.

She threw off her blanket and sat up and listened. She heard Henry, huddled under blankets, breath thick with sleep. And something else. She went to the edge of the porch and looked out past the curtain of rainwater that dripped from the eaves.

Down at the bottom slope of the land, barely visible in the gloom, a phantom writhed along the ground. Flashes in the dark. A trembling. The river had flooded its banks. The sound of angry surging water came clear and she could make out the crack and whump of wood—deadfall and whole trees torn from their banks sent crashing against rocks and other trees.

She fumbled for her coat and boots and then a light went on inside and her mother appeared with a kerosene lamp, robe held tight in front.

"Momma!" said Iris. "The river's flooding!"

"I hear it."

"The pears!"

"Iris." Her voice above the hammering rain and boiling current. Henry stirred. "We can't do anything about it. Just can't."

"We could build a dam. Shut off the ditches."

Emily's hand carved through lantern light. "I seen floods before. Nothing you can do. Can't stop it. Those trees are either gonna make it or they're not. God's will. Our concern has got to be the livestock."

Henry sat up. "Is it breakfast?"

"No, Henry. It's still night."

"What's that?"

"The river's gotten up over it's banks, but we're fine. That flood can't reach us up here. Iris, go get the dog and the horse out of the barn, just in case. See how far the river is from the coop, but don't get too near. We'll keep a close eye on it."

"I'm hungry," said Henry.

"Go back to sleep, Henry. We'll have our breakfast in a while." To Iris she said, "Go now." She handed Iris the lamp. "I'll light another."

Iris put on the slicker and hurricane hat and the lamp and set out toward the barn with the hard rain coming in slanted and the river churning at the edge of what she could see in the darkness. The night was a booming, roaring calamity. The air was vibrating. As she got closer to the barn she could hear the dog barking, probably had been at it a while but nobody could make him out. She couldn't see any trees. Rain wept down. Darkness above, darkness all around.

She wheeled open the sliding door and loosed the yipping hound from his kennel and he bolted right out toward the flood to challenge whatever invader was making all the racket. She yelled *Ajax!* and three beats later the Chesapeake came bounding back. Thank God for a smart dog. She got the nervous Percheron out of his stall and led him up away from the river and tied him to a post in Rink's old smithy shop where he was out of the worst of it. Then she went back to judge the distance from the chickens to the flood. Hard to say. The swaying light of the lantern made darting, coppery stripes on the river. Maybe seventy-five yards. She'd come back down in an hour and check it again. Then she led the Chesapeake up to the house and inside, out of the weather.

Seven a.m. Henry lay on the floor, asleep and swaddled in a plaid wool blanket, spine-to-spine with the dog. The skies were thick gray and they could make out the barn and the privy and the hurrying gray-and-foam colored flood beyond, spread out in unnatural places. Iris put on her boots and John Rink's old duster and her wide-brimmed hat and went out into a rain that had slacked to a drizzle.

She took the road that led along the back edge of the meadow, boots sucking in the bronze clay mud, and when she got down to the orchard everything inside her went sour. The meadow was drowning in hurrying, gray-brown water. Only a few forlorn pear trees remained upright. The dike that Rink had started had failed to hold the torrent. The irrigation holding tank was gone, as was the wagon they'd used to haul trees and manure. The orchard was all but destroyed.

It took three days for the river to return to its banks. The south bridge over the river had been knocked off its piers but the stout covered bridge at McKee survived, so it was possible for folks upriver to head into Jacksonville if they were willing to take the perilous East Side Road, a winding rock-strewn trail that edged along the steepest embankment on the entire river and was barely wide enough for a car.

Downriver the Purtles had lost a big chicken coop and thirty-seven hens; the Ryans their hay barn and a good dog swept away. Gardens and sheds and not a few privies and their contents had been carried off toward the ocean. Rumor was three whole houses had been washed away down towards Grants Pass, but nobody had died. People had said it didn't make sense to put anything worthwhile smack on the banks of the river and they'd been right.

When the water finally receded Iris and Emily and Henry went to the edge of the meadow. Henry sat on a blanket while Iris and Emily walked out into the field in their knee-high rubber boots. In places they sank a foot or more into mud, boots threatening to come off in the hungry ooze. The grasses and mustard were flattened and gray and pointed downstream, lacquered in place by the scouring waters and their load of silt. Here and there a mud-banked pear tree lay on its side, roots sticking up like a skeletal hand clawing at the air. Some leaned out at crazy angles. Only a half dozen or so remained upright. Strewn throughout were branches and broken boards and a man's undershirt and a whole glass bottle of vinegar and a sizeable piece of picket fence and a dead cat from somebody's place upriver.

They brought Parker down and the big horse was not happy to stand almost hock-deep in the sludge as they roped his harness to a tilting tree, nor was he convinced that a carrot and apple were good enough enticements for him to slog through the mire, although after much pleading and a bit of tasting he grudgingly plodded ahead and righted the leaned-over trees. They brought up thirteen trees that way, and when they were done the horse and the two women were covered with dark ooze and the orchard consisted of just nineteen trees with a chance of bearing fruit. The rest had been torn out and ravaged, or had been swept away entirely.

"Hardly enough for a pie," said Emily, wiping her already dirty forehead with a filthy wrist. "And a jar of jam."

They trudged back to the house around sundown. Iris took Parker to the barn and set him up with a bucket of grain while she brushed the mud off his wide gray chest and withers and the big stripe of cream that ran between.

Emily took Henry inside and started the wood stove. She opened the damper and meant to light the kindling but instead simply sat on the floor and stared. After a few minutes Henry went over and sat back-to-back with her and busied himself twisting the tips of his socks with his fingers. At last he said, "You are dirty oh boy."

She nodded. "I'm going to heat up some water and give myself a proper washing."

"I saw trees," he said."

"Yes."

"I'm hungry."

Emily nodded. "Well, that makes more sense than anything yet today."

Chapter Thirteen
April, 1927

EARLY SPRING. WILLOWS HANGING full green down by the river and fat-headed crocuses stuck out of the silt left by last year's flood. Up at the house Ajax had found himself a piece of sunlit porch floor and was dead to the world, snoring softly.

Emily sat at the eating table, hands folded in front of her. She'd said her peace already. *They ain't gonna hire you, Iris.* She knew that as fact. But her daughter was that head-strong age and sometimes you had to loosen the reins and give a horse her head, even if she runs into a tree.

On the sleeping porch Iris couldn't decide between the cotton church dress she rarely wore and her overalls. The one seemed too frilly but it was what girls wore, and the overalls were rough and patchy but they made her look like somebody who could handle herself in tough situations. At the last minute she took off the overalls and put on the dress thinking, *It's clean, let's get on with it.*

Iris drove the Packard into Jacksonville, the quarter panel Rink had secured with baling wire chattering like an angry squirrel. She parked on California Street and walked the last two blocks to the courthouse. It was grand, for certain. Broad-shouldered, big arched windows, white cupola against a pure blue sky. Her Sunday shoes landed flat and loud on the granite treads. Inside was a big hallway, the floor checker-boarded with squares of green and white stone, twin spiraling staircases of polished wood. It smelled oiled and clean and important.

Under each rising stairway was a desk. One desk was unoccupied. Behind the other was a young attendant. He had black hair and wore a white shirt with a black tie that disappeared into a dark green vest. On the wall beside him was a display case that held a stuffed bobcat and a red-tailed hawk and an assortment of rattlesnake rattles, some big as a pine cone. Across the way was a moveable bulletin board with wanted posters tacked to it.

"Can I help you?"

"I'm here about a job with the department of catching poachers." The words sounded small in the big hall.

The young man shook his head. "I'm sorry. Are you looking for the Oregon Department of Game and Fish?"

"That's it."

"The ODGF office is in Salem. And I don't believe there are any state jobs available here in southern Oregon. We're not a big staff and I'd know if we were hiring."

"Well, you're in charge of this county, aren't you?"

"We are the governmental and judicial bodies for Jackson County, that's correct."

"Then you got to have some kind of laws about game and fish, isn't that right?"

He squinted. "There are state laws governing game limits and fishing regulations, yes."

"Well then?"

"Well, what?"

"Well it sounds to me like you need a game warden. That's what it sounds like."

He scratched his ear. "I'm not sure…"

Iris held up a hand. "Who can I talk to around here?"

"Well," said the young man, drawing himself up, "I am the official attendant here. You can talk to me."

Iris looked over his vest and tie. "I don't think you're deaf. Are you deaf?"

"No. I am not deaf."

"Well?" Raising just one eyebrow. "Who can I talk to?"

"Look, maybe you should talk with the sheriff. Sheriff Kuntz. He's the law for Jackson County and he'll probably know about things like this."

"Where's he?"

"He's next door. At the jail house." The young man stood, paused. "Aren't you rather young for that kind of work anyway?"

"I'm old enough."

He shrugged. "I'll take you over there. He'll set you straight."

They followed the brick course between the buildings. The jail was a plain rectangular two-story with stucco sides and a clay tile roof. Behind was a board fence over which Iris could make out the top framing for the gallows.

He asked, "Where do you live?"

"Out on the Applegate."

"How come I don't know you?"

Iris shrugged. "I been around." Then she added, "I left school when I was twelve, and I just never went back."

He nodded.

"My Momma schooled me."

"Who's your father?"

"He passed. A while ago."

They went up three concrete steps to the front of the county jail. A thick oak door hung in the entry and the young man pulled it open and Iris walked inside. It was dim and then she could make out a plain desk to one side and a heavy door that led to a corridor. Through the narrow window she could see a row of cells and doors with iron bars.

"Wait here."

The young man went through a smaller door to their left. She was alone in the office. There was a telephone on the desk, a glass ashtray filled with cigar butts, and a few papers. A heavy locked cabinet that probably held firearms. Kerosene lamps, no electric ones yet. On one of the walls was a framed portrait of some famous stuffed shirt and then she realized it was a President of the United States, most likely the current one. What's his name? Hoover. Other than that there wasn't much to look at.

After many minutes the attendant reappeared with a tall man with an enormous drooping moustache, hair parted in the middle, and behind his suit vest a little round belly was peering over his belt.

"Sheriff Kuntz, this is the girl."

Sheriff Kuntz frowned, an unlit pipe secured between thin lips.

"I got to get back." The young man made for the doorway and was gone, the big door closing with a curl of warm air. Iris faced the sheriff in the dim interior of the county jail office.

He took his pipe from his mouth and pointed the stem at her. "Just what is it you wanted to talk to me about?"

Iris gathered herself, said, "I want to apply for the job of game warden for Jackson County."

The sheriff nodded ever so slightly. "That so?" He returned the pipe to his mouth and breathed in so the pipe gave a wheeze.

"Yessir."

"You got qualifications?"

"I lived around these parts all my life. I can ride. I can hunt with the best. I can outshoot anybody you know."

The pipe came out. "That so?"

Iris held her chin up. "Yes, that's so."

"You think there's a lot of shootin' going on with game management?"

"I'm just sayin' that I can handle myself."

"You gonna bushwhack in a dress?" Kuntz didn't try to hide the smirk curling his tobacco-stained lips. "Bull up some poachers in that pretty dress?"

"I got other clothes," said Iris, her voice low. "I got work clothes."

"So here's the deal, missy." Kuntz hitched his pants with his free hand. "You got three strikes before you even begin. And you know it's three strikes and you are out, don't you?"

Iris said nothing.

"One, you're too young. You gotta be nineteen to get a government job. Two, you're a girl. We don't hire girls. And three, you ain't finished high school. You gotta finish high school to get a government job."

"I'll be nineteen soon enough."

"Three strikes."

"I went to school."

"No you didn't. I know who you are. You're Iris Greenlee. Your daddy was Dexter Greenlee who got himself shot by that deer poachin' sombitch up near Trail. You got kicked out of school on account you beat that poor McClellan boy with an axe handle. You live with your momma and crazy brother up the Applegate. I know about you, Iris Greenlee."

"That Doren McClellan," said Iris evenly, "threw my brother, who can't swim, into the river."

"You're lucky you didn't get arrested."

"Look, Sheriff Kuntz, I'm here because I'd be a good game warden. It's in my blood. You said yourself."

"Well now, that's strike four, cause there ain't no job opening for game warden. Derek Mayfield has retired and the state has declined to re-fund the position." He shook his head, studied her. "What in the world makes you think you could waltz in here and be the game warden anyway? That ain't work for girls."

"Does the law say that?"

"I am the law."

"I mean the written-down law."

He hooked thumbs in his belt. He had a long-barrel Colt holstered on his hip. "How come you ain't thinkin' about gettin' a fella? Gettin' married? You're kinda a pretty in a way. A fella could like you all right. Put in a garden, grow petunias. Bake some cakes for the church raffle." The smirk was full-blown now, and the big moustache curved up like an otter sunning itself on a rock. "What's a girl want to be game warden for? That don't make sense."

"Makes sense to me."

"I don't care for sass in this office," said the sheriff. "So I believe we're done wasting my valuable time here." He turned and walked back through the side door and Iris stood there with heat rising up inside her. She thought of taking out her pocket knife and cutting the telephone cord, just to be ornery, but she didn't. Instead turned and walked back out the door, down the cold resounding steps of stone.

"Hey! Wait there!" The court house attendant came trotting up in his official vest and tie and suddenly she loathed being in her Sunday dress, its folds and the lace-front bodice. Anyone could tell she didn't belong in a proper dress.

"You're Iris Greenlee," he said. He had a triumphant look, as if he'd just made an important discovery.

"I don't think I need you to tell me that."

"Ha, well. Right." He nodded. "Your father was that game warden, right? Dexter Greenlee?" His cheeks were flushed. "The one got shot up near Trail?"

"Seems like everybody is awful concerned about my daddy all of a sudden."

"I figured out who you were. Are."

"Like I said, I'm well aware."

"You're kind of famous."

"On account of my daddy getting shot down? Is that the kind of famous somebody should be famous for?"

"Well, that, and for beating up that kid in school. Now I remember the stories."

"There's stories about me?"

"Some." The young man realized he'd let his enthusiasm get the better of him. He was embarrassing this girl. "You know, just stories. Lots of people have stories."

Iris looked off, thinking.

"Some folks say he had it coming," added the young man. "That fellow at school, not your daddy."

"He had it coming, all right."

"They say you almost killed him." Said it with awe.

"I tried to take his head off but missed and got him sideswipe."

"I'll be."

"He was all right after a while. He was dumb as a mule to begin with, so hittin' him didn't change much."

He laughed and showed nice teeth. He said, "So you haven't killed anybody?"

"It was my daddy got killed."

His smile left. "I know that. I didn't mean to be, ah…"

"It's all right." Iris said. "It was years ago. I was little." She nodded to herself. "Back in nineteen-fourteen."

"Oh, sure."

"That fella got off, by the way. He shot my daddy all right but they said it was self defense. So he got off. Even though there was a witness and everything." She gestured toward the western mountains. "Now he's roaming around out there somewhere, I suppose, still taking deer when he shouldn't." She looked at him.

He couldn't help himself and stuck out his hand and said, "Jack Dressler."

Iris considered his waiting fingers, several of which had ink stains along the tips. She shook the hand of this strange boy, his palm smooth, warm. A woman she did not know on the opposite side of the street gave them a long hard look. "Iris Greenlee, but you know that." She withdrew her hand, said, "Did you want something?"

"Well, I was just curious what the sheriff said. About being a game warden."

"He said they don't hire girls. Not the smart-ass ones, anyway."

"Oh. Well, I figured he'd say something like that."

"And I need high school."

He nodded.

Iris sighed. "Nothin' I didn't half expect."

"Yes. We don't…they don't hire girls for jobs like that. Guns and everything. It can be dangerous work. They just don't. Maybe they'll change that some day."

"I'm not holding my breath."

"Heck, they had a woman governor over in Wyoming."

"You got a particular interest in my business?"

"Oh, no I was just getting out for a minute. It gets stuffy in there sometimes." He gestured at the courthouse. "Then I saw you, so I thought I'd ask about it. Just being neighborly."

"We ain't neighbors."

"Well, friendly then."

"We ain't friends either."

"That's right. Not really. Then polite. Just trying to be polite."

Iris squinted at him, thinking. Then she nodded. "I'm going back to the courthouse."

She turned and strode off toward the big building, dress swishing. Jack Dressler had to trot to keep up. "What for?"

"I got to look at something."

"Look at what?"

"Those posters," said Iris. "Of wanted criminals. I want to get a look."

"You want to see criminals?" Jack Dressler was amused. "What you want to see them for?"

Iris didn't reply.

There were seven posters thumbtacked to the cork-covered bulletin board. Some looked freshly hung, others were yellowed with time, their dog-eared corners drooping. Three were for well-known criminals that often appeared in the newspapers.

Iris whistled. "I know him." She pointed at an older FBI poster for Al Capone that showed a grainy image of the mob boss in jaunty fedora with a cigar stuck in his mouth. The reward was $10,000. "Wouldn't that be something?" she said aloud but to herself. "Ten thousand dollars for Mr. Al Capone?"

"The Federal Bureau of Investigation is on his trail, I believe."

"How come there's no women criminals?"

"Oh, they come through now and then. Mostly women that killed their husbands. Not many women bank robbers and such."

She inspected each poster, turning her head this way

and that as she studied each felonious face, her hands clasped behind. She took a long look at:

OFFERED BY THE STATE
$300 Reward

No. 18664 Harold Smitts, alias Harold Jones, having escaped detention at the County Jail in the County of Jackson in the State of Oregon on March 16, 1927, having overpowered a Sheriff's Deputy and stolen a Horse from the State Livery, remains at large for the Crimes of Larceny and assault. The Reward offered in the case will be paid to the person or persons who cause the Arrest and the detention and turns the Prisoner over to the Authorized Officer of this Institution.

— Sheriff of Jackson County
State of Oregon

The man depicted in the mug shot photo had sparse hair and a hooked nose and eyes that were set close together so that he looked like a bird of prey. He was dressed in a rough coat and a tie.

Iris pointed. "This fella looks like he was born to trouble from the get-go. You know about this fellow?"

Jack Dressler nodded. "Well, not personally of course. But that's Harold Smitts. From up around Grants Pass. He robbed the assayer's office a couple months ago. Grabbed gold right off the counter. Maybe you read about it? They caught him down by Peterson's millpond that next day. They put him in jail but they underestimated him, apparently. A few weeks ago he said he needed to iron his shirt for the trial. A deputy gave him an iron and he hit the deputy over the head with it and got away. Not smart."

"Who's not smart, Smitts or the deputy?"

"Both not, I guess."

"So he got away?"

Dressler shrugged. "Sheriff Kuntz has made inquiries but..." he spread his hands wide, "...it's a big piece of country."

Iris nodded. "Who pays?"

"The reward?"

"Yes."

"The state of Oregon."

"How do you get the money?"

Dressler frowned. "Well, the man has to be brought in, of course. He has to be apprehended."

"Bring him where?"

"Right to the sheriff. Then they lock him up. Again." He paused. "Why do you want to know?"

"How often these outlaws get caught?"

"You'd have to ask the sheriff. But I suspect less than half the time, depending on what they've done. There's not that many law officers available to track down the wanteds. I guess you figured that already. Lots of those fellas just disappear into the mountains and you never hear from them again."

"That's so?" said Iris.

Chapter Fourteen
May, 1927

SILVER BILL'S PLACE was a tumbled board-and-batt shack that he had built near one of the springs feeding Corley Creek. It's where he got his water to make moonshine whiskey. Iris had been up there years ago hunting with John Rink and he'd showed her Bill's cabin off in the distance. An area that had a reputation for armed moonshiners and other unsavory characters, Silver Bill among them. Momma said lawmen didn't venture up there any more. Iris took the Winchester rifle with her.

She climbed up through white pines and manzanita to where the western ridge levelled out and Silver Bill's place peeked out through the trees a quarter mile across the Corley Creek valley. A curl of smoke lifted from the stovepipe; might be moonshine being cooked. She made her way down the steep flanks of the creek, fought through tangles of serviceberries, forded across shallow riffles, and hiked up the other side in boots cooled with creek water.

The cabin was half-surrounded by big firs, but a front area had been cleared and was sunny and from that vantage you had a good view of the tree-toothed ridge opposite. A grey mule stood in a picket corral and stared at her and twitched its big ears and she walked into the open. She didn't want Bill thinking somebody was sneaking up. She hefted the rifle over her shoulder and held it by the barrel.

On one side of the shack was a wet mass of old mash that gave off a powerful stink as it rotted in the sun, the pile alive with drunk flies and bees.

"Hello the house," Iris called out but there was only the thrum of the insects. She walked up the steps. On the narrow porch were two barrels that smelled of liquor, each capped with a whitish-brown crust. She poked at a crust and it wavered slowly up and down.

"When the cap sinks, the juice is ready," came a voice and Iris gave a start. How could anybody be so quiet and get so close without her knowing? Silver Bill was standing not ten feet away, a double-barrel shotgun levelled.

"Who the hell are you?" said Silver Bill, wrinkling his nose.

The last time she'd laid eyes on him was years ago in town. From across the street she'd seen him slide into an alley like a bobcat disappearing into the brush. He had thick white hair that hung down behind and a scraggly billy goat beard that wavered across his chest as the air caught it. Behind those gnarly whiskers his face was brown and wrinkled as dirt in a bucket.

"Silver Bill," said Iris. "It's me, Iris Greenlee."

Silver Bill worked his jaw like he was chewing a cud. "And just what the hell you doing up here, walkin' around with a carbine, scarin' law-abiding moonshiners? I was just about to separate you from the land of the living." He shook the blue-black barrel of his shotgun. "Good thing I seen yer hair and made you out for a girl, otherwise you'd been in pieces all over my porch."

"You know me?"

He nodded. "Iris Greenlee. Shit yes, I knowed you. Your daddy was Dexter. A law-abiding soul but I won't hold that against him. A good man wrongfully kilt. The time you was knee high to a duck."

"Yes sir."

"Your momma is Emily."

"That's right."

"A good woman, her." He did not relax his shotgun. "What you doing up here? You ain't scoutin' about for the marshal, are you?"

"No sir. I was lookin' for you."

Silver Bill shook his head. "Not many folks come lookin' for me."

"I was thinking you could help me."

He thought on that, jaw cranking back and forth sideways. "Your daddy and me was friends there for awhile. Did you know that?"

"You watched over me and my brother. During the trial."

Silver Bill snorted. "You remember that?"

"I do."

He stomped a foot. "You kicked that fella, that nogood shithole drunk Coldstone. Damn funny. You remember kickin' him?"

"He was making fun of my brother."

"What say we put away our firearms and have us a drink. I don't suppose you like white whiskey?"

"I'm not particular fond of it, no sir."

"Well, it's water or whiskey."

"Water then."

Silver Bill relaxed the shotgun and broke it open and took out the shells and put them in his pocket. He climbed up his sagging porch and pointed a finger at the top step. "Set here. I'll fix us up."

Iris eased down onto the top step and slid the Winchester over the side so the butt rested on the ground and the barrel poked up by her side. Silver Bill disappeared inside his shack and a minute later emerged with a tin cup and a glass jar full of clear moonshine.

"I usually don't drink before noon, but seein' as I got company." He handed the tin cup to Iris. The water was warm but tasted clean. Silver Bill nodded at her cup. "That's the sweetest water in the valley." Jerked a thumb over his shoulder. "Comes up right out behind the house." He tossed half his liquor down in one practiced gulp, held up the jar. "Makes the best damn sour mash whiskey." He put the glass to his lips and let the liquor slide into his waiting mouth. Then he sat heavy on the top step and Iris got a good whiff of the man, the heavy sour scent coming from inside his flesh.

"What are you doin' up here now?" he asked again.

"You know a fella name of Harold Smitts?"

He looked off toward where the far ridges met the sky in a haze. "I know him."

"You do?"

"He's my cousin."

Iris felt her heart sink. Kin! He's not going to give up kin.

"What's the matter?"

"Nothing."

Silver Bill let that set for a minute, then repeated, "What business you got with Harold Smitts?"

Iris sighed. "You promise you won't get mad at me? Shoot me or nothin'."

"Depends," said Silver Bill.

"You know he's a wanted man."

"I heard as much."

"Well, I was coming to see if you knew where he was at."

He frowned. "Why's that?"

"I aimed to bring him in for the bounty."

Silver Bill nodded. He didn't seem surprised. "How

much he worth?"

"Three hundred dollars."

He whistled. "I believe that's more than Harold has put together for himself in his whole life."

"I'm sorry. I didn't know you were kin."

"Well," said Silver Bill, picking at something in his ear. "We ain't exactly close, Harold and me. In fact, I don't much care for him."

"How's that?"

"Long story. Involves a mule." He looked off. "And a pearl necklace, if you can believe that."

"What happened?"

"Fact of the matter is, I don't recollect fully. But things sure got gummed up and that Harold, he's a lyin' som-bitch."

"So you ain't mad at me?"

"I ain't mad. Fact is, I don't care if that old shit gets caught." They sat silent, then Silver Bill said, "What's he done?"

"I guess he robbed the assayer's office. Got himself caught, then hit a deputy on the head with a smoothing iron and got away from the jail."

"I'll be damned."

"So you might say he's wanted a couple of ways."

Silver Bill nodded, stood. "Give me your cup."

Iris handed it up. Silver Bill went back inside, reappeared a moment later. His jar was full to the rim. He handed Iris the tin cup and she could smell the liquor in it.

"Have a drink with me," he said and the way he said it Iris knew she'd have to down the moonshine to get to the other side of whatever Silver Bill was thinking. The liquor burned in her throat and shards of flame curled up into her nostrils.

"That's good, huh?"

It took Iris a moment to get enough air in her lungs to make the words. "Damn fine," she managed.

Silver Bill nodded. "What makes you think you can take on a grown man? You're nothin' but a whelp. And a girl to boot."

"I'll get the drop on him." As punctuation she put down another swallow and let the burn roll up into her eyes and make tears.

"And if you don't?"

She looked him in the eye. "I will."

"How old are you, girl?"

"Eighteen this past March."

"Eight damn teen. How come you ain't married?"

"I ask myself that sometimes. I ain't figured it out yet."

He nodded at the snout of the Winchester poking up past the step. "You shoot that thing?"

"I can."

He pointed out past his little open meadow to an oak some fifty yards away. "See that sawed off limb? Right there in the lower branches you can see the square-cut stub of a limb poking out."

"I see it." Iris stood, walked down the steps, got the rifle, chambered a round. Put the stock to her shoulder, hoping she was a step ahead of the whiskey already winding its way into her head. Put the bead on the target, make it stay there. Breathe, hold, squeeze.

The limb shattered and the mule heaved up and down on its hind legs and brayed at the gunshot. The report echoed down among the ridges like a thing alive. A twist of blue gun smoke hung in the air.

Bill nodded. "Well now. There it is."

"There it is," said Iris, leaning the Winchester up against the porch rail, taking the tin cup. The burn of the moonshine was becoming more friendly.

Silver Bill sniffed. "I'm gonna tell you where old Harold is holed up. But there's conditions."

"What's that?"

"You don't tell nobody where you heard the information from."

"I wouldn't do that even if you didn't tell me not to."

"And I want fifty bucks out of the reward."

"I'd split it with you, Silver Bill."

Silver Bill snorted. "Damn cub girl come in here and turns the day upside down." He shook his head. "That is the damnedest thing. But fifty dollars will do me a world of good. That's all I need. If I was to go with you, we'd split the deal. But I'm too old for that now. Anyway, years ago your daddy did me right. He didn't have to, and he did."

Iris waited for more of that story but there was nothing forthcoming. "What he'd do, Silver Bill?"

"I swore I'd never tell. So I guess I better not."

"Must be years now. And my daddy's gone. I'd think it would be okay if you want to."

"Can't. Wouldn't be right. But I can square it now. With you." He looked at her. "Fact is, you comin' here is kind of a blessing. Yessir, it surely is. A chance to repay. Man's gotta die clean that way."

"All right."

"You know where little Cumby Creek runs into the river?"

"Sure."

"You go on up the Cumby road a good two miles, you'll see a big rock, looks like a damn rabbit. Got ears and everything."

"All right."

"Head north. It's plenty steep. You get up there straight north for a ways you're gonna see a big piece of cliff. Can't miss it. There's a pretty good cave in there, and

Old Harold is gonna be in there, waitin' for things to blow over so he can get a train to California."

"If you ain't seen him, how do you know he's there?" Her tongue thick and slow.

Silver Bill chuckled. "It's a place we mapped out a while back. In case things got bad. I ain't been up there in years. But if Harold Smitts is hiding in these parts, that's where you'll find him."

Iris nodded. "I'm gonna bring him in and I'll get you your fifty dollars."

"You can't go straight at him in there. You gotta come up from the east side."

"All right."

"Tell me, why you want to do something like this? Go off huntin' after desperadoes?"

Iris shrugged. "We need the money, and I ain't into sweeping floors or washing dishes."

"I'll drink to that," said Bill, tipping his jar.

"And I want to make my mark."

"Your mark?"

She shrugged. "I'm not sure what that is, I just know what it ain't. And it ain't what I been doing to this point. Maybe I just want to do something important."

Silver Bill considered, looked at his worn boot tips. "Well now there's something to do all right."

"You don't think that's right 'cause I'm a girl."

"I didn't say nothin'."

"Don't have to. I seen it in your eyes."

"That's not exactly it."

"What then?"

Silver Bill looked off. Put the jar to his lips, tilted back to let the last silvery drop of moonshine crawl toward his waiting mouth. Swallowed. "Hunting men." He choked a bit, cleared his throat, launched a gob of phlegm into the weeds. "That's a business."

"I figured it ain't like hunting frogs in the creek."

"Wouldn't want to see you to go and get hurt. Or, you know. Worse. On account of I know your people and all."

Iris nodded. "I appreciate that."

"There's somethin' else you should know." The wind came up sudden and heavy in the trees and limbs screaked.

"What's that?"

"Smitts ain't gonna be alone."

Chapter Fifteen
May, 1927

"YOU GOING TO GET UP after a known criminal on the sayso of some drunk moonshiner who knew your daddy."

"Made up my mind, Momma."

"Chasing after criminals up in the hills isn't the work for young women."

"Says who?"

"Says anybody!"

"What am I supposed to do? Sell eggs my whole life?"

"You're supposed to help out on this farm, yes. You're a farm girl."

"Well that's just it. I'm not all sure I'm a farm girl."

Emily spread her arms toward the walls of their cabin. "This look like Paris to you? It's a damn farm. And you just happen to be a girl on this farm. Therefore, farm girl."

"I'm doing this, Momma."

"You want a job? Go down to the Grange, they always need help at the counter. There's been some real nice gals that work down there, you know Medi and Camille."

"Good lord, I am not going to spend all day stuck inside the Grange with the likes of Medi Andersen."

"Well you sure as hell ain't no bounty hunter. Where'd you get the notion?"

"I can shoe a horse, split wood, I can track and I can hunt. I been doing rough things since I was little."

Emily snorted hard. "That don't count toward hunting a criminal man who's packing a gun and likely to do anything to escape the law. Official law or otherwise."

"I can't say I got a lot of faith in the official law around here."

"Well, there used to be some good law around here and he got killed off."

Silence.

"That's the past, Momma. And as bad as that was, it don't exactly bear on here right now."

"It has every bearing, Iris, and that's downright shameful for you to say other!"

"Momma, the money's gone. The pears are about worthless..."

"We'll get more."

"Where? Where are we gonna get more trees at two dollars and fifty cents apiece? And there's all of us and the dog and horse besides, and there's shoes, and lamp oil and gasoline for the truck. And what if there's another flood?"

"We can do without the truck."

"We're not going to be out here without a truck. Besides, everyone's got automobiles now. This isn't eighteen eighty."

"What do you care? You're gonna be up in the hills chasin' after criminals. You won't be here one way or the other."

"We still need money. Momma, it would help a whole bunch if you would just say all right."

"Who's gonna help me with Henry?"

"I'm not turning my back on that. You know that. But this isn't about Henry."

"I'll tell you something," said Emily, body all square and upright seated at the table, hands folded in front, "when you have a child, you make a bargain with the Lord.

You say: Thank you Lord for bringing this wonderment into my arms and I swear to do everything I can to keep this child from harm. That's what you say directly to God. And it may be the truest thing you ever say. That goes for Henry. That goes for you. Now you're asking me to go back on my word."

"I'm asking for your blessing."

"Blessing! To go out in the hills and get shot!"

"I'm not going to get shot."

"You don't know!"

Iris flashed hot, held her tongue.

"You got your head under this roof—my roof," said Emily. "I am the leader of this household, and what I say goes." Emily puffed up with bluster, hands clenched tight, white around the knuckles.

Henry came in from the back porch and surveyed the conversation and turned himself into a corner and said, "Where's Ajax?"

"He's either out on the porch or out in the barn, Henry. Why don't you go find him?"

"All right." He went to the front door, paused, hand on handle, said, "I can make gold."

"I know that. That's a good thing."

"Yes."

When he'd gone off Iris said, "There's Henry. That's one of the straws you picked for this life. I guess I picked that one, too. There's no changing that. And there's no fault in it, either. Short straw, long straw, crooked straw. It's what we drew. And I know you had your fair share of crooked straws. One of those is me. And I know it's not what you bargained for, and I'm sorry for that. I don't know the right of it, nobody does. But you gotta let a straw be a straw."

"Now what in hell does that mean? Straws bein'

straws?"

"All right, that came out funny. I guess I'm just not like most folks."

"There's an understatement."

"Maybe it's just in my blood."

"You mean your daddy?"

"I mean both of you. His whole lot of brave and your whole lot of stubborn."

"Damn you, Iris Greenlee."

Iris said nothing.

"I know what this is about." Emily sniffed. "You just don't want to turn out like me. Like a tired-out old apron hung up on a hook."

"If I turn out like you I'd be twice the woman of any other gal in this county." She stood up now, tall for her age, taller than her mother, streaked brown hair tied back and half-way down her spine, youth already rubbed off in spots, especially around the set of her mouth and eyes.

"Are you taking the truck?"

"I'm riding the horse."

"Well I appreciate you lettin' me know that you're taking our work animal."

"We'll only be gone a few days."

"How in hell do you think you're going to get this desperado without getting shot?" Emily regretted the words; it made her sound curious.

"I got a plan," said Iris. This was a bluff. For all she'd stayed awake at night thinking about it, a real plan hadn't made itself known yet. All she could think to do was sneak up on Smitts and trust that the muzzle of a Winchester was a pretty good persuader. If she needed to shoot, well, then there'd be no telling. "Silver Bill told me where this fellow was hiding and how to come up on his camp without being seen and everything. Said the fella probably didn't even have a gun." She left out the part about Smitts having accomplices.

"And just how drunk was Bill when you talked with him?"

"As sober as I'm standing here," lied Iris.

Emily threw up her hands. "You gonna walk that man all the way from God knows where to Jacksonville? At gunpoint?"

"If I have to."

"God," said Henry, who was sitting on the front porch with the dog, well within earshot. "God knows where to Jacksonville."

Iris put on John Rink's old boots that he'd patched with hide and glue. She'd cut new laces from deer hide and she'd tucked an extra five feet into a rucksack along with dried apples and jerky and two boxes of deer loads. Lord it better not come to that. She wore her overalls and a cotton shirt.

She left in the early afternoon and rode Parker along the new-paved road that followed up the river until the highway became gravel and Parker's hooves crunched into the day. Her bottom got sore and a mile from where Cumby Creek came in she found a flat grassy place and an eddy where Parker could water himself and she gratefully eased herself out of the saddle. There she settled in for the night, aiming for an early start the next morning. She took off the saddle and halter and hobbled Parker with braided cord. She ate her jerky and apples and offered an apple to Parker, which he took gently in his big wet rubbery lips.

The sun went down and Iris settled on her blanket and heard the swifts pattering and cutting through the evening air and as the light faded came the noiseless bats quick and gone into the dark and as the stars came out so did all the nagging things she'd been trying to keep at bay. She pulled her blanket up to her chin. Scattered thoughts were flying crazy every which way, just like bats. Why was a girl out hunting a man? It wasn't in accordance with the laws of nature. Stupid dumb farm girl. Was she crazy? Why the hell wasn't she thinking about getting married? Too ornery. Can't cook much. Just plain butt ugly.

The ground was hard underneath. There were stones in the wrong places and she hefted herself up to toss them away. Overhead the stars moved; she tracked them against the web of branches black against the night sky. She wanted to make everything stop so she could sort things out proper and at the same time wanted the morning to break so she would just get on with it. Wind in the trees. Smell of horse and mint. She reached over, pulled the rifle close.

So here it was: girl, horse, carbine. Would she really shoot Smitts if she had to? The thought that she could and would got iron-hard in her gut and she held onto it, didn't want it to soften up. What son of a bitch would try to outdraw a girl who held a rifle sighted in on his heart? One who thought she wouldn't really shoot, that's who. Hell, a squirrel in the road might go any which way—you never could tell. How many men were up there? Did dying hurt? Did her Daddy hurt when he died, or was it all over so quick that there was this world and then the next and nothing in between?

Three hundred dollars, she thought. Three hundred dollars.

The dawn came up steely pink and indifferent to her and she was glad to be doing and rid of the thinking. She got the big Percheron and with her palm followed the hide along his warm muscled shoulder and said I'm sorry to put you into this and saddled him up and topped off the canteen and checked the cartridges in the Winchester. She guided Parker up to where Cumby Creek bubbled through a culvert to pass under the roadway, then reined him up the dirt logging road that ran along the creek. The sun arched behind her. She looked hard for a rock that looked like a rabbit. She saw big moss-covered hunks of granite that looked like plain rocks and one that looked sort of like a boot and she rode on for nearly four miles, cursing Silver Bill's whiskey-filled head, and at last she came up to a six-foot-tall knob with a split down its top and staring at it saw the head and ears of a rabbit.

"I'll be damned," she said to the horse and patted his damp neck and Parker shook his head at the compliment. She rode partway into the brush and found a stout scrub oak and tied reins to a branch and watered him pouring from the canteen into her hat. It was a branch that would keep him from wandering but the big horse could snap it if something should happen to her and he got hungry and pissed off enough.

She slid the rifle from its scabbard. Parker nickered at the out-of-ordinary day. "Hush now," said Iris, and she undid the sixty-foot hemp rope that hung from the pommel and put that in the rucksack. She thought about eating some apples and jerky but she had no appetite so she gave the apples to Parker. It was right about noon and she got the sun behind her and started to move up the ridge, following her shadow, headed north. The idea was to come up in broad daylight when whoever was up there would be sitting around in the laze of the early afternoon, maybe taking a supper. If she got the drop on them, fine. But if they got the drop on her she planned to say she was out hunting a cougar that had been spotted around. Once the men had heard her story and relaxed their guard, she'd draw down on them and take her prisoners.

She moved quiet, pausing every few yards to listen hard and watch for movement up ahead. She'd climbed a good mile when the jagged edge of a cliff came into view over the tops of the trees. She closed her eyes and steadied her breathing and thought of Momma bare-kneed kneeling in the lettuces digging with her short-handled hoe and John Rink packing a deer on his stout shoulders and her real Daddy shot dead before she could know him and her brother innocent of all. Three hundred dollars. She'd take some of the bounty money and buy Henry his own teacher. What did they call them? A tutor. A tutor, by god. Then she squeezed all thoughts out of her mind until the only thing left was the ridge and the way forward and the carbine in her hands.

She moved along and caught the scent of a cooking fire. More of the rocky cliff cleared the tops of the trees and then fifty yards past a tangle of brush she saw the encampment. Three men sat on logs staring into a rock ring and the small fire inside of it. Over the flame roasting on a stick spit was a some skinned-out critter. One of the men reached out to give the spit a turn.

She'd been hoping for no more than one other fella; two swung the odds considerably. If there were any more off somewhere it could go badly. From her remembrance of the wanted poster Smitts looked to be the narrow-faced one tending the spit.

Momma, she thought, I'm seeing it through.

She had two choices. Circle right and close the gap by another twenty yards and pop out right on top of them. The risk there was being heard in the dry underbrush. Or stride right out bold as you please with the rifle at her shoulder, pull out the tale about the cougar and sell it hard. That meant she'd have to do some acting, and she was too nervous to pull that off, so she started out to her right and damn if she hadn't gone ten feet when she snapped a twig and the three boys heads went up like jackrabbits and they had their weapons in their hands.

She'd cornered herself with a dumb-ass mistake and now the only way out was to set it all on the line. She put the rifle over her shoulder and stepped out into the clear. She was hoping they'd see right off she was a girl and that would probably make them hesitate.

She called out, "Hey there fellas, don't shoot! I ain't no buck." She walked toward them like nothing and they had all drawn on her and were staring in disbelief. The bullets didn't come. Lord she was going to piss her drawers.

"Who the hell are you?" One of the men shouted and she could hear another one say, "It's a damn girl."

The one she figured was Smitts pointed at her and the finger was a warning and she stopped. He had what looked like a forty-five service automatic in his other hand. "What the hell you doing up here, girly?"

The ruse spilled out like she'd practiced. "We're down in the valley and a damn cougar got one of our calves last night and I been trackin' him up here."

The men exchanged looks. "A cougar?"

"That's right."

"You alone?" one of them demanded.

"Just me. What are you cookin' there? Smells good. Damn, I'm hungry."

She wanted to get them thinking and hesitating. She took a few more steps and then Smitts said, "Now hold it right there. This ain't a party and you ain't been invited." It was more or less a threat but at the same time one of the fellows put his pistol in his shoulder holster and sat back down on a log.

"There's no damn cougar around here," said Smitts'

partner. He held a double-barrel shotgun and Iris knew she was just within range. "What girl goes after a cougar all alone?"

"I been hunting my whole life," Iris replied, which had the ring of truth to it.

"Why didn't you bring some dogs?"

"Our dog ain't no damn good after big cats. We tried. He'd sooner chase squirrels."

The man with the shotgun looked her up and down. It was not a friendly look, but that hungry look that men can give women. Iris knew what he was thinking: this girl was alone, up here in the mountains, and that maybe they were about to have a good time. She came forward, twenty yards away. She was about squeezing the oil right out of the Winchester's stock.

"Maybe," said the man with the shotgun, "if we give her some supper, she'll show us a kindness in return."

Smitts laughed but it was clear the idea had appeal. The man with the shotgun seated himself and rested the twelve-gauge against the log.

"C'mon over here closer," said Smitts, "and let's have a look at you."

Iris moved closer until she was no more than ten yards away. They were dirty and undone and needing shaves. The shotgun man had on a suit with a vest and his shirt collar open at the throat and his right pants leg was torn from about the cuff. The second fellow had a collarless long sleeve shirt and held his pants up with rope suspenders and over that he had a shoulder holster with a buckle strap in front. He wore army-style boots. Maybe a deserter.

Smitts had on an ill-fitting suit and shirt and Iris figured he ditched his prison outfit somewhere and probably pinched the duds off a clothes line or maybe even right out of somebody's closet when they weren't at home. He'd put his automatic in his waistband but he stood a bit twitchy for the sudden appearance of this girl at his hideout and what to do about it. No doubt one option was to make this girl go away for good. His gun hand hung close to where the grip of the forty-five showed above his pants.

That was her opening. Iris swung the Winchester off her shoulder and levelled it at the men and now everything started to go hazy like just before you fall asleep. She heard herself say, "Harold Smitts I'm takin' you in to Jacksonville and the county jail. And the rest of you gentlemen as well."

The shotgun man moved first and Iris knew that would be the way it played out and she put a good bead on his left shoulder and the report blasted all the stillness and the man went ass-over-tea kettle behind his log chair and he screamed.

The man's shotgun flipped out of his reach and she levered in a new round and swung the carbine over just as Smitts was bringing out his gun and she shouted, "Hold right there, Smitts, unless you fixing to die right now." The voice was one Iris had not heard in herself before, a voice like an axe blade. Smitts stopped in mid-draw and Iris put the barrel of the Winchester square on his heart and kept an eye on the other man. A deep calm came over her, a certainty that she'd do whatever it took to get out of this alive and that to hesitate was to die and that she was not afraid and that to shoot either of these two men would be a simple thing.

"That fuckin' bitch shot me!" The shotgun man began caterwauling something awful. "I'm a dead man." Nearby a horse whinnied and Iris figured it was the horse Smitts had stole in town.

"I wanted you dead you'd be dead," said Iris flatly. To Smitts she said, "You bring that gun out with two fingers and throw it over here." She tapped the ground in front of her with her boot.

"I ain't doin' that," growled Smitts. "And I ain't going' back to Jacksonville because some little girlie with a big gun comes up here and tells me so. You gonna shoot me in cold blood? I don't think so." He still held his gun halfway out of his pants, measuring the situation. Iris could see he hadn't thumbed back the hammer.

The next shot was right between Smitts' knees and shattered the log behind. Smitts stumbled backwards, tripped over his log chair and fell on his backside.

Iris chambered a new round, moved quickly to her right, circling the trio, watching each weapon. The man with the shoulder holster eyed her with raw heat.

"Who are you?" he growled. "You're not the law."

"I'm a citizen of the state of Oregon," Iris said. "That makes me law enough for the likes of you." When she got around to where she could see Smitts' gun had come out of his pants and was laying in the dirt she stopped. "Get up," she said to Smitts.

"You fucking bitch!" screamed the shot man again. His shoulder was covered in blood and his face was clenched in pain and anger. He was out of the fray.

Smits propped himself up on his elbows, his automatic two feet away. If he made a move now Iris decided she would try to wing him, just as she had the first man. He wasn't worth a lick dead. The third fellow stood still and Iris could tell his shoulder holster made drawing his weapon awkward but he was still thinking about it. The only way they could outdo her now was if they both went for their weapons at the same time.

Smitts looked angry but he was beat in his eyes. He'd been beat before and he probably figured it was his natural due for his luck to run thin. He left his gun in the dirt and stood up, dirt and twigs clinging to his pants. The unturned critter on the spit was beginning to burn and the smell of scorched meat was strong.

"Sit down over there," she pointed the Winchester toward the other side of the fire ring and Smitts obeyed and sat down like a scolded schoolboy.

"Fuck fuck fuck!" The shot man began kicking at his log. "Don't nobody care if I bleed to death?" Iris used her foot to move the shotgun out of his reach. "Goddam, somebody shoot that bitch!"

"You," she said to the third man. "Take that pistol out of that holster and let it fall."

The rustling of the forest so loud it sounded like a hundred desperadoes were riding in to liberate their compadres. It was all she could do to keep from looking behind her. Sweat licked the back of her neck. The military-boots man was sizing up the situation, but the moans of the shot man were working in her favor.

The man reached into his jacket.

"Shoot her, Cliff!" yelled the wounded man.

The strange steel-hard voice came out of Iris, and she said, "Don't try it, Cliff. Just don't."

The pistol hit the dirt, a black snubbie with dark wood grips, and then there they were, three bad men and one girl bounty hunter. Her head was about to float off. She motioned for Cliff to join Smitts and he sat in the dirt, slit-eyed with evil. If he got half a chance, he was going to take it.

"Roll up your pants."

"What?"

"You heard. Roll up your pants to your knees."

The man named Cliff did so, slowly, and sure enough he had a big skinning knife in a sheath strapped to his leg. He grinned. "You think you're smart, don't you?"

Iris said, "Take out the knife and toss it."

He pulled the knife out by the butt, slowly, then suddenly flicked his wrist and the knife flew from his hand and she barely got out of the way as the blade flashed by. She raised the rifle and took aim but didn't fire. His grin got wider and uglier.

"That must have slipped out of my hand."

Iris said nothing but gathered up the weapons and put them to one side, all the while keeping the rifle on the trio. She slipped out of her rucksack and opened it and took out the length of rope and tossed it to Smitts. To the wounded man she said, "Get up."

"God damn the day women was made," said the shot man as he struggled to his feet.

"Tie one end around his waist," she said to Smitts.

The convict looked around as if someone was supposed to give him official permission. "How'd you know we was up here?" he said.

"I smelled you," said Iris. "Now get a cinch on this man, and make a good knot."

When the wounded man was tied, Iris had Smitts stand five feet behind and run the loose end of the rope inside his waistband and out one leg of his pants. She did the same with the man called Cliff. When all three were roped together like trout on a stringer she took up the loose end.

"Any of you men think of taking off your pants and making a run you better know you'll be dead before your drawers hit the ground."

She marched the three over to the horse, a stout pinto, and had them saddle and bridal the animal. The shot man plopped himself on the ground and moaned and the other two kept getting in each other's way and both men cursed each other's clumsiness and the girl with the rifle and the days they had been born. When they were done Iris had them stand away while she checked the cinch. Then she ran the loosed end of the rope through the front dee and under the fender and into the back dee where she tied it off good. She found a canteen hanging from a branch and tossed it to the wounded man, then had Smitts and Cliff help the shot man onto the horse while he complained bitterly about the manhood of his companions.

"You're a bunch of sissies the way you let this damn girl push you around. You boys outa put your nuts in a bag and throw 'em off a cliff. You sure got no use for 'em."

"Shaddup, Zinler," said Smitts. "You the one got shot by her."

Iris looked up at the man Zinler. "I'm right behind you. You try getting' away with this horse you'll be dead before you get ten yards and then the horse will go off and drag your other buddies through the buckthorn until their skin peels off. And they ain't gonna be too pleased with all that. So let's go on down nice and slow."

They staggered their way down the ridge under a washed-white sky with the wounded man groaning the whole way, although Iris could tell by the way he rode that he still had most of his strength and he wasn't in danger of bleeding out. When they made the logging road she mounted up on Parker and by evening they reached the main road. She had them sit on the embankment and gave them the apples and jerky she had in her rucksack.

After an hour a flatbed came clattering along and Iris flagged down the surprised driver, a sheep rancher by the name of Larson, and had him go into Jacksonville and fetch the sheriff. It would take hours, she knew. But she wasn't tired. In fact, she was bright as she possibly could be. She sat on the road with the Winchester across her lap and watched her prisoners a few feet away in the tall grass. She'd tethered the pinto to a nearby tree and untied the rope and had the wounded Zinler put the rope down his pants leg and she took up the free end and again tied it to the horse's saddle.

"Why are you working for the law?" said the man who'd thrown the knife. "What's the law ever done for folks except make it hard for a decent man to make his way? Can't piss here and can't shit there and can't even spit without running afoul of some goddam law. And what do you get out of it, anyway? Girlie? Huh?"

"I'm not workin' for the law. I'm workin' for me."

"A couple hundred bucks? Ha. I get outta jail and I'll make some real money. I got surefire ways to get rich. Make more money than you ever dreamed of. Isn't that right, Mr. Smitts?"

Smitts shrugged. "Sure," he said. "That's what you keep saying."

The shot man laid himself out on the rough grass with a hand clamped over his wound. "You fellas so smart, how come you got jumped by a girl? A damn girl." To the night stars he said, "Son of a bitch."

(from the *Medford Meteor*,
May 25, 1926)

Local Girl Captures
Three Desperate Men

*Daughter of slain Game Warden
takes the Law into her own hands to
arrest several criminals*

With a pluck and daring not seen in these parts since the untamed days of gold, when murderers and thieves freely walked the streets with preachers and shop keepers, a young local farm girl, Miss Iris Greenlee of Applegate, made her way into the mountains southwest of Jacksonville and single-handedly apprehended three of the most-wanted desperadoes in southern Oregon.

Armed only with a deer rifle given to her by her father, the late Dexter Greenlee, game Warden of Jackson County who was unfairly shot to death by a poacher in the hills outside of Trail in 1914, the young Greenlee crept up on the three as they took their supper whereupon a Fierce Gunfight erupted. After wounding one man and disarming the others, the young bounty huntress marched the nefarious trio at gunpoint down the mountain-sides into the waiting arms of Sheriff Gerald K. Kuntz, who brought the men into custody at the County Jail in Jacksonville.

The apprehended are as follows: Harold Smitts, who escaped the County Jail on June 15 and was awaiting trial for larceny and other crimes. James Zinler, wanted in Klamath County for cattle theft; and Prvt. Herman Beauchamp, a deserter from the United States Army who had been stationed at Camp Withycombe in Clackamas County.

Chapter Sixteen
June, 1927

IRIS STOOD IN FRONT of Sheriff Kuntz' desk in her overalls. The sheriff lit his pipe and leaned back in his squeaky office chair and regarded her through fantasias of tobacco smoke. If she had a gun right now she'd shoot him. Shoot him between those droopy eyes then take the hunting knife and shave off that droopy moustache and go unlock all the criminals back there in the cells and turn them loose on the state of Oregon.

"That's my money." Her words came out small and tight, squeezed down with fury. "I brought those men in. That's my bounty money, like it said on the poster."

"What poster?" Kuntz was enjoying her anguish.

"The damn wanted poster in the courthouse. Where all them wanted posters are. It said three hundred dollars for Smitts. He's in your jail right now. It was me that went and got him."

Kuntz looked off. "I don't recall any wanted poster for Harold Smitts."

Iris took a step. "It was there. I seen it. That's what made me go out there and get those fellas. You think I'd do that just for a la-de-da? Risk my life for a lark?"

The sheriff narrowed his eyes "Who's to say what a girl might do?"

"I'm saying it now. And you was there, Sheriff. You came out in your truck to where I had those boys tied together. You put them in leg irons and got 'em on the back of that hack and you hauled 'em off. So what are you saying? That you didn't see me?"

The sheriff rolled smoke out of his nose. "Well there you go. You said yourself you didn't bring them to the jail. I did. That's what a bounty is about. What brings them in gets the bounty. Far as I know, you found 'em there already tied up. And I'm obliged you sat with them a spell and kept 'em under watch. But I'm the one brought them in."

"You're a son of a bitch."

Kuntz ripped the pipe from his lips and leapt to his feet and smacked the desk with his free hand. "Don't you use that tone with me, you little pig scrap! I'll lock you up for assaulting an officer of the law!"

Iris didn't flinch. Her finger curled around an imaginary trigger.

"And don't tell me my business," Kuntz hissed.

"It was all in the newspaper. About me capturing those men. A newspaper fellow came out and talked to me about it."

Kuntz slit his eyes. "Newspaper men are full of shit. They make up stuff so they can sell their papers. It don't mean nothing. Now get out of my jail house." His pipe had gone cold but he put it back in his mouth and sat down and glared at her.

Iris tried to slam the door on her way out but it was big and heavy and the old hinges offered too much resistance and the door glided shut with a quiet thump. She charged across the open space to the courthouse and ran up the steps and into the big entryway, her boots cracking against the checkerboard stone flooring.

Jack Dressler looked up, surprised. "Hey there…" he began but Iris marched right past to the board where the wanted posters were tacked. They were all different from the last time she'd looked, and there was no poster with Harold Smitts' glum, narrow face.

"Where is that wanted poster for Smitts?" she demanded. "It was right here." She pointed to a spot now occupied by a man wanted in several states for bank robbery. "You saw it."

He shrugged. "Sheriff's been in here since then, changing them up. He does that now and then."

"He took my bounty money."

"What?"

Iris turned to face him. "That thieving excuse for a lawman claims he brought in Smitts and his buddies. And he took the bounty money."

"Aw, now. He wouldn't do that."

"He did do that." Looked up at the arched plaster ceiling, yelled, "What kind of damn law you got in this place, anyway?"

"I'm not sure what to say, Miss Greenlee."

"I don't expect you do."

A door at the end of the hallway opened and a squatty man in a three-piece suit walked out, a frown cut into his forehead. "What is all this commotion about?" he demanded.

"Your Sheriff Kuntz took my bounty money that I earned fair and square."

The man held up a pink palm. "What in the world do you mean, young lady?"

Iris walked up fierce and the man took a step back.

"I'm Iris Greenlee. You heard of me?"

He looked at Jack Dressler to make sure the desk assistant stood ready to assist if a physical altercation should ensue. "Iris Greenlee? Yes, you're that farm girl who found Harold Smitts hiding in the hills. Isn't that so?"

Iris leaned in. The man was rotund but not large, and

she had him eyeball-to-eyeball. "Let me tell you straight. I'm the *damn* farm girl who brought that *damn* criminal Harold Smitts down from his *damn* hideout on the business end of Winchester carbine. And while I was at it, I brought in his two *damn* friends, too. All of them armed criminals, all of them whipped puppy dogs when it was over."

"I see," said the round man, looking down at his shoes and faking a cough and taking another step backwards and out of reach. "Ah, well, the citizens of Jackson County commend you." Gesturing at the grand staircases as if the gravitas of the courthouse could ameliorate any circumstance.

"The problem," said Iris, cocking her head slightly, "is I didn't get my *damn* money."

"And what money might that be?"

Iris smiled, razor-lipped. "We know who I am. Just who might you be?"

The little man tugged at his vest bottom, inflated his chest. "I'm Terrance Joy, the prosecuting attorney for Jackson County." Saying it out loud helped Joy regain some aplomb. "This is the Jackson County Courthouse, and I keep my office in there." He indicated the door through which he had recently appeared. "It's a dignified place and we like to keep it that way. Can you do that? We don't tolerate rude-like behavior."

"Mr. Terrance Joy, we're about two ticks away from some rude behavior all right." Iris exhaled loudly through her nose, said, "Right there was a poster, on that board. It said a man named Harold Smitts was wanted for escaping the jail." She turned to Dressler. "You saw it."

Jack Dressler nodded. "I did."

Back to Joy. "And on that poster it said that whoever brings in this man would get a bounty payment of three hundred dollars. I went out and brought him in. That's my money. Three hundred dollars."

Joy frowned, said nothing.

"And now I got this sheriff of yours telling me there ain't no bounty money for me. I'm understanding that he's decided to keep it, personally, for himself. And he says in fact I don't deserve the money because after I brought those fellas down the mountain, he happened to be the one with a truck that hauled 'em into town, and he's the one who gets the money."

Joy took a pocket watch from a vest pocket, glanced at it, sniffed, and slid it back into its nest. "I see."

"You don't give a good goddam, do you?"

Joy used a stubby index finger to signal that Jack Dressler should come over, just in case. Dressler reluctantly got out of his seat.

"Perhaps," said Joy, "the poster was removed and the offer of a bounty rescinded before you managed to round up Mr. Smitts. That's the likely explanation. It happens." He nodded, agreeing with himself.

"So that poster was a lie?"

"Young lady, I'm in no position to judge what happened to you. And I can see you're quite upset. But the truth of the matter is, the State of Oregon offers financial recompense for certain acts, but these are not everlasting positions. They change on a regular basis, depending on the needs of the state. And I cannot vouch for every haw and gee that transpires in Salem. But I do subscribe to the idea that the legislators and other law creating bodies of our great state are hard at work to ensure the safety of every citizen. You, myself. Our Mr. Dressler here." Joy smiled at the attendant who now stood halfway between the two. "All of us."

Iris worked her jaw. "You got jackasses out there in the woods who don't give a damn about breaking the law and you got jackasses in here—in these dignified halls—who don't give a damn about keeping the laws and when you add it all up all you get is a whole bunch of jackasses."

"Are you quite through?"

Iris moved and Joy flinched but she walked right past him to the bulletin board where the wanted posters were pinned. She gave each a close look and finally pointed to one. "Look here."

Joy didn't move. He didn't care to be ordered about by a scruffy farm girl.

Iris removed the pin and brought the poster to the prosecuting attorney, held it in front of his face. "See it?"

He nodded reluctantly.

"It says this man here, Thomas Fogerty, is wanted by the State of Oregon for arson. Says he set fire to a lumber mill in Ashland. Isn't that what it says?"

"I have to be…"

"And the reward for bringing this fellow in is one hundred dollars. Isn't that right?"

"That's what it says."

She took the poster to Jack Dressler and held it in front of his face. "You seein' what I'm seein'?"

"Um, yes. Thomas Fogerty. One hundred dollars."

"You see it…" pointing to Joy, then Dressler, "…and you see it." She flapped it back and forth. "Now I'm taking it with me."

"You can't…" Joy began.

She cut him off. "I aim to bring it back. Until I do, nobody can take it away or say it wasn't never there in the first place. Not you, not you, not that weasel of a sheriff."

"Now that's uncalled for, young woman!"

"…not anybody. Until I come back with Fogerty."

Joy put a finger to the back of his ear. "Until you come in with this man, Fogerty? Is that what you said? You mean capture him?"

"That's what I said so that's what I mean. So I'm asking you, Mr. Prosecuting Attorney of Jackson County, when I bring him in, all the way to the country jail, do I get that one hundred dollars?"

Joy smiled. "That's really up to the circuit court. But I see no reason why…"

"You a witness?"

"Excuse me?"

"Are you a witness to this wanted poster and what it says?"

"I have no legal obligations in regards to your request but yes, I've seen what you've shown me."

Iris nodded. She turned to Jack Dressler. "And you?"

He grinned. "Yes, I have. I've seen it all. Tom Fogerty. One hundred dollars. Do you really think you can get Fogerty?"

"I'm gonna bring him in tied up with a ribbon and bow."

Sheriff Gerald Kuntz put his boots up on the desk of the prosecuting attorney. Kuntz knew it was all right to put his boots there because Joy had invited him to do so, saying his office furniture was property of the State, not him personally, and so why shouldn't men of position be afforded the simple luxury of putting their feet up in a comfortable position on furniture owned by the State? If that action should wear out the desk and make it untenable, why then the State could simply replace it. In fact, Terrance Joy at this very moment was smoking a cheroot and had his own smallish feet and shiny black leather shoes propped up on his desk, although he was careful to place them on the afternoon newspaper to keep the shoe black off the polished oak surface.

"That damn girl," said Kuntz, bringing a match up under his britches so the friction caused it to break into flame, then applying the fire to his hawkbill briar. "About as ornery as a tomcat in the rain."

"Indeed,"" Joy replied.

"Who does she think she is?"

Joy considered. "Perhaps it goes back. To her father being murdered and the killer going free. Freed at the hands of an inadequately prepared prosecution, I might add." He rolled his cigar from one corner of his mouth to the other. "Perhaps it's made her grow up hard and untenable."

"Un what?"

"Untenable. Difficult. Unreasonable."

"She could get herself into a whole heap of trouble, that's for sure."

"She's not without skill when it comes to the apprehension of criminals," Joy continued, watching his smoke ascend. "She found those boys before you could, Sheriff Kuntz."

"Oh, har de har har," said Kuntz. "I got other things going, you know. It's not like I can spend all my time traipsin' up in the mountains after petty thieves."

"She'd make a good sheriff."

"You're pushin' it, Joy."

"Not bad looking, though." Joy raised an eyebrow.

"Too skinny in them hips," said the sheriff thoughtfully. "I like 'em with a little meat on their bones."

They were quiet as the big wall clock chimed the five o'clock hour. Joy watched the swing of the pendulum. It was funny how all the education and the studies and the bar exam were so easily paled by the machinations of local politics, of those who held the reins, of who you knew and could talk to openly if not honestly. He shook his head. If his father could have known, he might have grown up as the son of a governor. "Perhaps we should have offered our young bounty hunter some portion of the reward. A token of our gratitude."

"That horse has left the barn, Mr. Joy."

Joy nodded. "I understand. When does the money arrive?"

"The judge said Thursday. Once it's approved. Lookin' forward to it. I need a new pair of boots." Kuntz, tipped the toes of his footwear to the side so he could see them better.

"I'd like to take the missus to a steak dinner. With a nice Bordeaux wine."

"I don't see how you drink that stuff."

"The girl says she's going to bring in Tom Fogerty now."

"The hell."

"She's quite determined."

"No shit…" Kuntz pursed his lips.

"What do you think about that?"

"Well, I think I better get a call up to Sheriff Morgan let him know what's goin' on."

Chapter Seventeen
July, 1927

THE EDGES OF THE NEWSPAPERS rattled in the breeze, Iris holding the pages against her lap so they wouldn't fly away. She'd gotten them from the *Medford Meteor*, which was only too glad to sell off some older copies from the storeroom. A Klamath woman with broad shoulders and a glistening braid of twisted black hair that hung all the way down the length of her back helped Iris find issues with mentions of the crime. They found two, Iris paid a dime, and took the papers and sat on a bench in a little park near the newspaper offices.

(from the *Medford Meteor*,
May 10, 1927)

Arson Suspect
Still At-Large

*Local Businessman Aggrieved for
the Loss of his Lumber Mill*

Local authorities are keeping a keen eye out for the man who set fire to the Pine Cone Mill at Nevada Street in Ashland, Ore., on May 8, causing several racks of drying sawn boards to go up in flames along with the mill structure itself, it contents of machinery and inventory, and several outbuildings. No persons were injured in the conflagration, but the mill itself has been described as "about all gone" by the owner, Mr. Andrew Stannard, originally of Macon, Georgia, who moved here with his family several years ago to seek his fortune in the lumber industry and was doing well in his business ventures until last Tuesday night when his dreams went up in flames and smoke, save for several stacks of sugar pine boles that were away from the heat of the action.

Spot fires and smoldering embers were still to be seen as late as Wednesday morning, long after Fire Chief Edmund Wentzell and his crew had applied powerful efforts toward extinguishing the blaze. In a testament to the extreme heat of the fire, it was noted that iron supports for the main rip saw collapsed, leaving the big blade tilted at a severe angle.

Fire Marshal Wentzell has a strong indication the fire was deliberately set, as a suspicious object in the form of a bucket containing kerosene was discovered in the nearby bushes, and the testimony of a transient man who was walking along the Southern Pacific line who claimed to see a man splashing a liquid on the sides of the mill buildings and setting all aflame. According to the transient man – "Bill" – there was a powerful smell of kerosene in the air. The perpetrator made his getaway riding a motorbike of powerful caliber.

(from the *Medford Meteor,* June 3, 1927)

Local Mills in Conflict; Warrant Issued for Arson

Feuding lumber mills in Rose-burg and Ashland may be at the heart of criminal activities

Jackson County Prosecuting Attorney Terrance Joy is seeking an arrest warrant for Thomas H. Fogerty of Rose-burg, in connection with the fire and destruction of the Pine Cone Mill in Ashland, Ore., on May 8.

The warrant request comes after certain evidence offered by Mr. Andrew Stannard, owner of the Pinecone Mill, who told the

Ashland Constable, Jason Barnes, that he had received threatening letters from the Fogerty family in Roseburg, in Douglas County, owners of the Fogerty Mill, a mill of long standing in the area, accusing Mr. Stannard of obtaining lumber contracts by grossly undercutting costs with the hopes of driving competing mills out of business.

Mr. Stannard, originally of Macon, Georgia, who moved here with his family several years ago to seek his fortune in the lumber industry, is of the strong opinion that the act of arson was committed by Thomas H. Fogerty, son of Roseburg lumber mill businessman Herbert Fogerty. It is Mr. Stannard's contention that the Fogerty team has taken up ill revenge in retaliation for what he described as, "very legitimate proceedings" concerning the contracts in question.

Mr. Stannard's umbrage is supported to an extent by the testimony of an iterant man – "Bill" – who has been "riding the rails" between Redding, Calif., and Eugene for more than ten years and has told Constable Barnes an eyewitness account of the night of the big fire that includes seeing a man leave the burning mill site on the seat of a powerful motorbike of which only three are registered in either Jackson or Douglas Counties, and one such device is registered to Thomas H. Fogerty says Constable Barnes, who has looked into the matter.

"This isn't the first time the Fogertys have resorted to destruction of property," Mr. Stannard mentions.

"Hey there, Sheriff Morgan."

"Hello yourself, Sheriff Kuntz."

"What can I do you for?"

"Just thought I'd call, let you know about a little deal we got goin' on down here."

"Yessir?"

"Somebody set fire to a mill here, the Pine Cone."

"Hmm. That a fact?"

"I suspect you know about it."

"I do."

"Well then you should know that there's an arrest warrant for Tom Fogerty."

"I'm aware."

"Well, I was thinking you might want to let old man Fogerty know what's goin' on. Tell him to keep a rein on his boy."

"I'm going up to the mill tomorrow, as a matter of fact."

"Another thing."

"Yup?"

"We got this ornery girl down here. A little farm girl cuss. Thinks she's Annie Oakley."

"That girl what brought in your jail escapee, Mr. Smitts, and those others?"

"I brought those men's sad asses into town, let's be clear on that point, Kirby. But yes, she's the one been stir-rin' the pot, trying to run down thieves and such, looking for the bounty money."

"I know where I'd look for that."

"If that's not the pot calling the kettle black. Anyways, I believe she's drawn a bead on the Fogerty boy."

"You think she'd come up here poking around?"

"It's possible."

"What's she look like?"

"She a rough thing. Plain. Like an old cast-iron pan. Wears men's overalls sometimes. I seen her in a dress and it wasn't a pretty sight. She likes to tote around a Winchester ninety-four. I seen her carry it right in town."

"Anything else?"

"Keep an eye out for an old Packard flatbed. That's her. If I was you I'd let her know she ain't welcomed in a territory where there's already enough law."

"My thoughts exactly. Don't make sense, though."

"How's that?"

"A girl huntin' after a man. No sense at all."

"There you go."

"Usually they just tryin' to hunt some man into a mar-riage."

"We oughta know."

"Amen, Gerald."

"All right, Kirby."

"I can't believe I'm a party to this foolishness." Emily put the dress on Iris' bed.

Iris took it by the shoulders and held it up. Dark blue, belted waist, puff sleeves, big yoke.

"It's quite something, Momma."

"That's four dollars worth of silk."

"I know that."

"Try it on."

Iris shimmied out of her old cotton frock and let it slump to the floor. The new dress slid over her head with a whisper and a sigh.

"It's what proper ladies wear these days for when they go to town," said Emily. "Although most of them ain't tot-in' firearms."

"I told you Momma…"

Emily waved her off. "I done my part. I suspect you'll look very nice in that dress when you're stuffed in a coffin."

"Momma…"

"Like what I think makes any difference."

Iris went to the mirror that hung over her mother's dresser. "That sure don't look like me."

"I believe you said that was the objective. But you look like a woman. You look fine. Put your hair up and keep those hands out of the truck for a couple of days." She paused, put a hand to her forehead. "Now why the hell am I handing out advice for this deal?"

"Because you can't help but tell people what they oughta be doin'."

"Well maybe if those same folks would listen I wouldn't have to keep harping on the subject of common sense."

"Thank you for this dress, Momma. I won't let you down."

"The only way you could let me down is by dying. I

don't care about much else except you and Henry. You ain't provin' nothing to me."

Iris turned sideways. Gussied up, she wasn't half-bad. A little serious maybe. Already lines across her forehead. "I got to do this, Momma. Sometimes in life you just gotta do things."

Emily almost said, *What do you know about things in life?* but she didn't say anything.

Iris took the noon Southern Pacific up to Roseburg. It was Friday. If there was a chance that Fogerty would show up in town, it was likely to happen either that night or the next.

For the trip she'd taken the stock off the rifle so it would fit in her valise with some rolled up undergarments and stockings, her overalls, and work boots and shirt, fifteen feet of half-inch hemp rope stuffed into a knapsack, and a box of deer loads. The train labored up Canyon Mountain and the trees moved past the window in slow procession, the valise clamped between her ankles and draped with the hem of the dark blue silk dress.

In Roseburg she got off the train and walked downtown and noted the location of the jailhouse and found a respectable-looking hotel, The Clayton.

"I'm supposed to meet my Aunt Elsie here," she told the hotel clerk. "She's on business and we're to be sharing a room before heading up to Salem. She was to have called ahead. She's coming in from Coos Bay on a private motorcoach."

"What's your aunt's last name?"

"Fogerty. Elsie Fogerty."

The clerk cocked his head. "Fogerty?"

"That's right."

"The same Fogerty as around here?" He waved a hand in the general direction of the street that fronted the hotel.

"Don't think so. You got some Fogertys around here?"

"Well sure," the clerk nodded. "Been in the area for generations. Run a lumber mill just outside of town up Buckthorn Creek."

Iris nodded. "That so?"

The clerk thumbed his reservation ledger. "No, there's no Elsie Fogerty that's called in. No Fogerty at all."

"Oh shoot."

The clerk tisked. "That's a bad road there from Coos Bay. I wouldn't be surprised if she'd be delayed a bit." He smiled.

"Well, then, I'm in a pickle. I'll need a room for the night."

He scanned his chalkboard. "There's a single on the second floor. Would that be all right? Bed's big enough for two when your aunt shows up yet."

"I'd prefer the first floor. My aunt's got some rheumatism."

"All right. Got one here on the south side. It's not bad. Got a bed and a cot."

"That'll do."

"What's your name?"

"Becky Smith."

"And Wesson?"

Iris froze. What did he say?

The clerk straightened. His smile faded. "Oh, I'm sorry. That's a joke. Somebody says their name is Smith and right away you say, *and Wesson?* Ha. Like the gun, you know? Smith and Wesson?"

"Oh, yes," Iris nodded, exhaling. "That's a good one." She put up a smile.

He took a key off its peg and handed it to her. "That'll be two-fifty."

"My Aunt. She was going to pay."

"Oh."

"Is it all right if I go ahead and take the room, and she pays up when she gets here?"

"Oh. Well, of course. But, ah, what happens if your aunt is delayed quite awhile? Perhaps the road is blocked by, you know, a landslide. Which would not be unusual."

"Then I'll pay, for sure. Although not for a double, you understand."

"Yes. Well, perhaps you could pay me now, and your aunt could reimburse you when she arrives. And everything is taken care of."

"Well, sir, since you put it that way, let me say that I don't have two dollars and fifty cents on my person, only two dollars. If I give you that, then I'll have nothing on me. And I don't think it's right for a woman to be alone in a strange city without the means to take care of herself, wouldn't you agree?"

"Of course, Miss Smith."

"And Wesson," Iris said, and the clerk laughed. "Say," Iris went on, "didn't I read about a Fogerty in the newspaper? Not too long ago?"

"Where you from?"

"Grants Pass."

He nodded. "One of the Fogertys, Tom, had a run-in with the justice system down there in Ashland. They said he tried to burn down a mill that was giving the Fogerty mill up here fits. They say the Ashland mill was underpricing contracts, trying to cut the others out of the business. So Tom took it on himself to square things up. Put a torch to a warehouse and the mill building. Now he skips around, keeping out of sight of the law…" the clerk raised his eyebrows, "…but it isn't really that much law here, if you know what I mean."

"Well, that's kind of a deal now."

"The family, hell this whole town, says he didn't do it."
The clerk glanced over his shoulder, as if checking for
spies. "Personally? I think he did it. But you didn't hear that
from me."

"So where do the Fogertys live?"

"Up Buckthorn Creek about six miles past the mill.
That's the ranch. But they also got a house in town here so
the fellas can stay in town instead of heading back up the
mountain after a night in some of the blind pigs we got
around here. That Tom Fogerty stays in that house a lot by
himself. Sometimes with his Indian woman. He's kind of a
no-count fella. Drives truck for his daddy's outfit now."

Iris nodded. "Where would that house be?"

"Three blocks up Spring Street. Big white house. You
can't miss it." He paused, then, "You planning on paying
those folks a visit? Seeing if they're relations?"

"Oh, no," she said. "That's not my bunch."

"Maybe your aunt will know them."

"So you think he's around?" said Iris. "That Tom
Fogerty?"

The clerk scratched his chin. "Well, I don't know
about that. But if he's around town, you'll see him on his
old motorbike."

"Motorbike?"

"Only one in town. Rides it like he's riding Twenty
Grand."

"Twenty Grand?"

"The Derby winner. The Kentucky Derby? The big
horse race? You didn't hear about him?"

"I'm not much on sporting news I suppose."

"Heck, Twenty Grand's about the fastest horse that
ever lived. That's what they say."

"Well now." Iris picked up her valise, feeling the heft
of the weapon and ammunition inside.

"I'll get that for you." The clerk started toward the counter opening.

"That's all right. I'm good and capable. Thank you."

He looked disappointed. "I'm Oris, by the way. You need anything, you just ask for me."

"All right, Oris. I appreciate that. She started toward the hallway.

"I'll let you know when she's here," he called.

Iris stopped, turned. "Who's that?"

"Your aunt!"

"Oh sure. I appreciate it."

"Welcome to The Clayton, Miss Smith!"

Iris could hear the expectation in his voice. She turned to see him grinning at her. "And Wesson," she replied, with as much cheer as she could muster.

The silk dress had two big pockets and one was regular and the right-hand pocket was a sleeve that went all the way down the inside of the skirt. Iris reassembled the Winchester and loaded it. There was a narrow window and she raised the sash and peered out onto a dirt alley. She was a good six feet from the surface—a fair distance to jump. She lowered the rifle with the rope and then turned herself around and went out feet first. Once on the ground she slid the rifle into the long right-hand pocket. She had to put a hand in the pocket and hold the gun up so the dress wouldn't look lopsided from the weight of the weapon. She was just a city girl out for an evening stroll; she figured the ruse was good enough to get her the few blocks to the Fogerty place.

The house was a plain four-square, two-story. White

clapboard and a granite block foundation showed gray in the evening light. Porch in front; stairs leading to a rear entrance at the back corner. Toward the front she could just make out the shape of a motorbike and her heart began to thump. A light on in a downstairs window. A few maples, not much cover. Bold would have to trump caution. She walked directly to the house and pressed herself into the shadows against the siding. She didn't see anybody nearby. She heard voices inside. A man and a woman for sure. She pulled the rifle up and out of its pocket and quietly as she could she levered a round and got the hammer back, ready.

She walked slowly along the side toward the rear entrance. Four steps to the small porch, wooden steps, careful to keep her weight over the outside stringer. The boards made sounds but not too loud. There was a screen door. She pulled it with her free hand and it opened. She eased the door aside and entered. A short hallway ahead, kitchen to the left. She moved into the hallway; the voices came from her right. A sitting or dining room off the hallway. A splash of light from the open doorway, three feet away. She went forward, a floorboard creaked, and she stepped through and leveled the rifle.

Fogerty and a native woman in a green dress sat together on a black velvet couch. They were holding hands. They looked at Iris calmly, as if they'd been expecting her. Iris put the bead of the barrel squarely on Fogerty's chest. A sizeable target.

"Tom Fogerty, I'm arresting you on behalf of the citizens of Jackson County."

Fogerty frowned. He looked like his poster picture but bigger, meaner. His beard hung around his chin like a skunk's pelt, glossy black with a streak of cream in the center. His black hair cascaded toward the back of his head. Eyebrows like fat caterpillars, and he knitted these furry critters together in disgust, as if strangers with weapons were frequent annoyances. "The fuck you are," he said.

"You'll accompany me to the jailhouse here in Rose-burg. That's all I got to say about it."

"Who the hell are you?"

"I'm a tracker and bounty hunter. And you been found."

"Get the hell out of my house."

"Law says I can enter if there's a warrant out on a fella. And there's one on you."

Fogerty shook his head. "I ain't going nowhere."

"You don't have much choice here."

"Well, I'm not Tom Fogerty." He smiled thinly.

"You are. I seen your wanted poster. You're a dead ringer. With that beard."

Fogerty stroked his whiskers with affection, flipped the end up to admire the unusual streak of color that ran its length. "It's quite a beard," he allowed.

"Let's go."

"I can't." He gestured toward the woman. "You see, I'm in love with Flora here."

"That don't have no bearing on your guilt."

"Oh, but it does," insisted Tom Fogerty, pressing the back of the woman's hand to his lips.

"I'm taking you to the jailhouse, Fogerty. That's the only story here." Iris held the rifle steady. "Move away from that woman."

Instead, Fogerty began to caress the woman's cheek with the back of his knuckles. "Oh, I can't leave her," he whispered. "She's beautiful. Don't you think she's a peach?"

The pistol came out of nowhere. In his other hand. The hand that was not caressing the woman's cheek. The deception smoothly played. The muzzle flamed and the first bullet took Iris above the left wrist and her arm snapped back off the Winchester like on a string. The second caught her in the left shoulder and she spun around and pitched face-first onto the dark wood flooring. She heard the rifle go clattering to the floorboards.

Tom Fogerty stood up, walked with loud, deliberate steps. Heel, toe, heel, toe. The sound coming not from outside but inside her head. Her whole body was ringing. She was thinking, *I've bloodied the dress and Momma's gonna be mad at me.*

Fogerty leaned down and put the hard round hole of his pistol on the back of her skull, like a devil's kiss. "You're lucky," he whispered. "Real lucky. I was aiming for your heart." Reached over, got the Winchester rifle, straightened, put the pistol in his waistband, gestured for his companion to move away, then fired the rifle twice into the davenport. He let the rifle clatter to the floor. "Keep your old deer gun," he said. "And if you don't bleed out, then don't come after me again. Ever. Hear me?"

Fogerty and the woman thumped off. Iris breathed like a fish on the bank. She heard an engine start up. Motorbike. Dark liquid began to ooze from under her numb arm. She watched, amazed, as her own blood curved across the floorboards toward her face.

Chapter Eighteen
July, 1927

SHE WAS IN A BED. In a room. With large windows. There were two windows to one side and two more in another wall, and they let in a great deal of light. Overwhelming light. Everything was filled with loud whiteness. She was in a bed. White sheets. A hospital. Her mother's face came swimming out of the light.

"Hello there, Wildflower."

There was faraway pain, but also warmth, peace. She nodded, fell back asleep.

When she awoke again the light had quieted, coming in flat and low and reached to the opposite wall where it floated a rectangle of orange. Maybe evening light. As she came awake her body did also and she began to feel the hurt. Like she'd been dipped in hell and then kicked by mules. So this is what it feels like to get shot. Hurts like a bitch. Maybe a twitch of sympathy for the fella she'd shot up Cumby Creek. What was his name? She shook her head. He had it coming.

There were two other beds. One was empty, and there was a figure on the other. Lying face-down on top of the sheets, bare feet bottoms upturned white and calloused. By the raspy cadence of the breathing, she knew it was her mother.

"Hey," she called but it came out a croak and she had to work up the moisture in her mouth to slick up the word,

"Momma?"

Her mother stirred and raised herself partly up with her hair all over. "Iris?"

"Momma."

Emily shook her head squint-eyed with sleep. "Hey there. How you feelin'?"

"I'm thirsty."

"I'll get you some water." There was a pitcher and a glass on a stand. Emily got up, unsteady yet as she roused herself, filled a glass, brought it over.

"I'll hold it for you," said Emily.

Iris gulped it down, cool against her sticky throat. When she was done she said, "I ache something awful."

"Iris…"

"How long have I been here?"

"It's Sunday. About two days."

"And I'm just now waking up?"

"You been in and out. They been giving you some medicines to make you sleep, take away the pain."

"There was a shooting…"

"I know all about that.

"It just came out of nowhere. So fast, I didn't see it. He had me pegged. I went down. Right down." She shook her head. "Like a shot goose. That's all I can remember. Water."

"Here."

"How'd they find me?"

Emily sighed. "There was a neighbor. Heard the gunshots, came over and looked inside and saw you there and called the doc. It took awhile I guess and they finally got you on over to the hospital."

"Where are we?"

"Roseburg. They got a little hospital affair here. Roseburg Baptist."

"You shoulda seen his face when I came around the corner. He about shit his pants. Where's my rifle?" She made to get up but Emily held her back.

"Slow down now, Iris. You don't know but you almost died. Your arm was shot up bad. Broke the bones, that's what they said. And hit some kind of vein and you about bled out."

Iris looked at her left arm, swaddled wrist to elbow in plaster, the fingers beyond dyed purple. She closed her eyes. "How'd you find out I'd been shot, Momma?"

"Well, the sheriff of Douglas County here figured out who you are and called that Sheriff Kuntz. Then some young fella from the courthouse came out to the farm and let me know."

"That Jack fella?"

"I guess. It got all a blur when I heard the news."

"Where's Henry?" Iris started to sit up but Emily again stopped her with a firm hand.

"Matter of fact him and the dog are out in the truck."

"In the truck?"

"Says that's where he wants to be and the dog won't leave his side so that's where they are, two peas in a pod. Sleep out there on the seat. I bring 'em a supper from the café and they got a bunch of bushes there where they can relieve themselves…"

Iris started to laugh but that riled up the pain. "Lord, I hurt."

"Well I'd like to say it about serves you right, but I won't say that." Emily shook her head. "I do not for the life of me understand and here…" gestured at Iris' arm, "…is why. That's the sense of tryin' to catch criminals."

"He said I was lucky. Tom Fogerty. Lucky that he didn't kill me."

Emily looked off. Out the window, she saw streets and

long-shadowed buildings and trees. It all looked so regular. Like if you could just step outside you could have a regular life like regular people. But her own life wasn't participating in regular. It was all gummed up. "Damn's sake, Iris," she said softly. "What the hell are you up to? Guns and shoot-ups?"

"I know, Momma. I'm sorry. I ain't looking to get myself killed, that's for sure. I was just trying to do a job."

"It's not a job," Emily said. "It's a fool's errand."

A nun appeared, face framed by a crisp white cowl. "Everything all right here?"

"It's all right," said Iris.

"Can I get you anything, dear? Water with a little lemon in it?"

"She's in pain," said Emily. "Can you give her something for the pain?"

The nun did not smile. She switched on the wall light. "Visitors should be out by seven," she said. "The doctor will be making his rounds about eight. She'll be getting her regular dosage then."

"She's in pain right now," said Emily, standing, hands on hips. "Right now."

The nurse narrowed her eyes, raised her chin. "I'll see what I can do."

"Thank you," said Emily.

The nun shuffled away. Emily said, "I've got to see to Henry. We got to get back to the farm, see to the animals. Let him sleep in his bed. Then we'll be back out. They say you'll be here another few days." Paused, then, "I want you to be all right. You understand?"

Iris said nothing.

Emily looked at her hard, whispered. "We're gonna get you back to the farm."

The next morning Sheriff Morgan walked into Iris' room with his hat held in his hand. He didn't care much for decorum or any place where he had to take off his hat. Meeting important people. Funerals. Un-hatted, his hair held a permanent dent that circumnavigated his skull.

"Iris Greenlee?"

"Yes."

"I'm Sheriff Kirby Morgan of Douglas County. I need to talk with you."

"All right."

He pointed at her with his Stetson. "You are damn lucky."

"So I'm told."

"You caused quite a stir around here."

"That wasn't my intent."

"Well now, what did you expect? Chasin' after grown men, getting' involved with gunplay and all. What's in your head, missy?"

"I was just tryin' to bring a fella to justice."

"Just tryin' to bring a fella to justice. Well now, I don't know how it is where you come from, but up here we got laws and we got lawmen to handle all that."

"You let your criminals run around town, come and go as they please? Is that the kind of law you mean?"

He took a step forward. The Stetson came up again. "Now don't you get fresh with me, young lady. I could put you behind bars for trespassing and unlawful use of a firearm."

"Law says I can enter if there's a known criminal inside."

"Don't lecture me on the law, little girl. I'm the law. I know what's what."

"I didn't shoot, neither."

"Well now let's cut the bull. I got your spent cartridges and the bullet holes to prove it."

Iris frowned. "That fella Fogerty whipped out his pistol and took me down before I could spit. Like he was all ready."

"Evidence says you fired your weapon, that's not in dispute."

"Well I'm disputin' it."

The sheriff's face went dark. "You walking on thin ice, missy. If you was a man, you'd be in a cell instead of this cushy hospital."

Iris stared past Morgan toward the doorway.

"Anyways, the owner of the property you shot up says he won't bring up charges. Says he just wants you out of town."

"What about Tom Fogerty?"

"What about him?"

"You gonna go catch him? He's a wanted man and you're the law, as you keep sayin'."

Sheriff Kirby smiled in a not-friendly way. "You just leave that to me."

Iris nodded slow.

Kirby walked to the door, turned back to say, "And go back home, missy, as soon as you're able. And don't come back."

Later that day Iris had another visitor. A young man showed up carrying her valise. He carried it with two hands held in front of him.

"Hello," he said.

Iris blinked, hazy with laudanum. "Do I know you?"

"Oris. The desk clerk from the hotel."

"Oris?"

He broke into a grin at the sound of his name. "Oris."

"Well hey, Oris from the hotel."

"I brought your things over." He hefted the valise.

"Oh, I'd forgotten all about that."

"Everything's in there," he said, raising his eyebrows. "Everything."

Iris nodded.

"I went to the constable's office. Mr. Halley. Nice fella. He knows me. Said I could take care of your things. You know. Your *things* and such." He winked.

"You got my rifle in there?" That made her about giddy happy.

"I do," he beamed. "I took it apart some. The rifle. I figured that's how you carried it. I hope that's all right."

"Long as you didn't lose any parts."

"Oh gosh no. I had Mr. Halley show me. He knows all about rifles and pistols and everything. He fixes them in his shop. How's your arm? I heard Tom Fogerty shot you. Well, that's obvious you got shot, you being here at the hospital. Well, maybe not. You might have broken your leg, possibly. And you'd be here then, too. But he got away. Tom Fogerty. That's too bad. Really too bad. He probably got the drop on you."

"You could say he did."

"Your name isn't Becky Smith, is it? It's Iris Greenlee."

"That's me. Sorry about that little fib."

He waved his hand. "No, no. that's all right. I mean, I read about you in the papers. They say you're a bounty hunter. Actually, they say bounty *huntress*. I guess that's what you call a girl bounty hunter."

"Bounty *huntress?*"

"You're kinda famous. Look." He set the valise on the floor and gave Iris a newspaper he had under his arm, the local *Roseburg Bee*, pointed to the front page:

(from the *Roseburg Bee,*
July 23, 1927)

Shooting In The City!

*Bounty Huntress Attempts to
Bring in Suspect; Gets Shot and
Is Left for Dead*

An Applegate girl has taken up the role of bounty huntress and sought to bring in a Roseburg man wanted in connection with an arson fire in the town of Ashland. The girl, Iris Greenlee, daughter of Deputy Game Warden Dexter Greenlee who was shot and killed near Trail in 1914, an incident that sparked an enormously controversial trial and subsequent acquittal of the man accused of the murder.

Iris Greenlee is daughter of Emily Rink of Applegate.

Apparently, Miss Iris Greenlee traveled to Roseburg from Medford with the express notion of capturing the purported arsonist, Thomas Fogerty, son of well-known lumber businessman, Rupert Fogerty, owner of Fogerty Mill on Buckthorn Creek Road. In the dark of night, Miss Greenlee tiptoed into the Fogerty house on Spring Street armed with a Winchester rifle. Seeing Fogerty taking his leisure on a sofa in the living room, the girl loosed two quick shots, both of those missed their target. Fogerty returned fire and struck the girl on her shoulder, sending the Bounty Huntress crashing to the floorboards. The girl is currently recovering in the Roseburg Baptist Hospital.

Sheriff Kirby Morgan has said that guilty or not of the arson crime, Tom Fogerty acted in self-defense and that no additional charges would be brought against him for the shooting.

Iris winced. "Well that's just horse manure there."

"What do you mean? Isn't that what happened?"

"No! Well, yes some of it. But I never shot at the man. He was too quick for me."

"You didn't shoot?"

"Never had a chance. He winged me and I was down."

Oris nodded solemnly, folded the newspaper and held it in front of himself with both hands. "Well, no matter what, that was just about the bravest thing I ever heard a girl do, that's for sure. Hell, that was brave if you were a man."

"Jury's out on whether it was brave or godawful dumb, but I appreciate you saying so."

He cleared his throat.

Here it comes, thought Iris.

"Well I think you're quite a girl myself. I don't care what they say."

"What do they say?"

He hesitated. "They say you're a no-count, trying to make money by messing with the lives of good folks."

"Fairly harsh. Seeing as how I ain't made a nickel off the effort."

Oris considered. "Don't matter to me," he said at last. "I like you."

"That don't say a lot about your judgment."

"That Tom Fogerty. He's the real no-count."

"He may be a no-count but he outsmarted me."

"If it's all right I'd like to see you again. I'd call on you. There, I said it right out."

"You'd call on me?"

"If it's all right with you."

Iris gave a laugh-snort out her nose. It made her arm throb. No fella had ever said he'd like to call on her when she was healthy and upright. Now that she was flat on her back with a shot-up arm and looking like a horse turd here was a fella saying he liked her. It was funny and sad all at once. "We live out in the Applegate Valley. It's a long buggy ride from here."

"I've got an auto," he said eagerly. "My uncle does. It's a Ford."

Iris hesitated. She liked the boy all right, but not in the way he probably wanted her to. She liked his plain self. He seemed honest.

"Look, I'm not thinking about anything but healing up right now. You understand? I got some complications I've got to figure out."

Oris looked down again, nodding. "Why sure. I understand."

"Hadn't you better get back to the hotel?"

"It's my day off."

"Huh," said Iris, thinking. Then, "Look, can you get your uncle's car? Like, right now?"

He looked up. "Right now?"

"I got a favor to ask."

He frowned. "What's that?"

"Would you drive me out to my farm?"

"To the Applegate?"

"Yes."

"Don't you have to stay here awhile yet?"

Iris looked around. Everything—walls, floor, ceiling—was square and hard and held no feeling. "I can't stay here any more."

"Why not?"

She looked at him. "I just can't. I been here days now."

"Well…"

"I'll give you some money for the gasoline."

"Well…"

"My momma's isn't getting back here until tomorrow. This would save her a trip and a whole lot of trouble. She might have you set for dinner."

He brightened. "That could be all right."

"It'll kinda be like you're calling on me. You can see the farm, and the river if you want. Meet my brother and my momma."

"I suppose."

"My overalls in that valise?"

"Um, yes. The dress, too. The pretty one. It's bloody though." He squirmed, knowing he'd seen her undergarments also.

"How long will it take you to round up your uncle's automobile?"

"An hour maybe if he's not riding in it."

"All right, I'll be out front in an hour."

"Is this like you're escaping?"

"Yup."

He grinned. "You just gonna walk straight out of here? Won't they try and stop you?"

"I'm gonna put on those overalls and walk straight out

of here carrying this valise and I guarantee you they won't stop me from leaving."

As Oris disappeared down the hallway Iris got out of her hospital gown and struggled with her bad arm to get into her overalls and plain blouse. Her left side just didn't want to cooperate. From the bottom of the bag the dismantled Winchester gave off a familiar oily, burnt-powder scent. The nurse had absent-mindedly left a bottle of laudanum on the instrument stand. Iris stashed that in the valise and walked out. The halls were empty. She thought she might have to bluff her way out but there was no one to question her. Her footfalls snapped off the linoleum.

The auto was a Model T roadster and Oris put the top down and let the wind billow through and around and Iris wiggled the fingers of her good arm at the hurrying air. They shimmied through the streets of the town and gained the highway into the Applegate Valley.

"We're escaping!" Oris shouted over the sound of the auto.

She smiled at him with her hair blown sideways across her grin and Oris felt a pang. How did he end up in this car with this amazing girl? Thank you Uncle Tobias.

After a while Iris said, "Where do you suppose that Tom Fogerty got to?"

"I don't know. For sure he's out of town. Maybe he's with one of the Fogerty's logging outfits, out in the woods somewhere."

"Where are they logging?"

He shrugged. "They always got a few things going. They just started a new operation up the Umpqua, I know that. It was in the papers."

Iris nodded, watched the countryside.

Oris shook his fist. "Hell, we're the escapees."

Iris smiled without turning to look at him. Somehow

the pain in her arm had toned down. Perhaps it was the drought of laudanum she'd taken. "Hell yes," she said as the little Ford tracked the curves of the two-lane and ahead the valley chevroned into a pure blue sky.

Emily and Iris sat on the back steps leading to the porch. It was night. Henry lay awake on a blanket they'd spread for him at the bottom of the stairs. He was trying to count stars. Iris had her wounded arm in a white cotton sling.

"Get me John Rink's tobacco and pipe," said Emily.

"Momma, you don't smoke tobacco."

"I can and I will."

"It's godawful old."

"Not going to make much difference to somebody who doesn't smoke."

"Shouldn't you be waitin' on me on account of I'm the one who's shot up?"

"I'm not catering to some fool who goes and gets themselves shot up. Now please. I believe I'd like to smoke some tobacco."

Iris went inside.

Emily looked down at Henry's shape on the blanket. "What do you see in the stars tonight, Henry?"

"A lot."

"Well like what?"

"A boy."

"A boy? A nice boy, like you?"

"Yes."

"You see things clear, you know that, Henry?"

"Yes."

"Here it is, Momma." Iris had the pouch and cradled

in her arm and the pipe and matches in her hand

Emily took the pouch and the stained meerschaum and filled the bowl and struck a match on the rough board step and fire blossomed white then yellow and the glow lingered on their faces. The tobacco sizzled orange and smoke curled out and Emily blew out a stream that melted into the night.

"That tastes like crap," said Emily.

"Don't smell no better."

"Ugh," complained Henry.

She took another pull and took the smoke into her lungs and then exhaled. "Nothin' to it," she said.

They were all quiet then, listening to the frogs and the river and every so often, the screech of an owl.

"That old barn owl."

"Thinks he's a dandy. Gonna get all the girls."

Emily said, "What about that boy? Oris? The one that drove you out from the hospital."

"What about him?"

"Are you interested in him?"

Iris shook her head. "Not like that."

Emily sighed. "He was kind of an odd duck."

"You could say."

"Well, you're a pretty girl and you don't want to lead a fella on, you know." Emily set the pipe to glowing.

"He's operating under his own steam," said Iris. "I'm not stoking his boilers."

"There he goes," said Henry.

"Who?" said Iris.

Henry was silent.

"So," said Emily. "Is there any fella you're interested in?"

"I don't know. Maybe."

"Whoo-wee! Who's that?"

"Now don't go booking the church. You don't know him. A fella down at the courthouse."

"That fella that came out here to tell me you was shot up in Roseburg?"

"That's him."

"What's he do? Is he a lawyer?"

"No, nothing like that. He's sort of a clerk, I guess."

"What's his name?" Emily knocked the last embers from the pipe, put it on the step.

"Jack."

"Jack What?"

"I'm not sure. Drummond. Not that."

"You don't know his name? You know anything about him?"

"Seems like a regular fella."

"That's what you like about him? He's a *regular fella?*"

Iris shrugged. "Maybe."

"Well?"

"I don't know. I just think about him. He's got a funny way about him."

"The Big Dipper," said Henry, pointing overhead.

"That's right. We read about it in the encyclopedia," said Emily, settling the pipe stem in a corner of her mouth. "There's the cup and there's the handle."

"Yes."

"All right," she murmured. "All right."

Chapter Nineteen
August, 1927

"MOMMA."

Emily came awake slow, heard the voice again and it came not from somewhere else but from inside her core.

"Momma."

That tone. Something was wrong. She got out of bed, went to the porch. It cool outside. Henry was snoring softly but Iris had thrown off her blanket.

"Momma."

Emily came to her, sat beside, a hand to her daughter's forehead said the girl was on fire. Iris' eyes were open but unseeing in the soft light of the quarter moon.

"You're burning up."

"I'm cold."

"Henry!" said Emily.

Henry did not stir.

"Get up, Henry! Get up!"

His humped up shape moved. He said, "It's not the morning."

"Get up and get yourself dressed. We got to help your sister. Iris is in trouble."

Henry kept his back to Emily. "Is she sick?"

"She's real sick, and I need your help."

"I don't know."

"It's easy. We're just going to take a ride in the truck."

His voice brightened. "The truck?"

"Yup. In the middle of the night. Can you do that?"

"I like the truck."

"Then please get yourself dressed." Emily went to the washstand, dampened a cloth, brought it to Iris' bed and laid it across her daughter's forehead. "Can you do that? Get yourself dressed?"

"Maybe."

"Say it, Henry. Say, *all right, Momma.*"

"Maybe."

"Well, that'll have to do. I'm going to get Iris out to the truck. You come along and we'll ride, pants or no pants. All right?"

"All right." Henry got himself out of bed, stood for a moment considering. He had been offered a choice, pants or no pants. He said, "I'm going to put on my pants."

"Good."

The surgeon, Doctor C.C. Cathcart, originally of Walla Walla, Washington, and educated at the School of Medicine at the University of Washington and now chief—make that the only—trauma surgeon at St. Bartholomew Catholic Hospital in downtown Medford, had a particular fondness for laudanum. Not to the point of incapacitation, of course. Never that. But a dram of the stuff pre-operation gave him foundation, steadiness needed to perform the most delicate maneuvers on the operating table.

From a locked drawer at his desk he took the dark brown bottle—his private reservoir—and pried off the stopper and took a swig bitter and tart as unripe cherries. He felt the drug in his gullet, slowly sinking along the length of his chest, until it arrived in the center of his being.

Like a light from within. He replaced his bottle, thought about a second sip—just a topper—took another quick swallow, hid the bottle in its nest and locked the drawer, strode confidently toward the operating room. He was so ready for surgery that he almost walked directly into the theater without scrubbing up! Imagine! He whistled while he soaped and rinsed and dried in the anteroom.

Waiting in the operating room were two stout nurses and an anesthesiologist who sat on a stool next to an instrument stand where four syringes had been arranged with military precision. The patient lay in familiar repose on the operating table that, according to Doctor Cathcart's instructions, had been leveled at seventy-eight centimeters from the floor. The anesthesiologist blinked rapidly above his surgical mask. At the edge of the bright operating lights stood an attendant with a rubberized disposal bag.

"Tonight we have a female," Doctor Cathcart began, talking while one of the nurses tied a surgical mask around his face. "Late teens. Local girl. Gunshot victim." Doctor Cathcart spoke the way he dreamed he would speak while lecturing in the twilight of his career at prestigious medical colleges throughout the country. With gravitas and excellent diction. Iris lay on the operating table, breathing loudly, eyes closed. She had been given a large dose of opiate tincture by the anesthesiologist, and her respiration had slowed and deepened. Her left arm had been strapped to an arm support that stuck out at nearly right angles to her body. She was loosely covered with sheets.

Cathcart slipped a triangle of sheet off Iris' shoulder and pointed. "You'll see an entry wound here, penetrating the deltoid and, miracle of miracles, passing between the scapula and the clavicle, leaving nary a scratch on either, and managing all the while to avoid the subclavian artery and vein, but just nicking the cephalic, causing near catastrophic blood loss, before exiting the infraspinatus. Fortunately, the vein was successfully cauterized. Despite the considerable amount of flesh removed on the posterior side of the wound, this damage is beginning to heal without evidence of dehiscence."

Then Doctor Cathcart pulled back the sheet to reveal the lower forearm. "Our real culprit is the second wound," he intoned with Shakespearean resonance, as if the narrator at the opening act of a dramatic play. "Major trauma to the forearm approximately thirteen centimeters from the carpals, the ulna and radius each showing multiple impact fractures, the bones have been set for five weeks now in a plaster cast. Crude but serviceable ligations..." and here Doctor Cathcart was taking a backhanded swipe at the work of his colleague of the Roseburg Baptist Hospital, Bjorn Svensk, a big-boned Swede from Minnesota who Doctor Cathcart was not particularly fond of on account of Svensk was considered to be something of a ladies man. Cathcart wished he would be considered as a ladies man, but he was dull and pedantic and he knew he was not a ladies man at all. But in the operating room, in the throes of a procedure, with a scalpel in his hand and his white-smocked attendants all around and a tad of laudanum to sharpen his focus, he felt resplendent.

"...to the radial artery and the cubital vein have adequately serviced the damage but unfortunately, as you can see, osteomyelitis has proclivicated throughout the ulna, quite likely due to unsanitary conditions in the initial operating room which, I believe we can all agree, is the plague of any rural surgeon who is obliged to operate in, shall we say, less than antiseptic conditions." Cathcart smiled at the murmured assents, the implication that the operating room at St. Bartholomew was anything but unsophisticated. "Further, the necrosis has not been adequately debrided, and we can all see the results, including several nascent neuroma.

"This morning I will be performing an AE acquired amputation of the patient's left arm in order to prevent migration of the sepsis. Pen." He held out his hand for the instrument and one of the nurses promptly placed the marking tool in his palm. "I'm grateful for the assistance of all of you." He nodded and then drew two Z-shaped lines, one on each side of Iris' forearm. "The incisions will begin approximately twenty centimeters above the distal end of the humerus." He frowned. Iris' sweaty skin had caused the ink to become blurry. He turned to one of the nurses. "Wipe off her arm," he said darkly, "and I'll thank you to attend with more alacrity."

With the arm dried, Cathcart redrew his guide lines. "I'll be employing the Wembley flap, which provides a more antiseptic closure."

Cathcart nodded at the anesthesiologist. "We'll be giving the patient intravenous thiopental, appreciated for its swift onset. My esteemed colleague Doctor..?"

"Ah, Grant. Howie Grant."

"Yes, Doctor Grant is our anesthesiologist of record." Cathcart pointed at the anesthesiologist's tray of syringes. "A slowly administered dose is required to prevent respiratory depression and the possibility of overstimulation. Don't be alarmed if there is a temporary apnea following an injection. It's quite typical, wouldn't you say, Doctor Grant?"

A muffled *Yes!* came from behind the anesthesiologist's mask.

"In addition, an opiate or barbiturate often precedes, in this case two milliliters of tincture of opium."

"Yes!" chorused Doctor Grant, enthused by Doctor Cathcart's narrative about anesthetics. "Administered not half an hour ago."

"Excellent. I'll now apply the tourniquet proximal to my little drawing here."

The nurse quickly loosened the arm restraint so the tourniquet cuff could be placed around her arm. Cathcart inflated the device himself, carefully watching the pressure gauge which was, at the moment, quite a charming face with a dial nose and grinning logo.

"Doctor Cathcart?"

"Yes?"

"Pardon me sir, but shouldn't the pressure be below seventy?"

"Of course," Cathcart replied with a touch of irritation. "I begin with a slight over-inflation and then reduce." This was not true. He had never overinflated before. "My method greatly reduces the chance of exsanguination prior to effective cauterization," he added, letting disdain drip into his vowels. He looked at the second nurse who had stationed herself by the cauterization generator. "Are you ready?"

"Yes," volunteered the anesthesiologist, and Cathcart frowned. "I was speaking to the nurse."

"Yes, of course."

"Scalpel. A three graduated, please. With an eleven." He held out a hand.

The nurse snapped the blade handle into his hand. He took it. As usual, the moment Cathcart positioned the instrument in his hand it seemed to melt into his fingers, as if there was no difference between steel and flesh. Everything became one entity—eyes, arm, fingers, blade. A ring of red sprung from Iris' skin as the scalpel encircled her arm. The nurse sponged, held a drain tray.

"Nuh," said Iris, shifting inside her drugged stupor.

"Thiopental," said Cathcart, his eyes fetching the anesthesiologist. The doctor readied a hypodermic.

The blade severed muscle, reaching progressively

deeper, the flesh opening like a sigh. Blood dripped into the tray. At the bottom of the cut the bone smiled. The stench of putrid flesh lifted to mix with the exorcising bite of sodium hypochlorite.

The surgeon lifted the flap of skin, removed the intrusive muscle around the humerus. The bone beckoned.

"Saw," breathed Cathcart.

The nurse complied. The attendant with the rubberized bag stepped forward.

"The Satterlee bone saw." Cathcart held it upright under the operating lights. "One of the finest surgical instruments ever created. This particular example is in my personal collection. I operate with nothing less. Single-piece construction exquisitely rendered in stainless steel by Hans Fischer of Munich." He moved the saw this way and that, watching gleams run along its edges. After a long moment, during which the nurses exchanged glances several times, Doctor Cathcart reached down and applied the blade to bone.

And Iris screamed.

Chapter Twenty
August 1927

SHE STAYED INSIDE for five days in an opiate-induced haze, mostly sitting in the kitchen chair looking out the window watching leaves move and the dog trotting in and out of her view. Pain came in hard waves of mean-spirited throbbing, twisting any spate of relief back into fresh pain, reinventing itself in new ways, sharper, heavier, moving along the length of her stump, up into her shoulder, sometimes coming from the nether regions of a limb that didn't exist any more. Pain filled her up to the point of being sick and then ebbed away, leaving her drained and pale. She thought about things she wouldn't be able to do. Tie her boot laces. Thread a needle. Hammer a froe. Saddle the horse. Everything. Everything.

On the sixth day Iris said she'd manage by herself for awhile if her Momma wanted to take Henry down to the river to pan for gold. When they were gone, Iris got up the courage to look at her stump in the mirror over the washstand. She peeled off her blouse and held the stump to the glass. She'd known it was there; she saw it glance-wise out of the corner of her eye, but she'd never taken a good long look at the thing. The end all lumpy red and the stitch line unnaturally square and the drainage hole staring back at her unnatural with its weeping eye. *There once was a hand there, a good hand. And now there isn't.*

She got her blouse back on and went outside and

stood on the porch. The loose sleeve waved loose in the moving air. There were finches in the trees. The big leaf maples drooped from the long dry summer but the sky was pale gray; there was rain coming.

She started down the porch steps and as she did she reached for the railing with a left hand that was nothing but deception—nothing at all—and her phantom hand passed through the rough wood bannister and she started to fall, slow as a big maple leaf loosed from its branch, her stump arm flapping with sad desperation. Her feet tangled in themselves and she fell and fell, put out her right hand to break her fall but still smashed her face directly into the hard gray ground. She lay stunned and bewildered at the bottom of the stairway.

She tried to pick up her head but her will power had left and she couldn't or wouldn't, only turned her face slightly so she wasn't eye-to-eye with the dirt. She tasted blood, probably bit her tongue and maybe busted her nose, stump arm rioting like somebody'd stuck a knife in it which, as a matter of fact, somebody had, and stupid was running out of her nose and down her throat and the end of what used to be her left arm. Stupid just oozing every-where. *What in the world made you think you could track down a wanted fella? Somebody dangerous like that? You dumb stupid horse turd. And now you've gone and made it worse for everybody. Dumb shit girl gone and fell down the porch steps, a freak show, a crippled mutt lying in the dirt with a stump arm, only two steps out of the gate and already used up and worthless.*

Then there was pain and anger and a haunting terror that life had changed for the worse and there was no going back. She was being cut away piece by piece.

She wanted to disappear. Vanish forever. Go down to the river and just slide in, clothes and all, let the water wrap its liquid jade arms around her, clear and cool and forgiving. She'd wash down on the flow, twirling rotating softly under the big alders, out into the riffles, into the pools. Everything would be cool and green. It would get quieter, then dark. She wouldn't fall down any more. Wouldn't bleed. Momma would be relieved not to have a cripple around, can't do this and can't do that, wouldn't have to take care of two out-of-sorts children all on her own. Henry would get on with it. That's just the way he was. And Momma would be unburdened, refreshed, probably get another good man—she'd picked well in terms of character but maybe not so much in terms of the long run—and they'd be all right, her and Henry. They'd just get on. And she—Iris—could drift away.

Maybe they'd write it up in the newspaper. *Worthless Bounty Huntress Girl Drowns in River.* Who'd care? The city boy Jack Dressler? That no-count Sheriff Kuntz? With his big fat moustache looks like he's trying to stuff a raccoon up his nose?

The thought of the sheriff got Iris' head off the dirt. That bull-shitting Kuntz sudden in her mind. She found her right arm and heaved herself up on an elbow, felt the world had tilted somehow. Or like it wouldn't stay still. It made her queasy. She took a deep breath, got up to sitting. She wiped her hand across her face and her fingers came away bloody. She looked at her stump, lifted it, the empty blouse sleeve crumpled and dirty and bloodied from its failed attempt to be a whole arm and she damn well better have not busted anything loose in there.

She gave her nose a tweak to see if it was broken, although it wouldn't make much difference one way or the other, given her state. Blood leaked and made dark splatters on the dirt. She got to her knees. Red, tear-shaped stains striped the front of her blouse. She stood up, waited until things stopped moving. Then she climbed back up the porch steps, careful to hold onto the railing with her good hand, the old wood splintery rough against her palm. The missing arm swung at her side; she could feel air passing between each ghosted finger.

Got a washrag from the kitchen, went to the washstand in her mother's room, the dark soothing walls, the faded calico curtains, the little curved tie-backs John Rink had made out of fence wire. She dabbed the blood off her face, took a couple of futile swipes at the stains along the front of her blouse. Her nose didn't look broken, just beat up. She rinsed the rag and set it across the back of a chair, took the bloodied water one-handed and made her way to the front porch and tossed the water into the bushes. Went back inside.

The laudanum was in the cartridge cabinet and Iris undid the latch and got the square brown bottle and had to sit down to put the bottle between her knees so she could unstop the cork and she took the bottle to her lips and let the bitter liquid work its way to her innards. She waited a good long minute, took another swig, another minute, one more swallow, put the bottle back and locked the cabinet. Just above was the Winchester on its pegs.

She stood for a long while in the dark quiet of the cabin watched dust float through window light and soon the laudanum was lifting her up and she took down the Winchester and went out to the porch and sat on the floorboards. She stared at the rifle as it straddled the caldera of her skirted lap and thought, *How do I clean you with one arm?*

She could probably unscrew the lever and get out the receiver all right. Maybe hold the butt between her legs so she could send a brush and a rag through the bore.

She was drifting. She could see perfectly but it was hard to focus. She picked up the carbine in her one hand, set the butt between her thighs, squeezed, tried to cock the lever but it pulled right out from her legs.

She stood. The board-and-batt siding of the cabin was waving. She put the stock between her thighs edgeways, right in the crook above her knees. It hurt that way but she had a better grip, and she reached down and racked the lever hard and the hammer went back and stayed cocked.

She took the Winchester in her right hand and reflexively her left arm came up, level and stiff. There was just enough length to the stump for her to set the fore grip on her bloody sleeve. It hurt to hold her sawed-off arm up that way. She settled the rifle, sighted down, lined up the bead on an old wren house nailed to an oak seventy-five yards away. Screw the pain. Breathe, hold, shoot. The firing pin snapped forward against an empty chamber.

"Bam," said Iris.

The screen door whapped in its dry frame and her mother was there.

"Iris, what are you doing?"

"Nothing."

"Why do you have the rifle? And good Lord you're a mess. You've got blood all over."

"I don't know. I fell."

"Where'd you fall?"

Iris pointed at the porch steps. "I fell right on my face. You should have seen it. It was a real comedy."

"You need to get cleaned up."

"I'm washed up."

"No you're not. You're hardly…"

Iris slipped to her knees, folded down like a marionette with cut strings. The rifle clattered to the floorboards. Everything was moving, swirling. Maybe she was already in the river. "Hold me Momma."

"I'll get a washrag."

"Just hold me."

Emily got on her knees facing her daughter and put both arms around her, careful of her stump, which felt hard and struggling under the fold of her embrace. Iris put her head in her mother's neck.

"I'm sorry, Momma. I'm so sorry."

"Nothing's your fault, Iris. Nothing at all."

"I made everything worse. And now I'm nothing but a cripple and a no-count and I can't figure how to feed the chickens, how am I gonna hold the bucket and throw the grain?"

Emily gave it thought. "You put the bucket on the ground. Move it along as you need."

"Momma."

Emily could feel the tears seep through her blouse. They stayed that way for nearly an hour, Iris sobbing twin circles of wet onto Emily's shoulder and then nearly fading away to sleep. Emily held Iris and tried to will the hurt out of the girl and into herself if need be. If that's what it took. *Lord let this child alone. Let this family alone. Enough of the trials and tribulations.* Emily could hear Henry as he sat inside and swept a wooden spoon across the floor in relentless arcs, the utensil clacking across the seams in the flooring like a clock with an engine of flesh.

Chapter Twenty-One
October, 1927

IRIS WAS UNRAVELING, like an old sweater. Each day a part of her loosened, undid itself, fell away. She sat on the front porch facing the road with the bottle of laudanum nearby. Sounds and smells and even the look of things were all on the other side of a gauzy curtain, a mist that obscured the day and blurred the night. She left her meals half eaten. She lost weight, her legs thinned. The dog's insistent, hopeful nose went un-stroked. The few chores she attempted often ended with her sitting on the ground, cocooned in her fog. Once Henry saw her there and went to sit with her back-to-back but he was now bigger than her, heavier, and she did not have the strength or will to support him and she slumped until he got up, confused, and went away.

Six weeks after the surgery Emily left Iris asleep on her bed on the back porch and took Henry and drove out to the road and down a piece and pulled over and waited. Mr. Hansen drove by and stopped and asked if everything was all right. Emily waved him on with a smile.

In about an hour the family doctor from Jacksonville came up the road in his swanky LaSalle coupe, making his rounds. Emily got out of the truck cab to flag him down.

"Mrs. Greenlee," said the doctor, leaning out of his auto, "I was just coming to see Iris."

"Yessir, Doctor Reese, and no offense, but we don't need you coming out here any more."

The doctor frowned. "Well why not, Mrs. Greenlee? Certainly the girl should be checked, routinely, make sure she's healing properly."

"She's healing, and she don't need the laudanum any more."

Another frown, a dismissive shake of the head. A fresh bottle of the drug—Iris' weekly prescription—was in a paper bag on the seat next to the doctor. "I'm sure she's in considerable pain. And another bout of sepsis…" he shrugged, "…could have dire consequences."

"Thank you all the same, Doctor Reese, but we'll make out. It's a family decision."

The doctor was nonplussed. He tapped a finger loudly on the outside of the auto. "You realize you're putting the girl in jeopardy?"

"She's in good hands, thank you."

He nodded, fiddled with the gear shift, then turned and said, "Be sure to wash the wound and keep it clean." Then he motored off.

Emily turned the truck around and drove home and found Iris sitting on the back porch facing the road. The dog lay a few feet away. Iris seemed to be staring at something in the nearby tree branches.

"Sit near your sister," Emily said to Henry, then she went inside and came back with a volume from the *Encyclopedia Britannica*. She sat with her back against a porch post. "Volume seventeen, Lord Chamberlain through Mecklenberg," she said. "A family favorite."

Henry snorted.

"Enough of that," said Emily. She split the volume open at random, scanned the pages. "Maine," she began, "is a state in the northeast portion of the United States. It was admitted to the Union in 1820 as the country's twenty-third state. It is one of the least-populated of all the states. It is known for its rugged, rocky coast, large forests, and many rivers and streams. It is a major supplier of lumber and seafood…"

⚜

Two days later Emily was feeding the chickens when Iris came hustling down from the cabin, the liveliest Emily had seen her in months. "Momma," she yelled. "Momma."

"What, Iris?"

"Where's that damn doctor and my medicine?" Iris came up, flushed and sweating.

"He's not coming out here any more."

"What do you mean, *he's not coming here any more?*"

"I told him to leave off bringing you the laudanum."

"What the hell did you do that for?"

"It's time for you to get past it."

"What the hell are you saying?" Iris was shouting. She held up her stump. "I'm in a world of hurt, don't you give a damn?"

"I give a damn. That's why I did it."

"Well hell," Iris snapped, "I'll just thumb my way into town and see the doctor myself." She turned and stomped off, but Emily ran ahead and stood in her way.

"That's not gonna happen." She was still holding the bucket of grains and scraps.

Iris clenched her fist. "Is that right?"

"That's so. And besides, that doctor can't give you any medicine unless I say so on account of you live on this farm and that means I'm in charge of what goes on here."

"You can't stop me."

"I can. You're wasted away. You ain't strong any more. I can wrestle you to the ground and hog-tie you in about two shakes."

Iris couldn't quite see. Things were moving when they shouldn't. She tried to blink clear. She felt her mother's hand on her wrist.

"Take a deep breath," said Emily.

Iris did; the swaying world slowed, stopped.

"Henry!" called Emily. He appeared from behind the coop. "We're going to the river."

"I don't want to go to the damn river," said Iris.

"We're going." Emily's hand did not leave her daughter's wrist.

They walked single file, Emily leading Iris, her daughter offering about as much resistance as a carnival balloon. The dog loped ahead and Henry trailed close behind. By the river's edge the air had cooled but it was warm in the swaths of late autumn sun, blushes of yellow in the trees and bushes, last bright red leaves of poison oak clinging to stems.

"Sit there," Emily said to Henry, pointing to a flat rock. "Turn your back."

Henry sat with his back to the river.

"All right," said Emily. She undid the front buttons of her cotton dress, let it fall in a heap. Took off her bloomers and stood naked in the sun.

"Momma." Iris stared. She hadn't seen her mother naked in forever. She was amazing, her Momma, with her white skin and browned forearms and neck and triangle of fluff at her crotch. Like some kind of farm mermaid. Brown hair, darker than her own and flecked with gray along the sides, reached halfway down her back.

Emily smiled, then she stepped to the water's edge and dove in headlong. She came up with water streaming across her grin. "Come on in! Oh my Lord it feels great!"

"I...I," Iris couldn't speak it, she was confused. About being at the river. What was her mother doing?

"What's the matter, you chicken?" taunted her momma, side-stroking in the green pool, yellow leaves scattered across the surface.

"I'm not chicken," Iris muttered. She was hazy. It was way too bright.

"Well?"

And yes, dammit, maybe she was scared. About swimming. With one and a half arms.

"Bwock bwock!" burbled Emily.

"Wack, wack," echoed Henry.

"Fuck," said Iris. She got after her own buttons. They were tiny, unmanageable. They slipped through her slow dumb fingers. Her right hand was a fool without its companion and her stump kept rising up like a thing with its own mind to try and help. She frowned and cursed. And then the buttons were undone and she stood in her knickers. Then those were off and she walked to the river and her body was sweaty and stupid and clumsy and she stood there, her toes clinging to the rough granite edge.

"You'll be fine," said her mother. "I'm here."

Iris didn't dive so much as fall headfirst into the early autumn water and it was colder than she figured and shocked her breath out and she surfaced and gulped and realized she was afloat and swimming of sorts, her legs and her hand and her stump arm churning. She looked at her Momma's glistening face not smiling now but calm and serene and watching her. Iris took a breath and dove under and the water was no longer cold, it was good and sharp and it peeled the haze off her skin and shimmered against her body, and her eyes came clear and she stroked hard with her one hand and kicked like crazy and in the slanted sunlight she saw the tiny darting trout and at the bottom of the pool the green nuggets of river jade.

Two days later Emily awoke to the sound of gunfire. A single shot. The sound in her dreaming but real as she came to. The daylight was bright; she'd overslept. The bedside clock said seven. She grabbed her housecoat and padded into the living room and saw that the Winchester was off its pegs. Out on the porch both Henry and Iris were gone, blankets turned back. Another shot cracked. She knew that sound. It was the Winchester, down by the river. Where John Rink and Iris would target practice. She went barefoot out into the yard and Ajax came bounding up with his loopy grin.

Iris stood in the clearing where John Rink had set up a little stand for reloading. Henry sat on his knees on a blanket nearby, hands on his thighs, looking down at the ground but facing his sister. Iris had on her overalls, stood sighting down the rifle, the stump arm up and supporting the stock, the loose unfilled sleeve of the blouse hanging limp, taking aim at a broke-off white pine trunk, nine feet tall and hoary with splinters and bullet gouges, some sixty yards away.

The rifle barked, Iris jolted back and Henry gave a squeal and a little jump up off his knees and clapped his hands. No telltale jump of shattered wood. A miss.

"Hell," said Iris.

"Hell," said Henry.

"What's this?" said Emily.

Iris didn't turn toward her mother. "Target practicing."

"I can see that. Why so early?"

She pointed at Henry. "That ornery critter there, he got me up."

Henry tried to make a disgusted face but couldn't control a grin. He pointed. "You don't have an arm." Rocked back and forth, smile stretched across cheeks fuzzed with young whiskers, pleased with the banter.

"At least you ain't mad at me," Iris said to Henry.

He shook his head.

"I was thinking you'd be mad at me on account of now I'm different and I know you don't like things to change much."

He thought about that, said, "No."

"But I'm different now."

"You're Iris," he concluded. "Shoot now."

Iris put the stock between her knees, got her fingers in the lever and racked hard and the rifle slipped out sideways. "Damn."

"I can do it for you." Emily took a step forward.

"No," barked Iris. "I'll do it." She wedged the stock between her legs, just above the knees. Fingers into the lever, hard snap and the hammer caught but the rifle dropped to the ground.

"Careful!" said Emily and regretted it.

"I'm careful as a cripple can be."

"Don't say that. You lost an arm. There's lots of people…"

"I don't want to hear about lots of people."

"Shoot now, Iris," Henry said.

Iris looked at her mother. "I aim to hunt deer and keep us in meat." She hefted the carbine, lifted her stump, set the stock across the ledge of flesh. The dog had come up and took a seat next to Henry and the boy put his arm around the dog like they were an old couple and the rifle cracked and the dog's ears went forward and Henry gave another delighted jump and Emily could swear her son's ears cocked forward too.

So here they were, a menagerie in morning light that had just lifted off the far ridges and now struck out across the valley in warm yellow, a one-armed daughter shooting at a broke-off tree and an addled boy and two dead husbands in the ground and a dog too dumb to know this wasn't at all like a regular family. And what was she? The sorriest ringmaster you could want. Truth be told she didn't know how to hold it all together, she was nothing but the last piece of thread in the britches.

The rifle barked and there was no *whap!* of bullet against wood. Another miss.

"Damn." Iris glared at her left shoulder and stump as if they were being disloyal.

Emily wanted to say, *What did you expect? You're two months out of having your arm sawed off and you got a bullet hole in the shoulder that's yet to heal and you got open wounds inside of you that will never close up no matter how hard you pray.* But she didn't. She said, "You get your fill of wasting good bullets here then there's eggs to gather and a horse needs grain and fresh hay and water."

Then she turned and went back up to the cabin.

Chapter Twenty-Two
March, 1928

IT WAS MORNING, the sun fully crested the ridges to the east. Iris was trying to teach Henry to split shingles. She'd set up a bolt of cedar and set the blade of the froe along the top and told her brother to hit down on the froe with a big oak hammer John Rink had made for the purpose. As Henry was inclined to let his eyes wander his aim was poor and several times he missed the froe and bolt altogether and came within a whisker hit hitting Iris in the knee. They finally cracked off a couple of good ones and Iris said, "We're quite a team."

Iris looked over to see her mother coming down from the cabin. She was carrying something. When she got close Iris saw it was a holster belt. The handle of a pistol curved out of the scabbard. Emily walked up to Iris and handed the rig to her. "Your daddy's gun," she said. "Your daddy Dexter."

Iris shook her head. "Where'd you get it?"

"I've had it. It's been in a secret place in the bedroom. In case we needed it, but really I think just to have a piece of him around. I didn't even tell John. I kind of regret that. But it's time to move ahead, and I think by rights and by circumstances it should be yours. So there it is. You take it now."

Iris stared at it, the wood-brown grip of the revolver curving out of the holster; the leather unscarred but gone dark red like an old saddle. She took it all in her hand, lifted it, judged the heft of it all, put it on the loading table so she could slide the revolver out of its sheath. The bite of the checkering was sharp against her palm. Barely used. Daddy's ghosted hand there.

"Cartridges," Emily said, putting a box on the up-turned cedar bolt. "They're fresh. I buy 'em every couple of years or so, to make sure."

"Why are you doin' this, Momma?"

"You know why."

"Put the belt on me."

"I was hopin' you wouldn't ask me that right off."

"Please, Momma."

Henry turned so he could peek out sideways.

Emily hesitated. She'd come this far with it, now she'd have to go all the way. Iris held up her good arm and her half arm. Emily took the belt and reached it around her daughter and threaded the belt tip through the buckle but there weren't enough holes in the strap to get it tight and it slipped over Iris' skinny hips down to her knees.

"I'll fix it," said Emily, and she unbuckled it and took the belt and went up to the work shed and was glad for the cool air and the murmuring trees and she got out the big awl and thought, *Dear Jesus if you're there, I need you more than ever.* And she laid the rig out on a piece of pine board and drove the point of the awl through the strap pushing with both hands, one atop the other.

Iris got where she could shift fast with her right hand while she steered the Packard truck with her thighs. Her thighs were almost as reliable as a hand, their touch on the bottom of the wheel true, working in tandem, one thigh passing the rim of the wheel to the other thigh as her feet pumped the clutch, brake, and accelerator pedals while right hand worked the gear shifter and the steering. If needed she could lean forward and steady the steering wheel with her stump. She could take an S-curve at good throttle, the wind billowing through the cab, Ajax leaning out the passenger window with jowls flapping. Alone and moving was relief from her own self. And gave her time to think.

On a Tuesday in March, the week of her nineteenth birthday and eight months after she'd been shot, Iris took the flatbed down to Jacksonville and had Bert Peeler the welder make quarter-inch iron bars into a grid of two-inch squares. The grid was sized to fit over the rear window of the hack and was held in place with bolts. There was no way someone riding on the bed could reach through the rear window and grab the driver, namely Iris. She told Peeler she planned to haul loads of cut lumber and didn't want the boards running through the back window if she made a sudden stop.

She had welder forge four stout tie-down rings and attach them to the floorboards with through-bolts, two toward the front of the bed and two near the back.

"Pretty stout tie-downs," he remarked. "You sure this buggy can carry the weight?"

"I'm sure," said Iris.

"How you gonna load this thing with one arm?"

She bared her teeth. "I'm gonna scare it up there."

He looked at the cab. "How you drive this thing, anyway? With that one arm? How you steer and shift at the same time?"

"I got a method."

Peeler shook his head. He'd heard stories about this girl. "That'll be four dollars."

"I'm going on a trip. For wood. I get paid after I make the run. Can you wait until then, Mr. Peeler?"

The welder squinted. "When's that?"

"One week from today. Can you let me go till then?"

"How come you askin' me after my work is done?" Peeler wiped his hands on his apron.

"You know I'm good for it."

"I dunno. What if something happens and you don't pay me back at all?"

"Then you can take my truck."

He looked the Packard up and down, squinted. "I drather have the four dollars."

On the last day of March Iris packed a rucksack with a blanket and dried apples and nuts, a canteen of catmint tea, binoculars, the handcuffs, fifty feet of quarter-inch rope, and boxes of cartridges for both her father's thirty-eight, the Winchester rifle, and John Rink's old fedora.

She put the revolver on the seat and the rifle on the floorboard and shooed the dog out of the cab and said her goodbyes without looking too long at anybody's eyes, hound included. She drove the flatbed down to Medford and then up the new highway up to Roseburg and on past to Sutherlin, then took the coast road west toward Elkton where the Fogertys had set up a logging operation on the north side of the Umpqua River. Dust-coated trees made it easy to spot the turn-in to the cutting site. She wheeled the truck around and drove half a mile to an old two-track striped into the trees and she drove in and found a flat spot and parked the truck where it couldn't be seen from the road.

She put the Winchester in a deerskin sheath she'd

made. It was a single-strap deal that went over her right shoulder and rode along her back. The sheath was angled so the butt of the rifle stuck up past her right shoulder where she could reach back and grab it easy.

She put the revolver into the rucksack and slung it over her left shoulder and held the strap in place with her stump arm.

The brush was thick and the going was hard, each step measured, and she stopped now and then to listen to the sounds of the woods and the rack of her breath. What if some choke setter had taken off to poach deer and wandered this way and found her creeping up the hill? What if such a fella thought she was a deer and let her have it? Could happen. The spring air was cool and bees were rioting in the manzanita flowers and there was the blush of green in the grasses but Iris' backside was streaming sweat.

She worked fifty yards off the road and followed it up toward the encampment. In about a mile, she found a copse of madrone twenty yards from the road and she nestled into the middle of the trees to watch. She figured the son of the local lumber baron wouldn't be setting chokers. If he was working for his daddy, he'd probably be a driver. And if Fogerty was a driver, maybe she could catch him in his truck without any of his buddies around. It wasn't much of a plan. But then plans could be overrated. She'd found out that much in the Fogerty town house. She took a swig of tea and settled in to wait.

Before long she heard an engine in the distance. The sound waxed and waned as the truck wound along the folds of the mountain. In ten minutes it appeared, a big rig with a long steel chassis and an extra set of rear wheels rumbled past carrying three boles of Douglas-fir, each five feet across, chained to its bed. She got a partial look at the driver as the cab flashed in and out of shadow but it didn't appear to be her man.

An hour later she heard a second truck bucking its way down the road. She got low and moved closer, this time crouched in a tangle of manzanita just ten yards from the road. As the big machine bullied its way past she could see, elbow and shoulder jutting through the open window, the black hair, the striped skunk beard. Tom Fogerty. Thin, pale, sun-struck dust curled behind the truck. It was a stroke of luck she'd spotted him right off. She'd need a few more pieces of good fortune before this was all over.

Two hours later the trucks returned, spaced an hour apart, driving crazy fast uphill with no loads, skittering the rear wheels on the washboard surface. Another couple of hours and the first truck came rumbling back down once more, piled with oozing fir. An hour later comes the skunk. In between Iris watched, listened. Crows and hawks and buzzards on wing, jays and squirrels scrabbling in the underbrush. She ate two apples, watched a brush lizard climb a gray stump to bob up and down in the sun. Late in the day the logging trucks returned, and just before dusk two hacks with maybe a dozen men rattled down the road toward the valley.

The sun settled and Iris gathered pine needles for a bed and pulled a blanket over her shoulders and watched the stars through a web of branches. She cradled the Winchester and wondered at why she felt so strong about doing something so foolish and was a rifle the only thing she'd hold onto in this life and what it would be like to have a real live man for the night and she knew that with her sawed-off arm her chances of that ever happening had diminished considerably, if not completely, and here she was not twenty and had never kissed a boy and how did life unfold for some people like a bolt of silk and how some had a scrap of burlap? She knew of girls from school days who were married off now and having children and right around midnight a trio of coyotes set up wailing like babies crying and she knew she'd never be a mother and she hoped Henry had latched the coop. She'd gotten good at shoveling chicken shit out of the coop with one-hand and her whole right arm was strong like a boy's. Henry refused the job even though he was partial to one of the big speckled Dominiques and once he said *No!* to something then it was pretty much over for that particular endeavor. Iris actually liked the job, the *shunk!* of the shovel and the sour aroma and chickens nattering all around. The coyotes chorused and her stump throbbed. Somewhere around midnight the stars disappeared behind clouds and an easy rain pattered down and she pulled the blanket over her head. She didn't sleep. She knew what her next move was going to be.

At first light Iris made her way back to her Packard hidden in the woods. She waited. The canteen was almost empty. She sat in the cab as the sun rose. She heard the first logging rig make its way down the two-track, engine whining in low gear. The engine sound tapered off as the truck made its turn onto the main road, then it revved hard and thundered past. Time to move.

She rattled out of her hiding place, drove the Packard up the main road and headed up into the mouth of the logging road. She went about a hundred yards, then turned the flatbed so it blocked the road completely, shut off the engine. Got out, raised the hood and set it up on the prop.

She leaned the Winchester against the rear wheel so it couldn't be seen. It wasn't the handiest weapon in her condition but she was glad she had it. She checked the cartridges in the Smith and Wesson, slipped the revolver into one of the big pockets of her overalls. She took her long hair and bunched it up inside the fedora which was a harder task than she'd figured on account of she kept pushing the hat off and didn't have a way to hold it and all the while her phantom hand kept trying to help. She took the loose left sleeve and stuffed it in the front of the overalls so she'd looked like a fella with his hand in his pocket. Then she took a dab of dirty grease from under the warm block and drew a line across her upper lip. A moustache. A bad fake, she knew. But Fogerty wouldn't be able to tell until he was close. And then she'd have him.

The sun rose thin behind a cloudy sky and the edges of the eastern ridges turned the color of a salmon steak. There was quiet, save for the sporadic snap and rustle as the forest gathered the light of day. An hour passed. She stood at the edge of the battered logging road. *C'mon, c'mon.* She was parched. She wished for one more swig in the canteen but it was done.

Then, the sound of an engine, fleeting and gone. Then, stronger. Fogerty on his way down. It damn well better be Fogerty. She rehearsed her speech. *Taking you in. Get down out of that cab. Shut off the engine.* Not in that order. But those were the main points. Big truck rumbling in the distance, the sound fading in and out, her heart going up a notch at each crescendo.

Inside the pocket of the overalls Iris held the grip of the Smith and Wesson, laid her index finger along the curved steel of the trigger guard, brought the hammer back with her thumb. *Of all the dumbest, stupid-ass schemes, what are you thinking?* She shook the doubt away. *There's no fork in this trail.*

She heard the truck gear down, the black nose of the hauler came around a last curve and headed toward her on a straightaway. The engine bellowed as the driver let off the accelerator. The brakes gave a long metal-on-metal screech. Fogerty all right. She kept her eyes steady, gave a wave.

The rig came to a halt thirty yards short. Rain-damped

dust folded out from underneath the big truck. She started walking.

Fogerty leaned his shaggy head and his skunk beard out of the cab. He gestured toward Iris' truck. "What the hell's this?" He sounded pissed.

Iris said nothing, kept walking. Closing the range. Head down. Twenty yards.

"You broke down? What the hell are you doin' out here, anyway?"

Ten yards.

"Hey!" shouted Fogerty.

At five yards Iris brought out the revolver and pointed it at the man. "Tom Fogerty, I'm arresting you on behalf of the citizens of Jackson County. Turn that engine off and get down out of that truck." Five yards. Won't miss from here.

Fogerty's mouth dropped open. "What the hell?"

"I'm arresting you on behalf of Jackson County."

"You can't do that."

"Law says I can."

"The fuck you can." Fogerty squinted. That wasn't a real moustache. And he knew the face somehow. "I'll be damned." It was the girl. The same damn girl he'd shot a while ago. With some stupid painted-on moustache. Sure enough. Come out of nowhere with a six-shooter. His own gun, a forty-five Colt, was under his seat. He sagged his shoulders, letting his hand drift to the floorboards. The sound of the big engine idling filled everything up. "I ain't goin' nowhere," he said.

"Turn off that engine and get down."

"I know you. You're that damn girl come into my house awhile back. Didn't you learn nothing?"

"I say get on out of that cab."

"What, you think you're some kind of bounty hunter?"

"I think I'm the one with the gun pointed at your head."

He looked at the flaccid sleeve tucked into a front pocket. "I heard they had to saw off your arm. Serves you right, don't it?" His fingers had nearly reached the big gun.

Iris held her revolver steady, the bead centered on Fogerty's face.

"How's that goin' for you?" Fogerty went on. "How's that work for cutting up a steak? What, do you hold onto it with your toes?" He grinned at his own wit.

"I'll tell you what it's like," Iris said over the hard burble of the engine. "It's like a part of you goes weak and useless. But then everything else gets stronger. Your other arm. Your aim. Your heart. Your hate." The dark eye of the Smith and Wesson stared out from her hand. "Do you know what I mean?"

"A girl bounty hunter with one arm is about the most pathetic thing I seen." He spat.

And her gun went off.

The shot tore through the canvas roof inches from his head. Fogerty went still as a photograph, fingertips half an inch from his weapon. The sound hung in the air, thick and heavy.

"Jesus Christ!" he said.

Iris was calm. Everything was clear and sharp; each branch and needle and squawk of scrub jay and hair of beard. She thumbed back the hammer and the cylinder notched over.

"That was shot number one," she said, her voice strange even to herself. "A miss on purpose. Number two goes through your left shoulder. If you're lucky, which I doubt, you won't lose the arm like this'n here." She lifted the stump, the extra sleeve hanging down. "You'll have to have your mother tie your bootlaces. If you ever had a mother, that is. Number three goes through your other shoulder, on account of I owe you a couple. Number four goes through your heart, although I'm doubting you got one. In fact, I might move number four up to number three, save a good bullet. Numbers five and six are just biding their time for all the others to do their talking. That's what."

Sap glistened on the fresh-cut ends of the boles resting on Fogerty's truck; air heavy with the scent of Douglas-fir and exhaust.

"Of all the dumb ass things," he said, shaking his head.

"Don't even think about reaching for your gun. I know you got one. And turn that damn motor off."

He hesitated. He didn't know just how plumb crazy angry this girl might be. The fact that he'd shot her and then she'd come all the way out here to hunt him down and now here she was pointing a pistol at his head said she just might be a gnat's ass from ending his days. He glanced down; the butt of his Colt peeking out from beneath his seat looked to be a long way off.

"Now don't shoot, all right? I'm turning the truck off. And givin' myself up." The engine clattered to an abrupt stop. The quiet of the forest took over.

Tom Fogerty eased himself out of the seat and down to the ground. He looked around. If he ran for it, would she shoot? Could she shoot true enough? He glanced back up the logging road. "There's another truck coming right off," he said.

"No there ain't. You're the second truck down. The other won't be back up for hours." She nodded at the flatbed. "Climb up on the bed."

"And if I don't?"

"Fogerty, I could shoot you in the back and bring in your dead ass body and say you tried to get away and they'd still pay me the bounty and give me a parade besides. You're a wanted man, there's an arrest warrant, and you're staring at a gun held by a girl you shot down and turned into a cripple, a girl who is now standing here looking at your ornery face and losing her charitability. So the only thing ain't settled is whether you're gonna get yourself up on that flatbed, or am I gonna start trimmin' body parts off you?"

He licked his lips. "You're still a fool for fucking with me, missy. You'll see. Your whole family is in a heap of trouble."

"From the looks of things, Tom Fogerty, you're the one that's in trouble."

"I can't just leave this load here," he growled.

"I suspect it'll be found before too long."

"I'm an innocent man."

"I don't give a shit."

"You gotta mouth for a girl. A one-arm girl."

"I may only got one arm, but you'll notice that arm is holding a Smith and Wesson thirty-eight pointed straight at your heart. So you best get up on that truck because this gun is getting heavy and then I'll have to make the decision, *Do I drop my arm or just go ahead and shoot this varmint and be done with it?* And under the circumstances, I'm leanin' toward the *just shoot the varmint* side of the decision."

Fogerty shuffled toward the flatbed and Iris kept five yards between them, far enough away to keep from being grabbed and close enough that she could drop him easy. Fogerty got himself up on the bed and waited with dark green snake eyes. She'd already set the handcuffs on the boards and she pointed to them with the nose of the revolver. "Hook yourself up to one of those rings."

"You gotta be shittin' me."

"I ain't."

He held out a wrist and gave her a twisted smile.

"Hook me up yourself."

The gun blast cracked the air. Fogerty froze, wondering if he would open his eyes to discover he'd been shot. Or maybe dead already. His ears rang.

Iris moved slightly to her right. "Two good bullets wasted," she said. "Can't afford any more misses. Just can't. So let's say you get those handcuffs on."

He fumbled with the cuffs, snapped one cuff over his wrist and the other around an iron floor ring.

"Give those shackles a yank."

He tugged at the metal feebly.

"Give 'em a real good yank."

Fogerty gave a hard jerk and everything held.

Iris sighed quietly, lowered the revolver.

"Why the fuck are you doin' this?" Fogerty snarled.

"I'll tell you straight. It's not about you, Fogerty. It's the money. The reward money. I don't give a damn about you. Who knows? Maybe you'll get a fancy lawyer and get free. Courts are a fool's paradise. But I get my bounty money and the rest of justice can jump off a cliff."

"Somebody heard those shots, they're gonna come running."

"Then we better get going."

On the drive back down to Medford Iris could hear Fogerty complain through the steel bars at the back of the cab. He was hungry, he was cold, he ain't never been shackled like a dumb animal, which probably wasn't true on account of he'd been locked up before. In Grants Pass she stopped at a filling station that was closed for the night but Iris roused the manager from his house and said she was a deputy marshal taking a dangerous criminal back to jail and that he'd better do the bidding of the state and pump her truck full, which he did, wide-eyed at the manacled man sprawled out on the floorboards and the one-armed girl marshal. The night was chilled so before they set out again Iris fetched the blanket from her rucksack and gave it to Fogerty.

"Thanks for fuckin' nothing," Fogerty said, but he wrapped the blanket around his shoulders.

When they reached town it was late and the street-lamps had been turned off. Iris drove the rattling hack to the east side and parked in front of a fine new house with a wide porch and big square columns. It was dark inside but she walked right up the steps to the front door and gave it a good thumping. A light went on in an upstairs window and the window raised and a man stuck his head out.

"What in the world is going on out there?"

Iris stepped back down the steps so she could be seen. "Mr. Joy, I'm sorry for finding you in the night like this but I got something I'd like you to see."

The little man shook his head. "This isn't an all-night diner. You can't just pull up in the dead of night and order services."

"Please, sir. It's Iris Greenlee."

The silhouette was still for a moment, then, "This better be good."

After several long minutes Joy appeared at the front door in untied shoes and pants with suspenders pulled up over a white undershirt. He was carrying a shotgun.

Iris held up her hand so he could see she wasn't armed. "I appreciate this, Mr. Joy. What I got is in the back of the truck here."

Joy peered into the gloom of the street, came down the steps, followed Iris around to the back of the Packard, the muzzle of his twelve gauge leading the way. Although it was dark, he could plainly see the striped beard and shaggy head of Tom Fogerty atop a cone of blanket.

"It's Tom Fogerty."

"Good Lord, so it is. What's he doing on the back of your truck?"

"I've brought him in for the bounty."

"Is he restrained?"

"Yes sir. Got him manacled to the floorboards."

"Truly!" Joy got up on his toes to get a better look. "How did you find him?"

"I tracked him to a Fogerty logging operation up on the Umpqua."

"Everybody can go to hell," Fogerty put in with a heavy sigh.

Joy looked at her. "You did this?"

"That's right."

"No help?"

"Nope."

"She bushwacked me. Took a couple shots at me but missed."

"If I'd been shootin' at you I'd a hit you."

"Well, this man must be taken to the jailhouse."

"Yessir. That's right. But I'd like you to accompany me to the sheriff's to vouch I brought this fella in all on my own."

"I'm not doing that," snorted Joy. "It's too late for theatrics."

"Please, Mr. Joy. I put myself at risk for the citizens of Jackson County. That should mean something."

He stared at her for a long moment. At last he nodded. "Oh bother. These are the affairs they don't tell you about when you take the job. Give me a minute to get properly attired."

"You got a spigot, Mr. Joy? I'd like to give the prisoner a drink of water."

"I'm workin' on a piss, too, by the way," said Fogerty.

"Yes of course." Joy pointed at the side of the house.

Iris found a spigot out back and had a long drink and filled the canteen and returned to the truck and tossed it to her prisoner.

"You gonna keep me handcuffed all night?" he whined. "I gotta piss bad."

Iris said nothing.

When Joy returned he was dressed in his suit and had even put on a tie. He had substituted a small caliber pistol for the shotgun, and he slipped that into his front coat pocket.

Then he reached inside his vest and took out some paper that he pressed into Iris' palm. Two twenty dollar bills and a ten.

"What's this?" said Iris.

"Let's just say I'm aware of the snafu that prevented you from obtaining the bounty for apprehending Mr. Harold Smitts and company. You deserve a measure of compensation for that. Now," he waved his hand at the truck, "let's go make sure Sheriff Kuntz incarcerates this fugitive and properly processes your reward."

"How much?" said Fogerty, peeking over the short sideboards. "How much is my bounty worth?"

"One hundred dollars," said Joy. "Actually, make that one hundred and fifty."

Chapter Twenty-Three
April, 1928

(from the *Medford Meteor*,
April 1, 1928)

Bounty Huntress
Brings in Fugitive

*Our Valley's one-armed
Bounty Huntress shows Grit in daring
capture of suspected Arsonist*

In a display of grit and de-
termination, a local girl, Iris
Greenlee, also known as "The
Bounty Huntress of Southern
Oregon," last Thursday apprehended and brought to authorities Thomas Fogerty of Roseburg, son of well-known Roseburg lumberman Rupert Fogerty, also of Roseburg, the former
Fogerty wanted on a charge of
arson in connection with the
fire and near-complete destruction of the Pinecone Mill in
Ashland. The feat is all the
more remarkable for the fact
that Iris Greenlee has but one
arm, her left arm having been

amputated following a gunfight with the selfsame Thomas Fogerty last July. Greenlee is the daughter of Dexter Greenlee, former Deputy Game Warden of Jackson County, who was gunned down in a shootout with a poacher in Dec. of 1914.

With guile and cunning, the Bounty Huntress tracked Fogerty to the timber country of Douglas County and took him at gunpoint, a revolver held in her good hand. This time she had the drop on her man, and fastened him with chains to the bed of her flatbed truck and proceeded to transport him to the County Jail in Medford.

"Thomas Fogerty is a wanted man and we are glad that he has been placed in custody," said Medford Mayor Herbert Hanson.

"I can't think of a way around it, Your Honor," said Sheriff Gerald Kuntz, both hands wrapped around a glass whose bottom held the amber traces of Kuntz' second whiskey.

District Court Judge Nathan LaMore leaned forward. "Have another," suggested the judge.

The two were convened in the back of a barn owned by a local farmer, Lucas Miller. Years before Miller had walled off a portion of the barn and turned it into a rough blind pig furnished with old oak school desks and a menagerie of wooden chairs. Despite the crude surroundings, Miller drew a distinguished crowd of local dignitaries and community stalwarts on account of the farmer on the eve of prohibition had bought up all the best whiskey he could find and now sold it at exorbitant prices that only the well-fixed could afford.

Kuntz nodded gratefully, waved at the barkeep—Miller's eldest son Jep—and pointed to his empty glass. "The girl delivered Fogerty directly to the county jail, all while that sniveling Terrance Joy was jumping around like a rat dog after a chicken bone. What kind of balls does Joy have, anyway? That money should never go to the tomcat girl. It's official State of Oregon business, paid to the office of the Sheriff of Jackson County."

"Actually," Judge LaMore said mildly, "it's paid to the county."

"Same difference. Truth known, I'd been more than halfway to getting up after that Fogerty myself once I took the time to figure out where he was hiding at. Which any fool coulda done. So the damn girl did it; anybody could of done it. Easy money."

"There may be a solution."

A third glass of whiskey chimed its arrival in front of Kuntz. "I'm listening."

"There may be certain illegalities associated with bringing Fogerty to trial. The circumstances surrounding the apprehension may run afoul of constitutional guarantees of due process."

"And?"

"The bounty would still be paid to the county for distribution, but until the legalities of Mr. Fogerty's arrest are fully examined, that distribution might never be made."

"You mean…"

"The money gets used for, ah, other purposes."

Kuntz smiled. "Damn, Judge. You know the law."

"Laws are malleable, my friend."

"How's that again?"

"We give laws their meaning. But we're just regular folks, after all. And there are multiple viewpoints on any particular nuance of the law."

"Whatever you say, Judge. But I'll tell you this—I'm buying the next round."

"Well then, I believe I'll refresh."

Two days later Iris walked into Sheriff Kuntz's jailhouse office dressed in her overalls. She had the Smith and Wesson holstered around her waist and she carried the Winchester rifle by the receiver, cocked, her finger aside the trigger guard.

Kuntz was bent to some wooden boxes. He was packing his things, getting ready to move to the new jailhouse that had been built in Medford. He was preoccupied and looked up slow. When he took in the visitor and her rifle he gave a start and nearly knocked over his lamp. "What's this, girlie?"

She kept the rifle muzzle pointed at the floor but dearly wanted to bring it up and put it square on his ugly face. "Sheriff Kuntz," was all she said.

"I don't take lightly to armed citizens busting in here." The sheriff was not at all sure of the mental state of the girl. Tried to calculate how quick he might get his sidearm out of his shoulder holster.

"Half this town is armed, sheriff. You got gentlemen in fancy suits walkin' around with automatics tucked in their breeches."

The big walrus moustache moved up and down. "I

think you better set that rifle over here." He indicated his desktop with a shift of his eyes. "It's cocked, you know. You just might blow your own foot off."

"That's not gonna happen."

He narrowed his eyes. "What do you want?"

"You know what."

"No. What?"

"This is the second time you've hoodwinked me out of my rightful bounty money."

"Nobody hoodwinked here." His eyes kept flickering toward her rifle. "The state hasn't paid the money on account of Judge LaMore hasn't approved the request. He's considering if the case against Tom Fogerty even gets prosecuted."

"That's bullshit."

"You better watch that damn mouth of yours, darlin', or else you're looking at disorderly conduct."

"You won't."

He snorted. "Why not?"

"Cause you got what you want. That's the game."

"No games being played here, girlie."

"My name is Iris Greenlee."

Tilted his head. "You think you're tough as a man, don't you?"

She let her stare fill everything up. Then she eased the hammer off, slow and deliberate, turned and walked out the door.

At the courthouse Jack Dressler looked up, wide-eyed, as Iris strode in. "Holy cow, Iris. You can't come into the courthouse with guns like that."

"Then let's go outside."

He looked around. The anteroom was empty save for stacked boxes of papers and official documents awaiting the move to the new courthouse in Medford. Jack got up and hurried the both of them into the gray light of an over-cast day. "What are you doing?"

"Where do you live?" she said.

"I have a little place. Over the Five-and-Dime."

"Take me there."

He frowned. "What for?"

"I want you to screw me."

His mouth dropped open. "What are you talking about?"

"You know how to screw a woman?"

"Holy cow."

"Do you?"

"Well..."

"Well what?"

"I mean, you can't just..."

"Can't what?"

"I'm working. Gosh."

"You can work any time. You only get a chance like this once in a blue moon."

"Are you all right? You fevered up or something?"

"I'm as clear as spring water. And I want you to screw me. You know how, don't you?"

"Well sure, but..."

"You think I'm too ugly?"

"No, no."

"Country hick girl in her dirty overalls?"

"I don't think you're a hick."

"You afraid of this?" She raised her stump arm. "What it looks like?"

"That's not the body part of you I'm thinking about at the moment."

She took a deep breath. "Then let's go."

They left the courthouse by the back door, Jack grinning with guilt. They followed the alleyways by instinct, not saying a word, walking then trotting until they came to the back stairs to Jack's apartment.

He stopped, rubbed his hands together. "It's up there," he said, still with a loopy smile on his face. "You sure?"

"You keep asking and I may just change my mind," and she headed up the stairway, Jack quick behind. Into a hallway lit by a small window at the far end. Four doors.

"This is the bathroom. This one is mine." Key rattling in the lock like a bell going off. He closed the door behind them, locked it with a slide bolt.

His room had a bed with a wrought-iron headboard and a nightstand and a parlor chair upholstered in dark green. There was a dresser against the far wall. He turned to her with a smile that was half excited and half confused. It was warm in the room; a low western light came in the only window. Jack went to the window and pulled the shade and the room filled with a reddish-tan glow.

"Kinda warm in here," he said. "but I think I'll leave the window closed, you know. We should probably try and be quiet."

"Why?"

"Well, some folks here might take objection to the fact that…you know…I mean we're not married."

"They can object all they want. But we're old enough and we can do what we want."

"We can do what we want, sure."

"We should take off some clothes."

He nodded. "All right."

Neither moved. They stood looking at each other. Then Iris put the Winchester rifle flat on the floor by one wall. She'd gotten good with getting the holster on and off, and with a hard tug the belt and the thirty-eight swung away from her hips and she put that on the floor as well. The boots were always a challenge so she steadied herself with her back against the wall and brought up each foot cross-wise and undid the clasp that the cobbler had riveted to her boot leather in place of laces. She let each boot fall with a loud thump and Jack took a deep inhale but said nothing. The overalls, with its two easy front buttons, relaxed from her shoulders and shimmied past her hips and rumpled up around her ankles. She stepped out and stood there in her knickers and her old broadcloth blouse with the one sleeve pinned up.

"You," she said.

Jack sat on the parlor chair and removed his shoes, put them quietly on the floor. Stood, took off his suit coat and folded it in half and placed it on the parlor chair. Had a brief struggle with his tie but finally pulled it off and folded that in quarters lengthwise and put it on top of his coat. Then the vest, again folded lengthwise and laid carefully on top of all. His shirt took forever to unbutton. He draped it on the back of the chair. "Iris," he said.

"Keep going." Iris decided he was handsome. He had nice shoulders and thick black hair that waved back from his forehead. He wasn't too skinny; he had some fine muscles for a fellow that sits behind a desk all day. Two good arms. Lucky him. She took a quick breath. The next few minutes were about to tell Iris a lot about life and men.

"You," Jack said.

She shook her head. "I'm down to two. Two to go. You got at least three. One more to even it up."

He narrowed his eyes, half smiled. His pants fell and he stood in his undergarments with black stockings up to his knees. There was already stirring in his underpants. Amazing.

She turned her back to him. "You'll have to unbutton me," she said. This was a lie. She'd gotten so she could bend her right arm almost all the way down her back. There were eight buttons. She could get six reaching over her shoulder, and the other two coming up from below. But now she stood quiet, facing the wall, waiting. If his first reaction was going to be one of disgust, she wouldn't have to see it. Not right off, anyway.

He came up behind, put his hands on her shoulders so his forefingers rested against the skin of her neck. She caught the scent of him; young man scent, washed, hint of pomade. The buttons slid through their holes, one by one. He lifted the blouse over her shoulders. She let it slide off and it settled on the floorboards, far away. She was glad to be free of the pinned sleeve. She felt her hair trickling along her spine.

For a long moment there was silence. Then Jack said, "Please turn around."

She faced him. This was only the second time she'd been naked in front of a man like this. The first one didn't count. This was different. She'd chose this. She held her arms still. Watched his eyes.

His eyes wandered her body. Lingered on her breasts. "Jeez," he said. He took off his undershirt. He had a patch of curly black hair on his chest. The bulge in his underpants was so close she almost reached out for it, just to see, but she didn't.

She thumbed down her knickers. Now fully naked. A first, for sure.

He took off his underpants. She'd seen hardons before. Henry had no shortage of them, especially first thing in the morning. But Jack's hardon was fascinating. And it was hers.

She couldn't help herself. She took it in her hand, felt it pulse, as if it had its own little heart. It was warm. Looked up at him. Said, "I want the truth. Are you bothered by my arm?" She could see her stump in her peripheral vision, her strange lump of flesh.

"Which arm are we talking about?"

"I ain't joking." She squeezed and he gasped. "I want to know."

For an answer he leaned over, kissed her. Wet and soft. All these firsts. All at once. The taste of him like clean river water. He pried her hand from his erection and led her to the bed. The springs creaked awful as they boarded. They lay on top of the covers on their sides, she with her good arm up.

For a long while they stroked each other, studied each other's face. He had greenish-gray eyes. Iris decided that greenish-gray eyes were about as good an eye color as an eye color could get. She'd never felt something as smooth as Jack's back. And the humps of his butt. Like silk. She wanted to tell him so but didn't. Were all men's butts this smooth? His fingers left heat trails along her back. No callouses, unlike her own farm-roughed hands. Hand.

"You didn't answer me." Let her breasts graze his chest.

Then they were kissing. He kissed her throat and her shoulders and then he was kissing her breasts and her whole body shivered of its own accord. Then his hand was down there, in her lower part, his finger cleaving her and slipping inside. He kept at it for a long while, his face buried in her neck, breathing strong, his fingers busy. She'd had her own hand down there before, even brought herself off that way, but having this man do it to her was scary good. Finally she said, "I thought you knew how to screw."

He pushed her on her back and then he was on top of her and sliding inside her and she hurt and gasped and she wanted it all and the hard pleasure that galloped out from her center. She blurted out *Jesus in heaven!* a couple times—couldn't help herself—and Jack yelped and moaned and the bedsprings put up a raucous chorus for a good long while.

***

"I didn't mean to hurt you."

She shrugged. "I wanted you to."

"To hurt you?"

"Yes."

"Why?"

"It's all part of it. I didn't mind."

"That's peculiar."

"I don't think so."

"But, did it feel good at all?"

"Yes," she nodded. "Yes it did. Real good."

"This your first time, isn't it?"

"Yeah. They say the first time hurts. But after that, it's easy as pie."

"Better than pie."

"Better than huckleberry pie?"

"That's a tough one. I might have to get a slice of huckleberry pie from Mrs. Gunder for a fair comparison."

"Is it yours?"

"What?"

"Is this your first time?"

"No. I've done it other times. But with just one girl, that is."

"Where is she?"

"She went off with her folks to St. Louis. Her daddy's job or something."

"Did you like her?"

"Not like I like you."

"You're full of shit, you know that?"

"So?"

"So what?"

"So you've never been with another fellow?"

"Actually hundreds, if you want the truth."

"Come on now."

"All right. You're the first."

"Well." He smiled cock-a-doodle-do.

"Oh don't be so proud of yourself. Since you're the only one I've ever been with how am I supposed to know whether some other fella might just be a whole lot, um, more fun?"

"I'm plenty fun, if you'd recall."

"And you weren't bothered?"

He knew what she meant. Jack shook his head. "Not in any way." Then he bent over and kissed her stump.

She jerked her stump away and then clubbed him on the head with it. "What the hell you doing?" she yelled. Her arm throbbed hot and achy from the blow.

"Jeepers!" Jack ducked out of range. "Hold on!"

"Why'd you do that?"

"What? What'd I do?"

"Kiss me there?" She held up the shortened arm.

"I don't know. I guess I wanted to show that I like you. All of you."

"That ain't proper."

"What, I can screw you but I can't kiss you?"

"Not there."

"That's bullshit."

"Not to me."

"I'm sorry, Iris."

"Say it straight out."

"Say what?"

She hesitated; didn't know how to say it herself. "That it was all right."

"You mean..?"

"Yes."

"It don't—doesn't—bother me. Your arm doesn't bother me. Your amputated arm doesn't bother me at all. It's part of you. I like you. That's it."

She stared at the greenish-gray eyes. "I got weapons over there that'll turn a liar into an honest man faster than you can say Jack Spratt. So you'd better be telling me the God's honest truth."

"You want the truth?"

"Yes please."

"I think I want you again."

She frowned. "You mean, sex like?"

"Yes. Sex like."

She looked at his crotch. There it was, already moving. Magic. She closed her eyes. "Well then, let's have at it."

Chapter Twenty-Four
May 1928

JACK DRESSLER SHOWED UP one afternoon, the rattle of the auto bringing the dog's yapping alarm. The gravel crunched and stopped. Ajax bounded and barked and put his big paws on the driver's door.

Emily went to the front porch and the screen door slapped behind.

Jack rolled down his window just far enough to stick a hand out, give a tentative wave, and withdraw before the dog could get at his fingers.

"Hello Mrs. Rink," he called, his voice muffled inside the cab. The dog made a quick move to the other side of the auto, looking for another way to get at the man inside.

"Who are you?" Not calling off the dog.

Jack put his face near the window opening. "I'm Jack Dressler. I'm a friend of Iris."

Out on the sleeping porch Iris sat on the floor cutting gloves out of deer hide, the skin pinned to a board and Iris tracing the outline with the tip of John Rink's old hunting knife. He'd showed her how to sharpen it just a week before he'd had his accident. *Especially the tip,* he'd said. *That's where the true craft is.* The two of them shoulder-to-shoulder as he swept the blade *shush sush* across the stone.

Henry sat cross-legged on the floor with his back to her. He was running a spoon across the seams between the floorboards, again and again, the sound like the click-clack of train wheels on tracks. Iris heard the crunch of the gravel under tires and the dog barking and she set aside the knife and got up.

"C'mon, Henry." Iris went into the kitchen and caught *I'm Jack Dressler* and stopped. *What in the world is that boy doing here?* Her body got warm.

"Are we having dinner?" asked Henry.

Iris smoothed her hair and walked out to the porch and Henry followed and the screen door whapped its familiar exclamation point.

Emily stood with arms folded. "That him?"

Iris nodded. "That's him."

"Unlikely looking fella."

"How is he *unlikely?*"

"He don't seem your type."

"Why? Cause he's got a job?"

"He's got a funny look."

"Good Lord, Momma, you can't hardly tell one way or the other from here."

"Kinda proper-looking."

"Anything wrong with that?"

Emily flicked her fingers toward the auto. "Why don't you call off the damn dog?"

"I will. In good time."

The women stood in the shadow of the porch, watching Ajax jump and paw and yowl. "I hope that fella of yours don't try and get out of that car. The dog is pretty riled up."

"He's not my fella."

"Iris, honey, you cast the line, and that's what you hooked."

"Can you get your dog? I think he's scratching the auto." Jack strained to be heard out the partially open window.

"Ajax!" said Iris and the dog looked over, surprised.

"Ajax!" she repeated, more forcefully, and the Chesapeake lowered his big square head and reluctantly came to her.

Jack got out of his runabout and the dog turned to him and made a low sound in his throat.

"Stop that, Ajax."

"Stop, Ajax," added Henry.

"Good dog," said Jack, not convinced.

"He won't bite unless he doesn't like you."

"Do you think he likes me?"

"We'll find out."

"Iris," said Emily, playing innocent, "you know this fella?"

"Yes I do, Momma. He's from down at the courthouse in Medford. You know him, too. If you recall, he's the one came out here to tell you I got shot up in Roseburg."

"Well what's he doing here?"

"He's standing right there, why don't you ask him?"

"This isn't about the taxes, is it?" said Emily to the visitor, frowning. "I'm gonna pay, but it's hard times for folks, you know."

"Yes," said Jack. "But no, that's not why I came out here."

"Well then why are you here, son? Speak up."

"I'm here to see Iris."

"What for?"

"Momma…"

"I met her—Iris—at the courthouse. And I thought I'd out come out and say hello."

"Uh oh," said Henry.

"Momma, this is Jack Dressler. This is my momma, Emily, and my brother, Henry."

"Hello, ma'am. Hello Henry. I hope it's all right I came out here today."

"Little late for askin' forgiveness on that score."

"Momma…"

"Are you going to marry Iris?" Henry wanted to know.

Emily waved a hand. "C'mon, Henry. I got some things to do. You can help." And she went inside, her son trailing behind, screen door punctuating their leaving. Ajax sat in front of the steps and dared Jack to mount them.

"Well," said Iris.

"Well hello."

Iris lifted her chin at the automobile. "That your daddy's coupe?"

"Oh, it's Mr. Joy's auto, actually. He let me borrow it."

"Fancy."

"I wanted to see you."

"You're seein' me."

"Maybe we could talk. I've got something to tell you."

"I'll show you around the farm."

"All right."

The dog trotted out in front, leading Iris and Jack around the corner of the house and past the chicken coop, down the grassy path that led off the upper ledge onto the floodplain, through willow thickets to the stone ledges heaped over the river.

"Iris," he said.

She held up a hand. "Don't say it."

"Say what?"

"I know what you're gonna say."

"You do?"

"You're gonna say something stupid. Something about us. About you and me."

"I was gonna say you're very pretty is what I was intending to say before I was so rudely interrupted."

She wrinkled her nose. "Well don't say that."

"That you're pretty?"

"Yeah that."

"Well you are."

She shuddered. "I'm not pretty."

"You are," he said.

"Stop that horseshit."

"Didn't anyone ever tell you that you were pretty?"

"Not really."

"Not your momma?"

"She says I look like a possum." She made the face.

"I can see the resemblance."

"Thought so and…" but her next words went directly into his mouth as he slipped an arm behind her back and pulled her to him and kissed her and for a good long time they stayed that way and she took it in, smooshy lips on lips, fingertips on the ridges of her spine, the soap smell, his hardness spawning against her belly. She was unsure what to do with her stump, leave it by her side or let it join the party? Would he feel the partial arm and be put off? What had she done with it when they had sex in his apartment? She couldn't recall.

She broke away. "Well now you've done it."

He nodded. "I suspect I have."

"What did you do that for?"

"I've been thinking about you. A lot."

"Thinking what? That you'd like to come out here and kiss some sawed-off country hick girl?"

"Not some country hick girl. A special country hick girl."

"Ha. That's funny. You can see I'm laughing so hard."

"You don't know how much gumption it takes to go on and kiss a girl like that. Fella might get slapped. Or shot."

"Those possibilities crossed my mind."

"Well I'm sorry if I offended you…"

"Shut up," she said and grabbed him with all of her arms and kissed him again.

They lay in the shadow of young willows. In a hasty bed made of their shed clothes. They stroked each other's back, brushed horseflies from each other's shoulders. The dog waited patiently several yards away.

"We better get some clothes on before Momma comes down here." She sat up. "Was there something you wanted to tell me?"

He smiled. "There's something, yes."

"I'm listening."

"About a job."

"Well? You want me to guess?"

"The deal is I heard they're going to be putting up a job for game warden of Jackson County."

Iris went quiet.

Jack said, "Remember when you first came in to the courthouse and you were looking for a job?"

"So I been down that road. It's a dead end."

"But it's different now."

"How so?"

"This time there's going to be an election."

"So?"

He sat up, held his hands wide. "So, holy cow. An election, people come out and vote for the person they like the best. And you, Iris, you've been in the papers. You're sorta famous around here. People know about you, where you've come from and your daddy, the one that was, you know, shot. And they'd vote for you. I'd vote for you."

"I don't want to be famous. And I wouldn't want anybody's damn pity vote on account of my daddy. Besides, there's bound to be no end to the folks who can do the job better than me."

"Nobody around here has done what you have, catching those men. And this would be a job. A real job. With pretty good money."

"Yeah, but they got requirements."

"You have to be at least nineteen years old, have been a U.S. citizen for at least seven years, and live in the state where the job is located."

"That's it?"

"That's it."

"Doesn't matter that I didn't graduate school?"

"Not from the requirements as I read them."

"But I'm a girl. They don't want girls. Especially girls that are crippled up and only got one arm."

"You do more with one good arm than most men do with two."

She shook her head. "It doesn't add up."

"But it's an election, you see? Anything is possible. You've got as good a chance as any. Better, I'd say."

They started to sort through their clothes. "So when's this all happen?" asked Iris.

"The election?"

"Yes."

"In five months. October. It's the first time the state has come up with the money to fund the position since Derek Vorhes retired. Some years ago. But now they're adding some twenty more game wardens all over the state."

"Don't I have to be certified or something?"

"I don't think so. Where's my other shoe?"

"Do you have to work in an office? In the city? She shook her head. "I wouldn't want that."

"Well, maybe. But you'd be out and about more than not. Where in the hell is my right shoe?"

Iris looked over her shoulder. "Dog's got it," she said matter-of-factly.

Jack got up, looked at the dog lying in the grass twenty feet away, front paws crisscrossed around some object on which he chewed contentedly.

"Damn!" said Jack and started forward.

"I wouldn't do that," said Iris.

Jack stopped. The dog was no longer chewing and was now staring over his short muzzle at him. "Well, could you please get my shoe for me?"

"Bring it here Ajax," said Iris.

The dog did nothing.

"Ajax?"

The Chesapeake got up, dropped the shoe, stretched, sat down on his haunches, the shoe right in front of him.

"There it is," said Iris. "Go get it."

"Ha ha," said Jack.

"All right," said Iris and she got up and walked to Ajax with only her blouse on which barely covered her bottom and she moved through dappled sunlight and as Jack watched her the thought came to him that there was immeasurable beauty to be found in this world.

Emily threw up her hands. "This is the biggest piece of horse manure I ever smelled in my life!" She walked down the steps and stood on the last one and pointed at the ground in front of her and Jack Dressler came up reluctantly to look her eye-to-eye. "You got yahoos and moonshiners and crustiest lowdown roustabouts that God mistakenly put on this earth running around the hills, carrying huntin' rifles and looking to shoot anything that ain't rooted to the ground. Why in the love of God would my child want to be the game warden of this lawless, good-for-nothing, piece of shit hillbilly county?"

"Well Mrs. Rink," said Jack, not sure of himself. "It seems Iris is good at taking care of herself. She arrested those fellows. She's done better for this part of Oregon than a handful of sheriffs. And you know there's a lot of those moonshiners cleared out these days."

"I know a few still around," said Iris dryly. "They're making a good livin', too."

"We had a game warden in this family..." Emily drove the heel of her boot into the wooden tread and the porch shook and dust shimmied off the girder, floating down in spectral tatters, "...and that one was enough."

There was loud silence. Jack started to say something, thought better of it, cleared his throat.

"Let me give you three big reasons why she's not going to ever be game warden of Jackson County," said Emily. A slender, dirt-knuckled finger appeared in front of Jack's eyes. "Number One: those ass-kissing boneheads they got running this county would never stand to see a woman be telling folks what they could or couldn't do. They'll rig the election." She turned to Iris. "Or they could hurt you. Or any of us." Back to Dressler. "And with that kind of a Number One, I don't need a Number Two or Three at all. And that's that." And she turned and went inside, giving the screen door a good tug behind her so it would crack loud and hard into its frame.

"Oh boy," said Jack. "I guess I didn't handle that very well."

"It's not your doing," said Iris. "It's just the way she is. My daddies getting killed gave her a rough edge. Hard to get around it sometimes. Don't I know it."

"I suppose," nodded Jack.

They stood a long while saying nothing. Jack put his

hands in his pockets. "Maybe you could talk to somebody about the election," he said. "Mr. Joy likes you. He's been in an election. He could tell you what it's about. How to do it." Jack smiled hopefully.

"I'll give it some thought," said Iris.

His automobile rumbled away into the late afternoon, sound of it cutting back and forth behind curves in the road, in and out, like the rhythm that lingered between her thighs.

Inside Emily rattled kindling against the iron insides of the cook stove. Game Warden! Of all the curses. The devil himself had set himself on the porch and was trying to orchestrate proceedings.

She rammed a piece of kindling into the box and it caught on something and stopped cold but her hand kept going and she ran a splinter the size of a sixteen-penny nail through the web of skin between her thumb and forefinger. She jerked her hand and broke off a six-inch piece. She stared at it in dull disbelief, a piece of shrapnel from a war she hadn't intended on fighting and seemed to be losing. Then the pain surged and she said *Oh damn!* through gritted teeth and reached down and grabbed the butt end and yanked it out and little arcs of blood pulsed from the wound.

Reflexively she pulled up the hem of her dress and wadded it fast around the puncture so Henry wouldn't see the blood and be upset. He was sitting on the floor with his back to her. She floundered to her feet and grabbed a dish towel off the kitchen table and used that to staunch the blood, all the while handing out little wheezy damnations, *Damn stove! Damn stupid cedar kindling! Damn city of Medford!*

when Iris came inside.

"Momma?"

"Well if it isn't Miss High-and-Mighty Game Warden of Jackson County."

"Momma, what'd you do?"

"It's nothing."

Iris took in the bloody hem, a smear of red on her mother's wrist. Motioned with her head to go into the bedroom. "Let's take a look."

"It's nothin'," said Emily but followed Iris into the bedroom. "Just a splinter."

Iris peeled back the towel and the wound hadn't settled yet and a spurt of blood leapt up. Iris clamped down. "Splinter! Looks like you ran a fence pole through there!"

"Just about."

"Let me get a proper dressing on that."

"I'm all right." Emily pulled her hand away. "I don't need you to coddle me."

"I ain't coddling you. Just doin' common sense. Now sit down."

"There you go!"

"Just do it."

"Use the clean rags."

Emily went to the creaky wood bed and sat on the edge and instantly wanted to lie down and go to sleep. She heard cloth being ripped into bandages. Iris came in with a damp cloth and cotton strips and mercurochrome. She unwound the dish towel to find the bloodletting had stopped. She tossed the rag to the floor, with the wetted cloth began to rub the blood off her mother's wrist and fingers, taking care not to disturb the clots. Within the pain, Emily felt soothed.

"This'll sting a bunch of bees," said Iris, dipping a cloth into the antiseptic. "That's what you always would say." She held up a finger swaddled in wet red cotton.

"I hate that stuff."

"Everybody hates it. It burns like hell."

"Let me," said Emily, taking the cloth. "It hurts less if you do it to yourself." She winced as she dabbed the puncture marks and the young clots dissolved and the blood came out but now not in little fountains.

Iris wadded one of the bandages and pressed it over the valley of her mother's hand and waited.

"You can't leave this farm, Iris."

"You're scared, I know."

"I ain't scared. I'm mad is what I am. I can't believe you'd do that to me."

"This ain't about you Momma."

"You're damn right it's about me. Sweet Jesus, Iris. I buried two husbands. I watched you layin' there in the hospital unconscious bleeding through your bandages. Ain't that enough?"

"It's a good job."

"That's no job. That's a one-way ticket to an early grave."

"It ain't as dangerous as bounty hunting, that's for sure."

"You tell that to your dead daddy."

Iris gave the injury a squeeze that made her mother squeak. "That's not a fair thing to throw at me and you know it."

"You want a job, we got plenty of work here on the farm."

"But there's more to it for me."

"More to what?"

"Everything." Iris began to bandage Emily's hand, wrapping between the thumb and forefinger, back around the wrist, repeat, her mother's fingers ruddy and calloused from trying to claw a living out of dirt and stone and wood.

"Sometimes life just doesn't spill out like that. Sometimes you gotta play the hand the Lord dealt you."

"Momma, I'm nineteen. I have to figure my own self out."

"There's no mystery."

"This game warden thing is just right there, starin' me in the face."

"It's devil's business."

"Let's be honest. The pears ain't going nowhere. We got doctor bills on account of my arm. We don't even have anything to barter except a few skinny chickens."

"You got a brother that needs you."

"Good morning," said Henry, lying on his back on the kitchen floor and looking up at the ceiling and the angles of the rough-pole trusses.

"Momma, I didn't make Henry. You did."

Emily shook her head. "That's not a fair thing to say."

"Well tit for tat then."

Emily sat on the edge of the bed. "I got real live people sprung from my own loins walking around this earth." She said it as if to remind herself. "Good people came from me."

"I know that."

"You can't know. Not unless you have your own. You can't know what goes on inside your gut, the part that doesn't sleep never. Always watchin' and trying to be ready. There's no man here. Henry's a man with the soul of a child. And he needs us. We got to protect each other."

"I don't shirk that. I'm good to Henry. But that surely can't be the all of me."

Henry got up slowly, hair askew. He turned slightly toward her, looked at the front door. "I'll pan for gold. You can watch."

"I'd like that."

"We need you around here," said Emily, her final try.

"He's here," said Henry.

Both women looked at him. Emily said, "Who's here?"

"Daddy."

"What do you mean, *Daddy?*"

"Yes." Henry nodded, pointed at the door without looking. "He went out. He left."

Chapter Twenty-Five
September, 1928

IRIS SAT IN THE SHADE of the gazebo roof at Milner's Park in Medford. A dry breeze lifted swirls of dust off the bare spots, and by noon the temperature had reached ninety degrees. The twenty or so folks that had gathered to hear her speak were restless, shaded their eyes, looked off toward the nearby drugstore with thoughts of ceiling fans and cool drinks, weighed their comfort against the novelty of hearing the one-armed bounty huntress say a few words.

Iris was sweating. Thank Jesus her hair was pinned up so she could get some air on her neck. They'd given her an old iron parlor chair to sit on. The velvet cushion was burnished to a sheen from years of wear, and a hard twist of wire nubbed up into her buttock from below.

"You can't say Jackson County isn't an interesting place…" said the County Assessor, Rolland Hammersmith, who stood before Iris on the gazebo platform. "…when we got a one-armed bounty hunter girl running for office!"

Some government employee of low stature usually was assigned these introductory tasks, and this was Hammersmith's turn. But Hammersmith did it willingly. He was flat-out curious, of course. Who was this young whippersnapper girl with the one arm? What business did she have trying to get a man's job? But mostly he was fond of theatrics, and found even the most humble stage to be an opportunity to present himself before an audience.

He looked enthusiastically at Iris, as if she was a prize novelty that the county had just acquired, like its very own elephant.

The crowd was silent. A few clouds scraped along the bottom of a white-hot sky. People fanned themselves with the small flyers Momma had passed out to folks as they assembled. She'd made them from stiff paperboard. In hand-inked letters the flyers said:

Iris Greenlee
Daughter of former Game Warden Dexter Greenlee
Of Applegate Valley
A Tried and True Friend of the People
Having Apprehended Several Criminals
And set Justice Straight
Is Running for the Office
Of Game Warden of Jackson County
In the Year of Our Lord 1928
Vote for Iris Greenlee

"So here she is everybody!" Hammersmith stepped out of the way with a master-of-ceremonies flourish. Iris wished he hadn't done that. It was like she was supposed to be important and maybe she wouldn't be as folks expected.

She stood. She wore her white cotton dress because, as her Momma had pointed out, it was what people expected of a young woman. It was cinched at the waist and Emily had sewn up the left sleeve nice and neat so it didn't have to be pinned.

Iris had her words written on a piece of paper so she could remember what she wanted to say. She decided at that moment that she'd rather be lying in a hospital bleeding to death than doing what she was about to do. How did she get here? That damn Jack Dressler got her all fired up, in so many ways, she could just about spit. And then he didn't have the time to come out and watch her make a fool of herself.

"I'm Iris Greenlee," she began.

"Boo!" said somebody. Iris looked the crowd over and couldn't tell who'd done it, all the faces looked still and shiny in the heat. There were three or four women in the audience, her Momma among them, and flyers were fluttering. Everyone's eyes were hidden in the shadows cast by hats and bonnets.

"I want to thank you all for coming out on this hot day to hear a few words. I'll be quick about it."

"Girls can't be game wardens," spat out one man who stood in the front of the small semi-circle of onlookers. He wore an old wool suit but he'd left off his vest and tie for the heat. Iris could see the butt of an automatic poking out of his waistband. He had a grey fedora with a black band, and he held his chin up.

Iris thought for a moment, then said, "Sir, have you ever looked down the wrong end of gun?"

"I have," he said. "In the Great War."

"Well then we've got that in common. We've both faced armed men. You in the defense of the country, and me in defense of the citizens of Jackson County." She held her stump up alongside her head. A brief puff of air made the fabric flutter.

"I've faced the wrong end of a gun and lost. But I haven't lost what it takes to make sure that the laws of this county are followed proper."

"Why ain't you married?" Another man called out.

"Too ugly," said Iris quickly and the crowd tittered. "But that don't mean I can't do the job. Half the men they got in this government is ugly as sin."

A few in the crowd clapped. The man in the fedora regarded the candidate. "You only got one arm, " he said. "How can you ride? How can you do anything?"

"I ride as well as any," she said, "and I'm not afraid to stand up to some fella that outweighs me by twice. And do you know why?"

The small crowd shook it's collective head.

Iris reached behind her. She had the revolver there, her daddy's thirty-eight, tucked into her waistband. She brought it out with flourish that Roland Hammersmith couldn't help but admire. Unloaded, it was light. She held it aloft. "Because I'll shoot his damn nuts off!"

There was a long moment of silence, a space of time balanced just so, weighed between what was appropriate for a candidate for elected office to say in public and what was not. Then the gathered people exchanged looks of surprise, then smiled and gave a smattering of applause. Even the man in the fedora grinned.

"You all have heard about me," said Iris, disregarding the words she'd written on paper. "That's why you're here. To see the one-armed farm girl. The bounty huntress, that's what they call me in the newspapers. I'm an odd duck, a duck with one wing, and you've come to see what's what. I understand that. If I were you, I'd surely do the same. So here I am. But you should know I mean what I say. I'll be the best damn game warden you ever saw. I'll do you proud. I'll stick up for the laws of this county and the state of Oregon."

There was some nodding of heads and a voice said simply, "Yup."

She put the gun in the front of her waistband so the handle showed. "This is my daddy Dexter's gun. He was a game warden, too." That's all she wanted to say about her real daddy. It seemed right, to say his name out loud, like he deserved as much.   She felt the heat of the day on her cheeks. She said, "I'm not going to keep you all here today. It's flaming hot and I've about said my peace. You know I'll work for you. If you got more questions, I'll do my best to answer them." The crowd stirred, exchanged thirsty looks. There were no more questions. Hammersmith jumped up and said, "All right folks. Thanks for coming out and doing your civic duty. Jackson County thanks you."

"Jackson County can kiss my ass," came a voice.

Hammersmith sighed and tossed a perfunctory smile at Iris before jumping off the stage and making a beeline for the soda fountain. In his wake were several members of the audience. The rest drifted into the heat, save for her Momma and a boy of about ten. Iris didn't remember seeing him, but then again it was all a fog.

The boy wore dirty overalls that hung on his skinny frame by just one strap. He was watching Iris. His right arm was missing and his white cotton shirt sleeve was pinned up. He stood in the shade of a big oak.

Momma walked toward her but Iris held up a hand. She was watching the boy. Iris said, "Hey."

The boy said nothing, didn't move.

Iris got down off the gazebo and walked up. "What's your name?

The boy said nothing.

"You come to hear me prattle on?"

He shrugged, kept his eyes averted.

"Where's your folks?"

He pointed in the general direction of the town.

"My name is Iris. What's yours?"

He shook his head. "I ain't supposed to talk to strangers."

"Well, I told you my name. So now you know me."

He squinted up at her. "You ever killed anybody?"

"I've had to shoot one or two in self-defense, but nev-

245

er killed 'em."

"You got a gun."

"I do. You want to see it?"

He nodded.

Iris brought out the Smith and Wesson, crouched down, held it flat in the palm of her hand. "You can touch it, it ain't loaded."

The boy put a finger on the barrel.

"You know," said Iris, "I see we're kind of alike, you and me."

"I'm a boy," he said. "You're a lady."

She smiled. "I don't recall anyone ever saying I was a lady."

He shrugged.

"How'd you lose your arm?"

"How'd you lose yours?"

"I got mine shot off."

"That's bull honey."

"It's the truth. I got it shot off in a gunfight."

"Right off?"

"No, not right off. It got infected, then a doctor had to cut it off."

He frowned, considering. "I got mine tore off by a combine."

Iris narrowed her eyes. "You cuttin' oats?"

He nodded.

"I'm sorry about that."

"I saw the bone. There was blood everywhere. That's all I remember."

"Mine hurt awful," said Iris. "You must be tough to have gone through all that."

The boy nodded but went quiet.

"You live in the Applegate?"

"Williams," he said. "Are you tryin' to be mayor or

something?"

"I'm looking to be the game warden of these parts."

"In Williams?"

"I think that's in Josephine County, next county over."

"They let ladies be game warden?"

"We'll see about that."

"I could do that," he said, brown eyes cool even in the heat of day.

"Can you ride and shoot?"

"Can you?"

"I can."

"So can I."

"Well then you'd make a fine game warden."

The boy started sudden, like a deer realizes somebody's right there. He took off across the faded lawn and called over his shoulder, "My name's Harney!"

Iris' opponent for the position of game warden was Clarence Dunn, a rough-cut ex-fisherman from Coos Bay who'd come to the valley to work in his brother's masonry business. He was thick-shouldered and mutton-chopped and a fierce opponent of government regulations. If elected, Clarence Dunn promised not to enforce any laws concerning the hunting and harvesting of wild animals in Jackson County, State of Oregon. The laws could be on the books, but he wouldn't lift a damn finger to prosecute any of them. As odd as that stance might have been, given the nature of the job to which he aspired, Dunn had an enthusiastic following. On Saturday nights Dunn's constituents tended to gather in town to get rowdy and drink illicit moonshine and walk the streets yelling a made-up campaign slogan, *What's Done Is Dunn!* while the night deputy stood off in the shadows of an alley and chewed a toothpick and watched.

One Saturday night some of Dunn's boys decided to pay a visit to the Greenlee farm. They came bouncing down the road in their trucks, spears of light leapfrogging each other, white whiskey bottles in hand. They ground to a stop fifty yards from the house. The doors creaked open, slammed shut. Six doors, one after the other. Footsteps on gravel; quarter moon cut into the sky. Dog in his kennel going crazy.

Emily came awake hard, sorting out the dream from the now. She swung her feet over the bed, had to pause to slow the spinning. Flapped in her nightgown and robe to the kitchen.

Iris was already there. "Did you hear that?"

"Wait here," said Emily and struck a match and lit the kerosene lamp, glanced quick at Iris, and walked out the front door.

Iris waited a heartbeat before getting the Winchester down off its pegs. In the darkness she undid the ammunition cabinet and grabbed three rounds and slid them into the chamber as fast as she could and cocked the rifle inside her knees and headed out the back porch, toe-heeled quietly down the steps. Henry was still asleep. Good.

At the front of the house a man was talking. He said, "Where is she?"

"She ain't here."

"We heard she was."

"You heard wrong."

"Get your daughter to quit it, Mrs. Greenlee."

"That's not gonna happen," said Emily, in a husky voice.

"We're telling you, this is the way it's gotta be."

Iris moved toward the corner of the house, lifting her

eyes over the top of a holly bush. At the edge of the circle of light cast by her Momma's lantern stood three men, faces half-melted into shadow. All carrying what looked like shotguns. Dressed in old suits, trousers limp with age, half-buttoned vests, one in a dusty newsboy hat and two in derbies. Emily stood in the middle of the lamplight, ghosted in her nightdress, lantern in her outstretched hand.

A fourth man emerged from the shadows. "I seen a holstered gun in the truck," he said. "She's here."

"Where is she?"

"You men get the hell off my property," said Emily.

"It ain't right for a girl to be takin' a man's job."

"*A woman shall not wear man's clothes.* That's from the Bible. What's that girl of yours doin' wearing' men's britches? If you folks aren't Christian then you're disciples of the devil."

Damn thought Iris. The Winchester felt hot in her fingers.

"Brother Dunn is a believer in the laws of God. *Every living thing shall be food for you.* That's the Bible, too. Genesis."

"We got families to provide for. Now she oughta do the right thing and quit tryin' to be the game warden. It's not right."

"Iris?"

The voice came over Iris like a bucket of ice water. She swung around low. "Henry!" she hissed. "Get back to bed."

"Is it the morning?" Henry came closer, stiff with sleep. When he saw light in the yard, he said, "What's that?" Before Iris could grab him he walked around the bush and into the yard in his long johns, toward his mother. The shotguns came up. *Shit!* Iris stepped into the open, rifle propped on her short arm. "Don't shoot! It's my brother!"

"There's the girl!"

"She's got a rifle!"

A shotgun went off, the bright burst shocking the darkness, buckshot slapping the side of the house. Henry's legs went out from under him and he fell flat on his face and lay still.

Emily dropped the lantern and it rolled and sent stripes of light across the dark undersides of nearby branches. Then everything went dark. There were scrambling sounds. A bottle broke. Iris lost her target, fired anyway, missed.

"Bastards!" Iris yelled and cocked the rifle between her knees fast as she could. Another shotgun burst tore open the night and shot ripped the leaves from a nearby oak.

"Leave it!" A man's voice yelled inside the dark. Truck doors creaked open, hammered shut; the engines started. Iris fired and heard the bullet hit steel. The trucks pulled away and their headlights bayoneted through the trees.

Iris ran to her brother. Emily was already there, down on one knee. "Is he hit?" shouted Iris.

"No."

"What?"

"He's all right."

"Henry!" hissed Iris. "Are you hurt?"

He lifted his head. "They shot me."

"Good Jesus, where'd you get shot?"

"He's all right, Iris," said Emily calmly. "He's says he's fine."

"Are you sure?"

"I fell," said Henry, turning onto his side, half his face dusted with faint starlight.

Emily sighed. "You got a bloody nose."

"Jesus Lord!" said Iris. "I thought you was shot!"

"I fell," confessed Henry.

Iris sat down heavy with relief. "Damnation!"

"I'm sorry, Iris."

Emily said, "We're gonna have to get some salt pork

on that nose." She looked into the darkness. "That shit-bag."

"He ain't hurt? You ain't hurt?"

"I fell."

"I seen that. But you sure you ain't shot anywhere?"

"I have a bloody nose."

"He stumbled," said Emily. "Thank God." She shook her head, shook a fist at the night. "That bastard come out here with all those dumb-ass boys like thieves in the night. I hope you got him."

"I missed, Momma. Probably just as well."

"I wanted to kill him, Iris."

"I know. I did too. Let's get inside."

"Shitbag," said Henry, standing up.

At the porch steps Emily sat and said, "Iris, for God's sake go get the dog and bring him on up to the house."

Ajax hadn't stopped his frantic barking. For his own good, they kept him penned at night so he wouldn't go chasing deer and or try to take on a skunk. Iris hurried to the barn in the dark, undid the kennel latch, got the dog by his collar, and let the powerful Chesapeake drag her up to the cabin.

Iris sat on the front steps with the rifle, watching the layers of darkness. She brought the dog out and tied him to a thirty foot rope that he'd explored the limits of and now sat poised in the darkness, ears forward, the rope nearly taut behind him. Out beyond the unseen river hussed and chafed.

An hour gone, Emily came out to join her.

"Thought you passed out," said Iris.

"Couldn't sleep. I'm thinking about Henry. And everything." Emily sat with her back against a railing post.

"Me too."

"Jesus lord, what a world we live in." Emily slapped at her thigh. "You shoulda shot the lot."

"We were lucky they weren't that good of shooters to begin with."

"I'll tell you what, daughter. I'd just about go for a piece of good luck that was real honest good luck, not just feelin' lucky because we didn't get killed."

"Clarence Dunn boys there. All skunked up on a Saturday night."

"That bastard."

"Momma?"

"What?"

"A couple of times you said, *That bastard.* Did you know one of those boys?"

In the dark Emily nodded. Sighed heavy. "I'm sorry to say I do. So do you. One of those men was Jasper Hibbard, the man who killed your daddy."

The next morning when Iris came into the kitchen Emily was sitting at the table, a square of young sunlight on the smooth oak surface. "Iris," said Emily. "Sit here."

That tone. Iris sat.

"I don't want you to be game warden."

Iris nodded, slow. "You want to kowtow to those men?"

"It's not kowtowing if it's the right thing to do."

"What's right about lettin' those fellas trying to scare me into giving up?"

"It's the right thing."

"Why?"

"Because then we'd survive."

Iris stared.

"You'd let it all go and there won't be any more trouble." Emily with hands clenched together.

"So that's the way it is," said Iris.

"That's the way I feel all right."

"Somehow I pegged you for a stronger woman than that." The words fell hard.

Emily stood. "I do what's right for this family. I protect us!"

"And what's right for this family? Letting lyin' murderers tell us what to do?"

"It's no sin to keep your family from harm. You want it different, go pray to Jesus Christ himself. But don't go expecting no miracles. Apparently, they're in short supply."

"And if I don't quit? What do you think is going to happen?"

"Nothing good, child. Nothing good."

(from the *Medford Meteor*,
September 19, 1928)

Bounty Huntress
Wins Election

*One-armed Bounty Huntress voted
the next Game Warden of the County*

The local girl known as "The Bounty Huntress," Iris Greenlee of Applegate, has won the recent public election for the position of Game Warden of Jackson County against opponent Clarence Dunn of Talent.

The vote was 364 votes for Iris Greenlee, and 347 votes for Mr. Dunn, a difference of a mere 17 votes making a quite narrow margin of victory.

State Game Commissioner Wayne Boscum made the announcement yesterday from Salem. In a telegraph, the Commissioner said that he expected Iris Greenlee would "do nearly as well as a man" in the position as far as he could tell, and that the citizens of Jackson County should surely support the daughter of Dexter Greenlee, murdered Game Warden of Jackson County who was cruelly executed in a heinous murder that occurred in 1914.

Sheriff Gerald Kuntz told the *Meteor* that he doesn't believe a woman should be in the position of the Game Warden.

"It's dangerous and hard work and if I were an ordinary citizen of the County I am right doubtful of the Greenlee girl to be able to uphold the laws. After all, she did get herself shot up," said Sheriff Kuntz.

Miss Greenlee will receive compensation from the state of approximately $55 per month. She will maintain an office in Medford.

That damn Jack had been right. People must have known about her, read about her in the paper. And maybe people were bored. Voting for her was a lark. They said *What the hell* and voted for her. And she won.

She sat on a cloud, for sure. Momma, for all her reservations, was pleased. Something good had happened. It was a miracle. They had half a bottle of medicinal gin that nobody'd touched for God knows how long and Emily brought that out and they drank it dry and sang, *Makin' Whoopie* until Henry asked them to stop because they were *hurting the dog* and they looked at Ajax in one corner with his paws over his ears they started laughing and couldn't stop.

Chapter Twenty-Six
April, 1929

THE COUNTY OBLIGED Iris with an office location that was nothing but a closet in the railroad station in Medford. There was a chair and an old side table for a desk. There was no telephone. If she needed to call, she had to beg use of the phone from the station master, a crusty old tomcat named Bradford Buck who had no intention of ceding any privileges to a girl, no matter if she was the Virgin Mary.

Iris did, however, have access to the state motor pool, which consisted of a two-seater Buick that always seemed to be checked out to one of the state police officers. Otherwise, there was a horse. She had her choice from three down at the livery. She took a middle-aged, cream-and liver mare named Mayjune.

"What kind of name is that?" she wondered aloud as the stable keeper bridled the mare.

He shook his head. "Seems they never could settle on when she was born. So they compromised."

"Who did?"

"Dunno."

One horse and one woman to cover some twenty-eight hundred square miles.

She tacked up a Foster Shoe calendar on her office wall and divided her work into segments. One week in the field on Mayjune tracking down reports of poachers and squatters and claim jumpers, and the next week in the small office writing reports in her clumsy, uncertain hand and sending telegrams to Salem if any situation warranted, which few did. In her first six months she made eleven arrests which led to five convictions, the best success rate in the state. The head of the Fish and Game Commission in Salem sent Iris a telegram of commendation that Bradford Buck intercepted, crumpled up, and threw in the trash.

In August of that year Iris rented a small house in Medford and stayed there three nights a week. With her job she could pay the rent and give the rest to Momma. It was a big help; there'd be no more fretting over selling eggs.

She rode Mayjune out to the farm on a Sunday to gather a few things for the move into town. "I'll be out on Thursday through Sundays, and when I get a day off," she said, tightening a canvass bundle across Mayjune's hips. Parker whinnied questions from the barn. "You know they're bringing in electric and telephones all the way out here. Maybe next year."

Momma stood on the porch with Henry. She had a hand on her hip. "Don't be making me into a grandmother now."

"Momma! Why'd you say that?"

"I know why you're going to town. It's because of that Jack."

"That's not so. It's just easier to work my job."

"He's going to have your knees up around your ears every chance he gets."

"Jesus Lord, Momma! Stop."

"You're gonna look like a frog."

"Is there a frog?" Henry wanted to know.

"Bull frog," said Emily.

Iris took a two-room cottage near the business district. A little picket fence and a crooked magnolia. Half a cord of pine was outside piled against the sun-grayed shingle siding. Inside was a small tin wood stove that was the only heat source. There was a single bed and a little bathroom with a sink and a real flush toilet that gave Iris endless amusement and satisfaction. Iris could walk to her office in the train station in ten minutes.

And Momma was right. She and Jack screwed like rabbits. It was pure craziness, a craving that wouldn't stop for rhyme nor reason. Although the county seat and Jack's job had moved to Medford, he kept his apartment in Jacksonville. He bought himself a used automobile, a little black two-seater Tin Lizzie with a soft top, and if Iris was at her office they'd meet at noon and drive the five miles over to his place and sneak up the back stairs. Two shakes after the door bolt slid into place they had their clothes off and were going at it. A half hour later they'd emerge—drained and stunned and shiny—and they'd drive back to Medford while they munched on dried sausage and bread.

In the evenings after work they'd do it again.

She thought about Jack at odd moments. Like while at her small desk, staring at the Foster Shoe calendar. She could see Jack shedding his shoes with a flick of his leg, letting them spin into the air and then thump hard on the floor. As she rode the mountain paths, on the trail and watching for sign, she heard the noisy bed in the plod of Mayjune's hooves and the rhythmic rub of leather. The bare madrone trunks were thighs twined naked and smooth in places and sweaty in others and stinky good. The feel of him inside her. Sometimes when her mind got elsewhere like that she had to rein the mare back around and retrace the trail to make sure she hadn't missed anything.

In spring Iris went out after a poacher up near Butte Falls. She brought Mayjune up easy along the edge of Billets Creek, the stream running hard with late spring runoff, the tumbling water masking the sound of the horse's hooves. Dressed in a new drab green shirt and denim trousers, John Rink's old fedora tilted high up off her forehead, hair in a single braid down back, leather vest with loose cartridges in the pockets. Winchester in the deerskin scabbard on her back, revolver in a holster at her left hip, butt backwards. Badge on her chest was a brass circle with a star cut into the middle. Stamped letters around the edges said, *Game Warden State of Oregon*. Smell of horse sweat and pine. Hawk cry overhead.

Halfway up the sound of an explosion, muffled with distance. The good horse not startled but swinging her ears forward, interested but not put off. Iris patted the wide damp neck. "That's right, girl," said Iris. She liked this horse's steady character.

In a quarter mile she dismounted and tied Mayjune to a madrone where the horse could find some graze, and she went on up on foot, following the big creek. The sound of her footfalls were well-masked, not that they needed to be. From what she'd heard about this particular poacher, John Blackstone, he was likely as not to be stone drunk.

After a quarter mile the land flattened out and the pines gave way to a small meadow cut down its center by the hurrying creek. There was a lean-to built there out of limbs and scavenged boards with a tin stovepipe tilted out of one side.

A man was standing creek-side, knees slightly bent, arms dangling loose. He was staring into a deep pool in the creek, a hole made deeper by a crudely built rock dam that reached halfway across the waterway.

Iris was eighty yards away. She walked into the open

where the man could plainly see her, but his focus was elsewhere. John Blackstone struck a match on the backside of his britches and put it to something in his hand. A thin line of smoke drifted out. Dynamite.

"Stop!" yelled Iris. "Stop right there! I'm a warden!"

The man turned, squinted. The creek was full of surging riffles and sounds could be easily misinterpreted. He took in the approaching figure, made to throw the bomb. Iris slid the rifle out of its sheath but before she could level the barrel the stick of dynamite was cartwheeling through the air, trailing a spiral of smoke, to land *keerplunk!* in the pool. There was a long moment when nothing happened, then a deep-throated *whumph!* The middle of the hole swelled up, a quivering mound of translucent green water that hung, poised, before exploding into a towering crown of white.

"Yee-hah!" shouted the man, lifting one leg for emphasis. Water pattered down all around.

Iris started walking, barrel pointed straight up—easier to carry one-handed—finger alongside the guard. "Hold on, mister. I'm the game warden here. And I'm telling you to hold up!"

"What in the hell?" John Blackstone turned slow, scrunching his eyes.

Sixty yards. "Game warden!" she yelled.

Blackstone dipped down, came up with another stick of dynamite.

"Put that down right away!" Iris commanded, bringing the rifle smoothly down to rest on her short left arm. Fifty yards. The first time she'd had to aim a weapon at a man in her whole time as warden, some twenty arrests.

"Who are you?"

"Like I said, I'm the game warden of these parts. And I'm arresting you." Still coming forward.

"The hell," he snorted. "You're just a girl! No such thing as a girl warden."

"There is these days. I was fairly elected by the people of Jackson County. And one reason they elected me is that I vowed to shoot the nuts off any poacher I find violatin' the laws of our fair county." Thirty yards. There was a small wooden box near Blackstone's boots. Inside were brown sticks of dynamite. Iris could see the fuses sticking out.

Blackstone shook his head. "You got a mouth for a girl."

"I got a gun, too. A Winchester Model ninety-four loaded with one-hundred forty-grain thirty caliber cartridges and it's aimed right at your soul. So you best not do anything unless I tell you to do it. You understand?"

"Hell, there ain't no such thing as poaching. The Bible says so."

Iris pointed to the pool where half a dozen good-sized trout floated lifeless, then to the long-handled net by the creek bank. "There's a law against using dynamite to harvest fish," said Iris.

"Aww, shit. It's just quarter sticks."

"It's against the law. Law of the State of Oregon. And it's my sworn duty to protect those laws."

"Laws." Blackstone shook his head. *The profit of the earth is for all.* That's the Bible. Ecclesiastes," holding up the dynamite like a finger. "*The earth is pre-furred over all things in this life.* All things. That means you and your badge and that pea shooter..." he waved a hand toward the forest, "...and whatever else son of bitches you got in them woods."

Iris watched his hands. "You alone here?"

"You want a drink?" he asked.

"No I don't. Are you alone?"

"There's a whiskey drink in the shanty."

"Would you put that dynamite down?" She tried to will

him to do it; she sure as hell didn't want to shoot anybody today.

"It's warm these days."

"Mister…" Twenty yards.

With a magician's slyness, he opened his other hand— the hand without the stick of dynamite—to reveal a flame flickering in his palm. A lit match. He touched the match to the dynamite fuse and set it to sparking and sizzling.

Iris was stunned. He'd done it so fast. Blackstone could now do one of two things. Throw the dynamite into the creek, or throw it at her. She sighted him up, curled her finger around the trigger.

But she was wrong. There was a third possibility. John Blackstone let the dynamite roll off his fingers and fall into the box at his feet.

He smiled, said, *"Woe unto them that join house to house, that lay field to field, till there be no place, that they may be placed alone in the midst of the earth.* That's Isaiah." Smoke curled around his ankles. "We shoulda had that drink."

"Run, mister!" she yelled. "Get…"

There was a great rending of everything, of air and sky and creek and grass, and an enormous unseen fist punched her hard all over and she tumbled backwards. For a long time dirt clods rained down and nothing made sense and she lay there while things whirled. At long last the spinning stopped and her eyes came clear and she realized the poacher John Blackstone had just blown himself to King- dom Come. He really had. *Sweet Jesus!*

She sat up, looked around. There was a thrumming in her ears. Her chest ached. The rifle was missing. Got to her feet; hadn't lost any more body parts; found the Winchester thirty feet away. Put it in the scabbard on her back. Went to the spot where Blackstone had stood. There was a dark crater there, eight feet around and a foot deep. A whole side of the dynamite box was there, miraculously intact, with a gaily colored logo printed on its side, *James Brothers Chemicals and Explosives*. And Blackstone's boots. Only not just his boots, but leg bones sticking out. Smoke twisted out of the depression.

Iris looked around. Against her will she identified pieces of clothing—and worse—in the nearby grasses and floating out on the pond. She took a few steps and vomited, wiped her mouth on her stump sleeve. It was over and done here. The state troopers could come collect the remains, but animals would probably get to everything first.

She went to the shanty. There was a blanket on the floor, an old bolt-action single-shot rifle, and a half-full bottle of moonshine whiskey. Not much else. She uncorked the hooch, had a swig. Set the bottle down, took up the rifle, went out, thought better of it, went back inside and took the bottle of whiskey, too.

On the ride back down the mountain she gave the mare her head and they plodded along while Iris drank moonshine. At one point she swatted at some bug on her cheek. But it wasn't a bug; it turned out to be a twig stuck there. But it wasn't a twig, either. It was white. It was a splinter of bone.

Chapter Twenty-Seven
May, 1929

IRIS FILED HER REPORTS and telegraphed the Salem office about the incident and got a telegram back from the regional supervisor telling her that copies of the report would go to the FBI and the Northwest offices of the Department of Justice. The telegram went on to say that she had been put on a temporary leave of absence pending an investigation. She went to Jack's apartment in Jacksonville and took a bath and then stayed there three whole days and refused to go out so Jack brought in apples and jerky and hard rolls and they ate and talked how just about the whole world had gone crazy and then their clothes inevitably came off and their musky scents filled everything up so that nothing else could get in.

The fourth day was a Sunday and she told Jack she was going out to the farm and stay there awhile. She didn't know if her momma had heard anything about the man blowing himself up but she supposed the newsmen had driven out there looking for their "Bounty Huntress" so they could get a few of her spoken words in the articles. She hadn't seen the newspapers herself. Had no desire.

Jack offered to drive her but she declined and took Mayjune out of the state corral without official permission but the stable master helped her saddle up anyway and she rode the mare up the highway to the farm which took about all day. Every so often things came at her with sudden clarity. The way the grasses bent under the blast, rippling toward her. The force of it pressing against her skin. The smell of the smoke after. The leg bones sticking out of the boots.

By early evening she and the horse had made the river road, the twisting waterway below glowing silver in the twilight, frogs and crickets just starting up. She found her mother on the front porch, huddled into her knees, as if she had been waiting for Iris. At the sight of her daughter Emily stood. "There's trouble, Iris," she called out.

Iris rode the mare all the way to the porch. "Look, Momma. That wasn't any my fault. That fella just went right out and killed himself."

"No. What?"

"He must have been crazy."

Emily looked at Iris with a blank stare. She said, "Not that. It's Henry."

"Henry? What about him?"

Emily shook her head. "It's my fault. I shouldn't have taken him."

"Taken him where?"

"To town. It went all bad."

"What did?" Iris slid out of the saddle, held the reins.

"Mrs. Cooper came by today. Said she was going to town, would I like to go? I figured good, we'll get away for a bit. I said I'd have to bring Henry, I figured he'd like it, and she said all right. We piled in her automobile and Henry came along just fine, he seems good with Mrs. Cooper because she just treats him like he's regular and makes all her chitter-chatter about jams and her cousin Gabby and my Lord."

"What happened, Momma?"

"We were in Tomkin's store looking at some cotton cloth, I was going to make a new blouse for you, with a special sleeve and all, damn fool notion, but Henry pulled out a bolt, you know, from the bottom and the whole pile came down which wasn't nothing, really, not that much of a commotion. But Henry got spooked good, he went off rushing out the door and runs right into Pamela what's-her-name, from the bakery…"

"Oh no."

"Pamela Bachman. Knocked her clean to the ground and she broke her wrist or some damn thing…"

"Oh God."

"…and they took Henry away and put him in jail and they want to have him examined."

"Examined for what?"

"To see if he's crazy."

"He ain't crazy for crissakes!"

"Some folks say otherwise."

"This can't be happening, Momma."

"We'll have to get him, Iris. They got him at the jail. He doesn't understand. He might hurt himself in there. I tried to talk to that sheriff but he don't listen to anything. Nobody wanted to hear it was an accident. They want to ship him off to Salem and the insane asylum is what I got the impression."

"All right, Momma. Let me put up the horse. I'll take the flatbed into town. You take care of things here."

"Iris?"

"What?"

"Did somebody kill themselves?"

"The damnedest thing. I'll tell you about it after I put up the mare."

By the time she got to the county jail it was late in the

night. A deputy was there, a young man not much older than Iris, seated at the front desk reading a beat-up dime novel. He said Henry was locked in a cell and there wasn't anything he could do until the sheriff returned in the morning.

"I want to see him," said Iris.

"Can't open up until morning. That's the rules."

"Deputy, you know me. I'm the official Game Warden of Jackson County, and I'm asking you to let me see my brother."

"That's not how we do things."

"Well then I'll just pay Sheriff Kuntz a visit and ask him myself."

The deputy smiled, put one booted foot up on the desk. "You ain't going all the way out to Shady Cove tonight and you know it."

"Look, is there another empty cell in there?"

"They're all empty, 'cept the one your brother is in."

"Then lock me in there with him."

He laughed. "I can't do that."

"That's no criminal in there. He's like a kid. He's scared. He doesn't know why he's here. I'm not gonna bust us out or anything. I don't have a weapon. You can trust me. Just lock me up for the night. I'm asking you please."

He exhaled long and slow, eyes on her shortened arm. "You really get that shot off? Is that true or is that a made-up story so you could get elected?"

Iris looked at her stump, held it up. "Two bullets and a shitty surgeon."

"You blow up anybody lately?" he smirked.

Iris set her jaw. "That fella did it to himself."

The deputy sniffed, gave a crooked smile. "I heard you got a fella in town." He raised his eyebrows. "Ooh la la."

"That's nobody's business," she said low and quiet.

"Fornication is a crime you know."

"You got a point to make, deputy?"

He nodded. "Just that maybe you ought to get used to being behind bars."

She let it lay. Shrugged, said, "Maybe that's so."

Done with needling, he nodded. "I'll tell you what. I'll let you stay until my shift is about up. The sheriff comes in around six. You gotta be out by five. You don't, and I'll just leave you locked up for Sheriff Kuntz to figure out what to do with you."

"I'm obliged."

He stood, fished the keys out of his pocket. "You got any knives or picks or any tools on you?"

"No."

He led her up a stairway of the new jailhouse, brought her to a passage door, unlocked it, showed her inside to the row of cells. Henry was in one cell huddled on the floor.

"Henry!"

He raised his head, said nothing.

"It's Iris. I'm here Henry. I'm going to be right here with you for the night so there's nothing to worry about."

"I want to stay right here in front of his cell so he can see me," she said to the deputy. "You can lock the door."

"There's a blankets on the cots. The other cells are unlocked. You have to go you'll have to use one of the pots, like anybody."

"All right."

"Five o'clock." He went back out, locked the passage door behind him.

The cell rooms fell quiet. The moonlight fell thin on the concrete floors. Iris got a blanket off the cot, spread it by Henry's cell. Sat there.

"Henry. Come over here where I can scratch your back. Would you like that?"

He sighed. Iris could tell he was about drained of everything. She wondered if he had struggled, if they had been rough with him. He sat up, not looking at her, inched his way toward the front of the cell until his back rested against the bars. Her broad-shouldered brother, nearly six-foot tall, a young boy betrayed by a man's body, a body that had everyone believing he should act like a man, be a man. She rubbed at the parts of him that pressed between the iron bars. She felt his heavy breaths. She wanted to say *I'll get you out* but she didn't want to say anything that might not be true. She said, "I'm here, Henry."

After a while he slumped and his head drooped and he was asleep sitting up against the cell bars. Iris put her back to his, the fleshy parts and the iron bars between, trying to think of what to do, and finally drifted off.

In the morning the deputy clanged open the guard door and called out for Iris to *Get the hell out of my jail!*

Iris got up stiff. Henry had folded himself up on the concrete floor. "He needs looking after."

"He's our prisoner. We'll do the looking-after."

"That's what's got me concerned!"

The deputy narrowed his eyes. "You can visit him on regular visiting hours."

"How about nights? Like this here? I won't be no trouble. I'll sleep on the floor, locked up." She reached down and picked up her blanket, shook it out, squared it up, and folded it over her outstretched stump, walked into the next cell and set the blanket neatly on the cot.

"We'll see," he allowed.

He led her out, locked the door.

"Deputy, we're on the same side of the law, you know?"

"Darling," said the deputy, smiling, "we ain't on the same side of anything."

Three days later a doctor came down from Eugene whose job it was on behalf of the state to evaluate the sanity of prisoners held in Jackson and Josephine county jails, usually at the request of local authorities or a family doctor. Doctor Warren was well-dressed and polite, requested a few moments to converse with Henry through the bars. Sheriff Kuntz supplied a three-legged stool and stood in the open doorway to watch. Henry lay on the floor curled up on his side. He had taken off his shirt to use as a pillow. The doctor placed his hands on his knees, smiled at Henry's rounded back. On the floor to one side of the cell was a pungent, ominous puddle.

Doctor Warren asked several questions. Henry said nothing. The doctor nodded to himself, rose, and walked wordlessly past Kuntz into the office. The sheriff retrieved the stool and followed.

"He's a real loony, that one," Kuntz told the doctor. "He's done other things."

Warren paused. "Such as?"

"He's got himself kicked out of school for causing disturbances."

"That's in his report. I have the state records."

"Well, there's other things that's not in the records. Such as he was caught looking into some girl's window when they lived here in town."

"If I'm not mistaken, Sheriff Kuntz, the boy would have been about seven years old then. Hardly an age for promiscuity."

"Well, that's my point. That boy's not right."

"Did you complete a report on that incident?"

"Not for that. Not for others. Some things you let pass. It's a small town. Folks gotta work together."

Warren gave a small nod. "Thank you, Sheriff." He left the jail, walked down the big granite steps. At the bottom of the stairway he stopped and squinted at a vivid blue sky. In his report he would, of course, request that Henry Greenlee be committed to the State Mental Hospital in Salem. He'd recommend a metrazol treatment to induce beneficial convulsions. And perhaps electroshock; the latest experimental results looked promising, and there was a rumor that the state would be purchasing the equipment.

Doctor Warren took a deep breath, slowly exhaled. Good vapors in, bad vapors out. It was, he noted, an exceptionally blue sky.

Henry was bussed to Salem on a Tuesday. He kept his eyes shut tight through the entire process—being leveraged out of his cell, handcuffed, and led stumbling to the waiting vehicle—so that the attendants from the State Hospital had to handle him as if he was blind. They were not pleased, and more than once wrenched his arms back until he grunted in pain.

That same day Iris met with two Justice Department investigators and recounted the events leading up to John Blackstone's death. The investigators were patient, thorough. But they were perplexed why a man would be throwing explosives at fish one minute and then taking his own life the very next.

"Did you threaten Mr. Blackstone?" they wanted to know, both leaning forward, resting their elbows on the table that separated them from Iris.

"No. Like I said, I told him to put the stick down. But he just fired it up out of nowhere and dropped it into the box. He knew what he was doing."

"Did you fire your weapon?"

"No."

"Why do you think he did such a thing?"

"He was plumb crazy. And drunk. I don't know."

"And he said what?"

"It was something from the Bible, about *There's no place on the Earth you can go.*"

It was all a formality. The investigators packed up their notes and their satchels and headed back to their offices in Salem. Iris was reinstated. But she was not the same.

Chapter Twenty-Eight
September, 1929

IN SEPTEMBER the fire marshal, the State High Commission, and the Fish and Game Commission merged with the Oregon State Police. The new Southwest District was to organize itself in the Hanley Building in Central Point, north of Medford. The Commissioner sent Iris a letter requesting that she establish her personal office at that location. She was to report to the District Captain of the State Police, Charles LeBlanc, and act under his direction.

She gathered her Foster Shoe calendar and pencils and a paperweight that was a small hunk of river jade she'd fished from the bottom of the Applegate and put them in an old pear box she'd found. She put her badge in the bottom and folded her service revolver and holster on top. The station master Bradford Buck did not look up as she left the train depot.

She had the Packard flatbed and drove to the Hanley Building, a big rectangular block of a structure, plain limestone walls, little ornamentation. Windows were small and narrow. The main walkway led from a gravel parking lot to the front steps and along the way curved around a circle of grass with two flagpoles at its center, one flying the stars and stripes and a shorter one with the dark blue flag of the State of Oregon. Both flags jostled in a whisper of breeze.

Inside was a counter that spanned the entryway. At either end of the counter were walls with doors leading inside. Beyond the counter were desks and boxes and a great deal of activity as officers and workers moved filing cabinets and lamps and typewriters. The reorganization was well underway.

Seated behind the counter was a large woman with red hair. She did not have on a uniform but she did wear a distinct air of authority. She squinted at Iris. "May I help you?"

Iris nodded. "I'm the Game Warden. I'm to set up in here."

The woman frowned, took in Iris' missing arm as confirmation, nodded. "You're Iris Greenlee. I'll get the duty officer."

Iris set her box down. After a long ten minutes the woman returned and said, "Officer Barton will be out here in a minute."

"You got a place for me in there?"

"Officer Barton will explain."

There was no place to sit down. Iris moved her box to one side and leaned up against the wall and watched the activity. After twenty minutes she was about to bust inside and go find this Officer Barton herself when a stocky state trooper appeared from one of the doors. He wore a military-type coat that was belted up high, sidearm holstered butt-out on his left hip, jodhpurs, black knee-high half-chap boots, and a jaunty police cap. Despite his riding gear Iris figured the only time he'd be on a horse is the Fourth of July parade. Star badge pinned high above his left breast pocket with some kind of medal underneath. Trimmed moustache. Big sideburns. He did not look pleased.

"Iris Greenlee?"

"That's me."

"I'm the duty officer, Officer Barton." He looked her

up and down. She was dressed in her green shirt and denim trousers, work boots, no hat, single braid behind.

"Where's your badge?" he wanted to know.

She hesitated. "Lost it in the dynamite explosion. You heard about that one?" The lie just came out—the badge was in the box at her feet.

He nodded.

"Never could find it."

"All right." Paused, scratched delicately at the edge of one nostril, said, "See here, things are changing."

"That's what I understand."

"The Fish and Game Commission is now under the direction of the state police, as are various other departments."

"I've heard."

"That means that all enforcement officers have to meet the requirements of the Oregon State Police."

"Uh huh."

"Yes. We have strict requirements for officer enrollment. And quite frankly, you don't meet the requirements."

"Because of my arm?"

"That's one. The requirements specifically state that an officer must be able to 'shoot with either hand.' That's exactly how the requirements are written."

"I can shoot better than any officer you've got."

Barton drew himself up, slit his eyes. "I seriously doubt that."

"What else?"

"The police academy does not accept women."

Iris nodded, long and slow. "You know I was elected. There didn't have to be tests or anything. All fair and square."

"I'm sure," said Barton.

"I am the official Game Warden of Jackson County.

I've worked hard. I've made arrests."

He scratched an eyebrow. "Yes, it's a bit complicated. I've written to the Commissioner for confirmation."

"So I can work?"

"Actually, I'm recommending that you be discharged."

"You saying I'm fired? Just like that?"

He shrugged. "You don't meet the most obvious of requirements. And quite frankly, I doubt if you could pass the written exams."

"I want to see Mr. Charles LeBlanc. Is he here?"

The officer glanced over his shoulder. "He is not here."

"When is he back?"

"He's in Salem. He'll return next week."

Iris indicated her box of effects. "I got a letter in here from the Commissioner saying I was supposed to show up here and report to Mr. LeBlanc."

"Like I said, things have changed."

"What if the Commissioner writes you and says I can stay on?" Beyond the counter out of earshot two officers were looking at Iris and talking.

Officer Barton smiled, shook his head. "I wouldn't count on it if I were you."

"So I *am* being fired."

"Discharged," said Barton. "General discharge under honorable conditions. But, to be fair, we'll wait for confirmation from the Commissioner." Said it like he knew the Commissioner personally. Probably did. It was a done deal.

Officer Barton left by the same door, hard heels clacking the tiles. Iris heard a bolt slide into place.

The red-haired woman had her eyes down. Iris took a deep breath, thought a moment, walked over and said, "My future as Game Warden doesn't look so good."

The red-haired woman looked up, said nothing.

"I'd like to write up my resignation."

"And?" said the woman.

"Would you be so kind as to lend me a couple of pieces of that official paper?" Iris pointed to a neat stack of ivory-colored stationary. The sheets had the seal of the Oregon State Police in one corner and a replica of the state flag waving in the other. "I'd like what I got to say to be on real official paper."

The woman gave her three sheets of the stationary, didn't say another word.

"Thank you," said Iris. She put the stationary in the pear box and hefted the box onto one knee so she could get her right arm under it. The red-haired woman watched.

Iris got out to the flatbed and set the box inside the cab. There was a police auto that had parked next to the truck and on the front seat was a state policeman's hat. Iris looked around. From the Hanley Building you could hardly see the police vehicle behind the old flatbed. Quick as a rattler Iris' hand shot out and in two shakes she was wheeling out of the parking lot and turning up the highway with an official state policeman's cap on the floorboards.

She drove straight over to the newly built courthouse in Medford. Inside smelled of damp plaster and wax and fresh varnish. She found Jack Dressler typing at a small desk in the foyer.

He smiled. "Iris, hey!"

"Hey yourself."

"I can't get away right now, Iris. I got to finish this pile of stuff."

"That's all right. I'm still sore from the last time. But I need you to help me." She held up the pieces of stationary. "I want you to help me type up a letter."

Chapter Twenty-Nine
October, 1929

BEFORE DAWN IRIS DROVE the old flatbed out of Medford and onto the state highway that ran up the mountains and into big tree country, past Grants Pass and then Roseburg. The clouds hung low in the mountains and a fine mist covered the windshield and Iris had to reach up every few minutes and work the wiper mechanism. Up to Eugene where the land leveled into hills spotted yellow with big leaf maples and grassy fields turning green with the warm wet fall. All the way to Salem. Eleven hours at the wheel, the four-cylinder engine making a scant fifteen miles an hour climbing the high passes, three stops for gasoline and two for a pee by the side of the road. It would have been easier to take the train, but the flatbed was familiar. That would be important.

At three in the afternoon Iris was parked in front of the Oregon State Hospital in Salem. It was unlike any building she'd seen. Red brick, huge across the front, four stories tall at the center and three stories each on the two enormous wings. A big white steeple stuck up in the middle like here was the center of everything. Some of the windows in the wings were covered with iron bars. Iris reckoned there could be a thousand people in there. Henry and crowds weren't a good mix.

She got out of the truck, stretched. She had on her green shirt and a pair of men's jodhpurs she'd found at the second-hand store and damn if they didn't fit. She couldn't find any half chaps, that would have been something. But she did pick an old pair of black leather cowboy boots out of the bargain bin. They looked the part. The boots were too loose so she used her old trick and wound some cloth around her feet to get them snug.

Iris cinched the holster around her waist, passed her hand over the grip of the Smith and Wesson. She reached under the front seat, pulled out an old rag, unwrapped her brass game warden's badge, pinned that above her left breast. Then, the topper: a real state policeman's cap with its shiny black brim and silver badge.

She walked to the front entrance thinking, *Lord save me from having to walk into these big government buildings ever again.*

Inside there was a central atrium and a long, curved walnut counter. Behind the counter were three blue-smocked attendants. Against the back wall were several rows of benches, and here and there folks sat, some alone, some in pairs, each somber as hell. They seemed to be waiting for something to happen. Each floor above had been built with a large central opening so you could look up past three floors of curved railings to the inside of the steeple. Daylight flooded down.

There was a roped-off area behind which visitors waited to be summoned to the curved counter by one of the attendants. Iris stood behind three other people and when it was her turn she walked up and said, "I'm here on official state police business."

The attendant, an unshaven man of about forty with gray-streaked hair combed straight back, said, "What do you mean?" He was staring at her sewn-up sleeve.

"I'm here to take one of your, ah, patients into the state police headquarters. It's believed he might have information about an important case we're investigating."

"I don't think we release our patients without permission from one of our doctors," replied the attendant, but the tone of his voice said he was unsure.

Iris handed him the letter that Jack had typed. It was on official state police stationary, with the seal of the Oregon State Police in one corner and a replica of the state flag waving in the other. It said:

```
October 9, 1929

To:
Oregon State Mental Hospital
Salem, Ore.

From:
The Department of the Oregon State Police
Salem, Ore.

It is requested that you release the pa-
tient Henry Greenlee into the temporary
custody of the officer presenting this
letter. Mr. Greenlee is required for fur-
ther testimony at State Police Headquar-
ters, and will be returned to the State
Hospital facility the same day.

Your cooperation is greatly appreciated,
Captain Thomas Banks, OSP
```

The attendant gave the letter a shake. "Let me get Mr. Vogelpohl."

A few minutes later the attendant returned with another blue-smocked man. Mr. Vogelpohl was impressed with Iris' mission. "We don't often have these types of things." He held out his hand. "Stanton Vogelpohl. I'm the Assistant Director here at the hospital."

She took his hand. It was soft and bloodless and dry. "I'm Emily Rink. Officer Emily Rink."

Vogelpohl seemed amused by the one-armed female officer in her cowgirl boots. That such a thing existed. He said, "What's this all about?"

"It's a murder case."

"Ah. Was it that awful tragedy out by the bridge?"

"No. It happened in Jackson County some time ago. But this here Henry Greenlee, we figured he might know a few things."

Vogelpohl shrugged. "You know, your Mr. Greenlee isn't responding to treatment."

"How's that?"

"He remains uncommunicative. He doesn't talk. At all."

The attendant, seated once again, nodded vigorously and added, "At all."

"What kind of treatments?"

"Metrazol. It's a medication that induces mild spasms that are beneficial to the body system. It can help a person regain control. With persistence, that is."

"And it's not working?"

"Unfortunately, no. But we have new equipment that's being installed. For electroshock therapy. It's the most advanced technique available for treating someone like this person you're after..."

"Henry Greenlee."

"Yes. Anyway, the initial results are quite promising. But I'm afraid you won't get what you need from that man..."

"Henry Greenlee."

She said it too hard. Vogelpohl looked at her amputation and then back to her face with a question in his eyes.

"Yes. Henry Greenlee. If you can't get what you need

by questioning Mr. Greenlee, then perhaps electroshock can help. When it's installed, that is."

"I'm thinking we'll get what we're after today."

Vogelpohl frowned. "Aren't you that bounty hunter girl? The one who lost her arm?"

Iris shook her head. "Lot of folks say that. But we're no relation. She got her arm shot off, and I lost mine to a combine."

"Oh dear."

"I could see the bone. Then I passed out."

Vogelpohl gave the letter a little shake, cleared his throat. "So, I assume it's about some kind of poaching incident. That's why a game warden is here."

"Maybe you heard. It's all new. Fish and Game, Fire Marshal, all work for the state police now."

"Right. That's right." Tapped his cheek, remembering.

"Well, we're hoping he'll talk to us," Iris said, conjuring a smile. "This Henry Greenlee. We need to ask him a few things. Bring him over to headquarters. And, if you don't mind, I see that the day is going by. We'd like to have him back in your care by later today."

"All right." The Assistant Director bit at his thumbnail, looked at the letter again. "I'll have one of our attendants fetch him. Mr. Coswell, get Doyle." Coswell nodded and turned to the wall behind him. He pressed a button on a small metal panel and spoke into it, "Mr. Doyle, please present yourself to the front desk. Mr. Doyle to see Director Vogelpohl at the front desk." His amplified voice resounded down the corridors.

"If you don't mind," said Iris, "I'd like to go along. I'd like to see where he spends his time."

"There's not much to see," said Vogelpohl.

"I'd like to see it."

Vogelpohl shrugged his indifference.

"Can't bring a firearm inside," noted the attendant.

Iris unstrapped the Smith and Wesson and handed the rig over the counter. "Can you hold this for me?"

The attendant's eyes got wide. "Of course," he said, clearly pleased to be entrusted.

"Keep a good eye on that," said Iris, "it's my daddy's gun."

"Put it in the safe, Mr. Coswell," instructed Vogelpohl.

"Right. Of course."

She held out her hand. "The letter?"

Vogelpohl started to give it to her, then thought better of it. "Perhaps I should show this to my supervisor."

Iris kept her hand out. "That's my copy to file. There's another coming to you by mail from the department. For your records."

He reluctantly put the letter in Iris' palm and she stuffed it into her pocket.

The man named Doyle arrived. He was medium height and stocky and had thick forearms. His smock was white and had faint ghosted stains of liquids that the laundry had failed to completely remove. He looked capable of handling a physical altercation, which Iris assumed was one of his main duties. He squinted at the sight of Iris but said nothing. The Assistant Director did not offer introductions.

Vogelpohl took them down a long corridor. There was distant yelling, some of it strangely bestial. Strong smells. Antiseptic. Alcohol. Bleach. And underneath, the odor of unused flesh. Sweet and thick, the byproduct of rot. The taste of it on her tongue. There were benches along the corridor, and on them were huddled an assortment of creatures in thin gowns, holding their knees to their chest.

Help me said one, looking Iris right in the eyes.

Kill me implored another, hands clasped in prayer.

Vogelpohl looked at Iris and shrugged. "They all say

that. They don't mean it."

The walls were a pale cream color above and a green below, poorly plastered shadowed cracks and unsmoothed places and the tile floors were white with squares of brown at regular intervals. Doors, some open to small cots, a short table. Other doors were shut and probably locked, heavy screen mesh over the insides of small glass windows. The air unstirred.

"Almost there," smiled Vogelpohl.

It was a large room. Tall ceilings. Windows with thick wire screens. Maybe twenty patients, all men, and several attendants in their pale blue uniforms. Benches along the walls and men curled up holding onto their legs with feet drawn tight and several in the same position only lying down. A small bookshelf in disarray. Men in cotton smocks stained brown and yellow in obvious places moving slowly; men still as tombstones attached to walls. That smell. Someone lying on the floor.

Henry was by a window. Tall enough to see over a fellow patient who was staring out the same window only a step closer to the opening. Henry was dressed in dark blue pants too big and a green shirt too small. He was barefoot; all the patients were barefoot.

"Henry!" she blurted out.

He didn't turn. Stood fixed on the window, or something beyond. Not the trees. Not birds. Something else.

"Do you know him?" asked Vogelpohl, surprised.

"I've dealt with him before," said Iris. She'd almost given herself away.

"I'll get him," said Doyle.

"No," said Iris. "Let me talk to him first. He might remember me. It'll help us get him to talk."

"He doesn't talk," growled Doyle.

"Henry Greenlee," she said and walked to his side and

looked at his face, unevenly shaved so a swath of long stubble darkened one cheek. His blue eyes out there, not here, hair mussed, the shirt fabric stretched at the buttons, cuffs undone, him now so much taller and yet smaller than she.

"Henry." Now looking away, her voice soft as moss.

He said nothing. Somewhere someone yowled like a tomcat in heat. It sent a chill up her spine.

"Henry Greenlee," she said again, hoping she still had sway. "You need to come with me."

He didn't move. Iris looked at Vogelpohl, who shrugged as if to say, *I told you so.*

"Let me talk to him a minute, all right?" Iris said to Vogelpohl.

"All right," he replied. He pointed at Doyle. "Doyle here can help you if you need, ah, assistance. I'll be in the hallway." He left.

Iris moved closer to Henry. She didn't touch him, kept her eyes down. She spoke so Doyle couldn't hear, "Henry, this is Iris. I've come to take you home. You don't belong here. Now, it's real important that you do what I tell you to do. If you'd like to go home. You'd like to go home, wouldn't you? To the farm?"

Henry stared out the window.

"Now, you've always been real good about doing what I ask you to do. So I'm going to ask you something. You don't have to answer. Just do what I ask. We're going home. We won't be coming back to this place."

She saw his shoulders loosen.

"You just follow me. I won't look back at you, I promise. You follow me. I might have to talk with some people. You say nothing. If anybody asks you something, you don't say a word. Ajax would really like it if you'd follow me."

He licked his lips.

"You thirsty? Maybe we can stop somewhere and get us a root beer. But you gotta come with me and not say a word, let me do all the talking."

Iris didn't know if she'd got to him. Maybe he didn't even hear her. She'd never seen him like this and it made an ache in her gut. "Like we've always done. Me leading, and you be my shadow. Like always. Can you do that?"

He said nothing. Time was slipping away. She didn't want Doyle to get involved, it could go badly. So she turned and thought *Sweet Jesus!* and said out loud, "Okay here we go." And she began to walk back the way Vogelpohl had led her. For a long moment there was nothing, and then she could feel him behind her, the dark padding of his bare feet. Doyle fell in line behind.

Vogelpohl was waiting in the corridor. He saw Henry following along and he marveled, "Well look at that."

"Doctor Vogelpohl," said Iris, "would you be so kind as to retrieve Henry's shoes?"

He flashed indignation, then cocked his head, flattered by the misnomer—*Doctor*—although he was neither a physician nor a committed academic. He was about to correct Iris, thought better of it, nodded and said, "Mr. Doyle, please get this man some shoes."

Iris led Henry to the atrium. Henry stood and looked up at the light above. After an eternity Doyle walked in with a pair of shoes, one clutched in each hand.

Iris took them and tucked them under her short arm. "I'll have him put these on outside," she said. She went to the counter. "My weapon?" she asked the attendant with the gray-streaked hair. The man disappeared into an interior room and returned with the holstered revolver.

Iris slung the belt over her shoulder. "Let's go, Henry," she said, and she strode through the front doors and held her breath and *thank Jesus* Henry came right behind. She put the shoes on the top step and sat down several steps lower. The letter was in her pocket, scrunched up. No matter; she wouldn't have to show it to anybody again.

"Put on your shoes, Henry," she urged. She stood off to the side and listened to the rustling of his efforts. When he quieted she said, "Here we go" and led them out to the parking lot and the flatbed Packard. Iris opened the passenger side door and Henry climbed right in. There's another little miracle she'd have to pay back to Jesus some day. But for now…

Iris got in the driver's seat, started the engine, and steered the Packard out to the main street. She aimed to put as much distance between them and the State Hospital as possible. She'd drive all night if they could find the gasoline. Would they arrest her for springing a lunatic out of the loony bin? Was that an actual crime? Would they come get Henry? Not if she could help it. He was never going back to that place. She'd shoot any blue-smocked sonofabitch she saw.

They reached the outskirts of the city and she began to relax as the buildings eased away the shadows of trees and the sun shot low under the cloud cover and streaks of light flashed across the windshield.

"Damn it's good to see you!" she sighed.

Henry stared straight ahead.

"I can't believe how they treat people in there," she said.

He closed his eyes.

Wrong topic. Iris said, "Momma misses you awful."

He said nothing.

"I miss you awful, too. So does Ajax."

He opened his eyes, looked straight ahead out the windshield to the road curving before them.

"I thought it was a shithole in there."

He sighed.

"Did you think it was a shithole?"

Nothing.

"I'm breaking you out of there, do you know? I'm sorry you got there in the first place, but there wasn't anything we could do. But now we're outlaws, you and me."

They drove in silence. The drone of the motor and of the wheels on the road sounded hopeful. After half an hour Henry said, "Shithole."

Iris sighed. "Dang, you *can* talk. Geez Louise, I thought maybe you'd gone deaf or something."

Near Corvallis Iris found a late-night gasoline station and filled up the flatbed's tank and bought four sticks of jerky from a jar at the counter. She gave two to Henry. "Eat," she said, and he began to gnaw. "There's water in the canteen."

Half an hour back on the highway Iris said, "You know, I lost my job as warden."

Henry said nothing.

"So there's no job and it's back to the poorhouse for all of us." She caught herself. "I mean it's back to the farm for all of us. Not a lick of money, though. Just eggs."

Henry looked out the side window and said, "Eggs."

"You hungry?"

Henry was quiet for a while, then said, "I'd like a root beer."

Iris smiled. "Henry, you're a regular chatterbox. Damn it's good to hear your voice."

Outside of Eugene they stopped at an open gasoline station and Iris bought two bottles of root beer and gave one to Henry and he drank it straight down in a series of noisy gulps.

They drove on in silence for another hour until, at the crest of the Canyon Creek Pass, the Packard pressing hard,

Iris rolled the truck off to the shoulder and stopped. She turned off the motor. "Henry, we're gonna let the truck rest for a while. You gotta pee, do it now right out there."

He immediately got out of the truck and stood in the open doorway and urinated for a good long while like he hadn't released in days. Then he got back inside.

"Thank you," he said.

"You're welcome."

The cooling engine ticked. In the far distance a pair of headlamps were coming toward them from the opposite direction, beams roving back and forth, another lonely night traveler. Henry was leaning forward and staring up through the windshield at the night sky. She looked out the windshield too. The bright moon was waxing fat and cast a glow around slender islands of iron-gray clouds. She said, "If I was rich I'd buy Momma a new dress. Like you see in some of those magazines."

Henry looked at the night.

"What would you get her?"

"A radio."

"A radio! That's a good one, Henry. What made you think of that?"

He shrugged, said nothing.

"I bet she'd really like that."

"Yes." He leaned back into the seat and folded his arms across his chest.

"All right. Well you're my brother and I'd surely like to hug you but I won't. I promise. But how about I give you a scratch, like you give Ajax? I'll give you a scratch on the back. Would that be all right?"

He lowered his head and hunched his shoulders, like a man expecting a stunning blow. But he didn't try to squirm away.

She reached out and got her fingernails between his

shoulder blades and gave him a gentle scuffing. It was nice to feel his big back, to know they were headed home.

"I'll tell you what," she said. "When we get back to the farm, we'll go pan for gold. All right?"

"All right."

"All right," Iris smiled and she fired up the engine and put the truck in gear and wheeled the truck back onto the highway.

Earlier that evening at the State Hospital Assistant Director Vogelpohl had pointed straight up in the air. A thought had occurred. "Coswell," he said. "What was the name of that odd girl they had down there in Medford? The bounty hunter girl."

Coswell smiled. He enjoyed it when his supervisor asked him a question he could answer. "Iris Greenlee," he announced. "The one-armed bounty huntress."

Vogelpohl pursed his lips. "Greenlee. Wasn't that the name of the patient we just released to the State Police?"

Coswell's smile faded. This was a question to which he did not know the answer exactly. He shook his head. "I don't think so," he said. "It was something else. Reed, maybe."

"Reed. Hmm. That doesn't sound right. Well, looks like the police are running late with our patient, whoever he is. I want you to stay until they bring our boy back. Make sure he gets into his room. Have Doyle help you."

Coswell looked at the wall clock. Surely they'd return within the hour. If not, it could be another stretch of overtime with no overtime pay. "Very well," he sighed.

Chapter Thirty
October, 1929

THE NIGHT WAS COLD and Emily built a fire and brought the dog in for company. Iris had gone hell-bent for the State Hospital and God knows how that would go. Emily could only hope and maybe add a prayer for whatever good it might do. *Anybody listening up there?* The fire snapped and popped and a spark vaulted the screen to land on the dog but he wouldn't move and didn't seem to mind any more than the sting of the hornets he snapped out of mid-air.

She had a lamp at the table and was writing a letter to her sister in Wisconsin but the words weren't coming right and she thought it was probably because she was worried and everything she wrote sounded false. *When does the worry ever stop?* Maybe never. Maybe worries were the stitches that held everything together, and if you stopped everything came unraveled.

The fire was trailing off and she was about to let it go out and put into bed when the dog came all the way upright and faced the north wall and began to growl from deep in his throat. Emily went to the bedroom and got on her knees and pulled the old Stevens double-barrel from under the bed. Took it into the light and clicked it open to see the brass butts of two fresh shells. Snapped it shut. Considered whether to let the dog out, decided against it. If there was a big cat out there it might go bad for the Chessie.

The dog began to bark and whine. A mixed signal, Ajax being fierce and unsure at the same time. Could be a cougar. She took up the lamp, then put it back. Holding the shotgun needed both her hands.

Emily opened the door to the back porch just enough to squeeze through so Ajax couldn't follow. *Stay* she said and she closed the door and he pawed at it from the other side and kept barking and whining.

At the top of the back porch steps she waited and listened. Under the sounds of the night and the protests of the dog was another sound, faint. She went down the steps and tiptoed out a ways, wishing for the lantern now as it was a clouded-over new moon and dark as could be. A big cat could walk right up to her and she wouldn't see it until the very last.

But that noise. She moved forward and as her eyesight adjusted she got her bearings among the trees and the chicken coop and seventy-five yards away the hulking shape of the barn. And there, in one corner of the barn, faint through the gaps in the boards, an odd light. A moving light. The barn was on fire.

She dropped the gun and ran for the barn but caught her foot on something and fell ass-over-teakettle and scraped up her arms and whacked a shoulder on something hard and when she'd righted herself there was a rustling and then the dark shape of a man standing over her.

"What's your hurry?" said the man and from the voice alone she knew it was Jasper Hibbard. In his hands he held the shotgun she'd dropped.

"You," she rasped. "What the hell are you doing on my property?" Emily tried to get to her feet but the shadowed shape reached out and pushed her back on her rump.

"Sit there and don't move," said Hibbard. "I already shot one Greenlee. I could make it two just as easy."

"You set the barn on fire, you bastard."

"It's an eye for an eye."

"Get off my farm!"

"I don't think you have much to say about it."

"You'll be going to jail."

"You don't understand," said Hibbard. "You ain't the law. That girl of yours ain't the law. The people are the law. There's no hidin' behind a badge or a piece of paper. When we say you leave it, you leave it. I mean, what's wrong with you people? Christ almighty, there's a special hell for tax men and game wardens."

"I got to get the horse." Emily tried to get to her feet again but Hibbard shoved her back. The flames were now outside, reaching up along the corner of the barn. In the growing light she could see Hibbard's hairy face, the hollowed-out eyes. She felt a pang for her first husband, Iris' father. He'd been at the end of a gun held by Jasper Hibbard, and he'd felt the slug enter his body. *Dear Dexter help me now.* Ajax in the house barking nonstop.

"Don't kill my horse," she said.

"Well now I'm thinking that's a fair trade given that my friend went and got killed on account of your daughter."

"If you're talkin' about that old drunk who blew himself up, I say the world is a richer place because of it." She closed her eyes for the blast of the shotgun. It didn't come.

"Brother Blackstone was a patriot and a true believer. The world needs more of him and less of the likes of you Greenlees."

The beams and the siding of the barn were dry with age. The flames were getting to the eaves and embers wove into the night. The fire rumbled and light rode the smoke as it billowed up and out. Inside the barn, the horse had begun to whinny. Another man's voice came shouting out of the darkness. "It's a goner. Let's go."

"We got neighbors who'll see that fire and come over lickety-split."

Hibbard looked up. He knew she was probably right. He said, "Tell your whore daughter it's time she quit tryin' to be a man."

"She doesn't have to be a man to be more of a man than you. You're a no-count murderin' son-of-a-bitch..."

There was a horse scream from the barn and then a crash and the big Percheron burst from the barn and fled out the open door at full gallop up to the road and into the night. He'd broken out of his stall. Hibbard, frustrated that the animal had escaped, raised the shotgun and aimed for the horse. Emily scrambled upright and launched herself at the man but he saw her at the last second and swung the butt of the gun around and caught her square on the jaw and she went down hard.

The world went whirling, all unsettled and out-of-kilter. Ground and barn and flames all turned around each other. There was flickering darkness and the sound of the horse's hooves on the road pounding away into the distance. She tried to make sense of it, could not. The blow had made her sick to her stomach and she fought the urge to retch. She held it back and willed the world to come to order. Which it did. Slowly, the spinning replaced piece by piece with pain. She worked her jaw. It might be broken somehow, hard to tell. She heard the burning barn, could feel the heat on her face. There was a tremendous light. She had to get some buckets of water. But it was hard to get to her feet. She looked up at Jasper Hibbard, but he had disappeared.

They turned onto the river road under a dark-clouded dawn. As they got close to the farm, Iris could see an unnatural glow ahead, a ghosted, dancing light. It was a fire, and a sudden panic and dread nearly closed her throat and she swallowed hard and fought for breath and hit the accelerator. The old truck rattled and bucked and the rear tires skittered out on the curves.

As they pulled up to the farm she saw the barn had nearly burned to the ground, collapsed and charred timbers stuck up at angles amid still-churning flames. But thank God the house was standing untouched. There were two other vehicles parked there, and fifty yards from the fire Emily stood with some folks who lived nearby. She held a cloth to her face.

At the sight of the flatbed Emily ran up to the road. "Iris!" she said, her voice made small by her swollen jaw. "Iris, is that Henry?" She came around to the passenger side of the truck. "You did it," Emily breathed. "You got him. Oh, Iris, what a night!"

"Momma! I got him out all right. But good God, what happened here? Are you all right?"

"They burned it down, Iris."

"Who?"

"Those same fellas. With that damn Hibbard."

"They burned it down?"

"Yes."

"Are you all right, Momma?"

"I got banged up some."

Iris got out of the cab, glared at the men, too riled to recognize them as neighbors. "Who are those fellas?"

"Oh, that's Jed Colbert and the Schmitt fella. They came over when they saw the fire. Too late. It was a goner. It was Hibbard that done it. He was aiming to kill the horse and I tried to stop him."

"Are they all right? The horse and the dog?"

"The dog was up at the house. The horse kicked down his stall door and got out. That bastard was aiming to shoot the horse so I jumped him and he whacked me good. But he didn't get off a shot." She waved her hand in the direction of the surrounding hills. "Now Parker's up there somewhere."

Iris came around to look at her mother close. "Let me see. Oh, that's not good." About half of her momma's face was swollen and plum-colored. "We gotta get something on that."

"It rains and shines at the same damn time," Emily sighed. "Damn, it hurts to talk. But you got him. You got Henry. They didn't catch you. Henry, I'm so glad you're here!" Emily had to stop herself from grabbing her son and startling him. "So glad." And she put her hands on the side of the cab and sunk her forehead into her arms and began to cry.

"Momma," said Iris.

One of the upriver neighbors, Henrich Schmitt, came up with his hat in his hands. "Miss Iris. We came right away when we seen the flames," said Schmitt. "We were too late. Thank God it wasn't the house."

Iris stared at the burning remains, the gray smoke curling up and disappearing into the gray dawn.

Jed Colbert walked over and said, ""Damn that's all a shame. You want to try and get water on it?"

Iris could tell his heart wasn't in it. She shook her head. "It's not worth the sweat, Mr. Colbert."

"How'd it start?" Schmitt wanted to know.

"It was deliberate."

Schmitt's eyes held flickering reflections. "How you know that?"

"I know it."

"Who'd do it? You know 'em?"

"I know 'em."

"Who are they?"

"They're dead men," said Iris.

Chapter Thirty-One
November, 1929

Iris drove northeast out of Medford and up through Shady Cove and into the Cascades, into the big trees, crowns waving against the sky, the road following the Rogue River all the way up toward Trail. The Smith and Wesson on the seat beside her; Winchester rifle and a box of cartridges on the floorboards. She had on her green shirt and overalls and had pinned up her hair and wore a beat-up Stetson she'd bought at the second-hand store. She'd left the warden's badge back at the farm. No need for that now.

Half a mile from Trail she turned off on a two-track logging road and drove for a hundred yards until she found a flat place where she could pull off. She unbolted the license plates and stashed them and the wrench nearby. There was nothing inside, no papers or do-dads to give an indication of the owner. If somebody stumbled upon the old truck while she was up in the hills, there wouldn't be anything to tie her to what she was about to do.

She had dried pears and jerky in her knapsack and a canteen of water. Enough for two full days. A wool serape for the night. It was going to be a hike, probably ten miles over steep, rough ground. Iris put the revolver and holster in the knapsack and slid the rifle into its scabbard on her back. Got her bearings from the sun and surveyed the way ahead. There'd been some logging here some years ago and there were still plenty of big trees but the understory had filled in thick. She settled the old Stetson on her head and started off.

It took until nightfall to reach the cabin. She crested a ridge and spotted it, hazy in the twilight. Maybe three hundred yards away. Here abouts was where her daddy Dexter had died. Too dark to try and move forward, no need anyway. Tomorrow would be good enough.

There weren't any lights at the cabin but she could see deer carcasses hung up nearby. Jasper Hibbard was either bedded down or was someplace near. No matter. She'd wait. He wouldn't leave his deer meat out too long. She could see her breath in the cooling air. She put on the serape, took a couple of bites of pear leather. The night came and she didn't sleep. Wasn't tired. A light went on in the cabin and didn't stay on but fifteen minutes. Then all was dark. Barred owl and coyote serenaded the spinning stars. Iris willed the dawn into play. *C'mon, c'mon.*

At last the ravens brought up the dawn and the first light crept over the ridges to dissolve the blue-black night. When she could see well enough Iris stuffed the serape in her knapsack and made her way down the slope toward the cabin. There was plenty of cover, big trees and brush, and her footfalls were hushed by her calf-high buckskin moccasins—she'd sewn in triple-thick soles—the leather quiet over twigs and leaves, each step a subtle shift of body parts and then a full stop. It would be hard for someone to pick up her movements with a casual glance. At seventy yards there was a tall timber stump next to a towering sugar pine. A fair distance, but a good rest for the rifle. A clean shot.

She settled in and steadied herself with her left shoulder against the standing tree. The rifle was already chambered. She eased back the hammer, slid the barrel slow and easy over the top of the stump, figured the range, adjusted the sights. The dawn bled strong pink, then yellow.

Hibbard came out in his long johns, stood on the porch looking around. His back flap was open. He looked like a drowned muskrat. He stepped to one side of the porch and opened his front fly and took a piss in the duff. He stood there, put his head back. His stream steamed in the morning cool. Iris sighted him up. Her finger on the trigger.

Then he shook himself off and shuffled back inside. Iris breathed out through her nose. She could have shot him right then, right there. She should have. But not with his back turned. Not while relieving himself. *Patience.* He'd come out again. He'd tend to his poached deer.

In ten minutes there was a movement in the trees behind the cabin. It was Hibbard, now dressed in trousers and overcoat. He'd gotten out of his cabin some back way and was hurrying up the ridge, rifle in hand, zigzagging, putting as many trees as he could between himself and what had spooked him. The bastard either had good eyes or was in league with the devil. Probably both.

A shot now would miss. It would also give her away. She got up, sprinted thirty yards to her left. Stopped, listened. Nothing. Took off the pack, got the revolver out and strapped it on, took up the rifle, left the pack, ran another thirty yards and came to a dead halt and listened hard. Ran thirty more yards to a four-foot-wide fir, froze. This time there was a following sound. It was close. It could have been a ground squirrel, but the noise had stopped sudden. Would Hibbard have hightailed into the woods? Or was he nearby, listening for her as she listened for him?

Iris got low, took off her hat and set it aside. A slight wind came up and got the fir needles to sigh. She was stone still, Winchester level and resting light on her stump arm. More ravens, now way off. Relaxed her eyes to watch for movement. Caught something to her right. Eased the barrel around. Waited.

The sun crested and threw hard light through the boughs. Warblers and thrushes chitted and flashed. The forest woke up, crackling as it warmed. She'd picked the shade side of a tree, in decent cover. Waited.

He stepped into a stripe of sunlight and stopped twenty-five yards away, shaking his head like a buck in the rut. His mistake. She leaned into the Winchester, aligned the sights. A strange thought occurred to her.

She thought: *A-B-C.*

Chapter Thirty-Two
November, 1929

NO ONE CAME OUT to the farm to get Henry or to arrest Iris for whatever crime it was she'd committed by spiriting blood kin out of the State Hospital. Maybe the whole thing got lost in the shuffle. It was government, after all. Or maybe that fellow Vogelpohl let it go on account of he didn't want his boss to know he'd been duped. She figured to let Momma handle the situation if any state police or goons from the hospital showed up. Tell them her fool girl and insane son had hightailed it for Mexico. But nobody showed up.

A Western Union telegram arrived by mail truck, dated three days earlier than the delivery. It said:

```
SALEM OREGON NOV 28 1929

IRIS GREENLEE

YOU ARE HEARBY RELIEVED OF DUTY AND
DISCHARGED FROM THE SERVICE OF THE
OREGON STATE POLICE EFFECTIVE
IMMEDIATELY. YOU ARE INSTRUCTED TO
SURRENDER YOUR STATE ISSUED FIREARM
AND BADGE TO OSP HQ IN MEDFORD. YOU
WILL BE DISCHARGED UNDER HONORABLE
CONDITIONS.
```

```
THE OFFICE OF THE FISH AND GAME
COMMISSION
OREGON STATE POLICE
COMMISSIONER ALAN MACDOUGAL
```

Across the bottom of the telegram in fine print was, *The quickest, surest way to send Money is by Telegram or Cable.*

"Well that tears it," said Iris.

"It's what you thought would happen," Emily said, speaking low through her lips, unable to move her swollen, purpled jaw. "What next, my daughter?"

"I'm working on that," said Iris.

It was a mild afternoon so Iris went with Henry to the river, weaving their way along the path, the grasses tan and stiff with brown and yellow leaves snared in the thin stalks. She brought his pan and set him up by the river's edge so he could pan and for several long minutes Henry did nothing but squat on his haunches and stare at the moving line where the water slipped in to touch the sand, the pan beside him. Iris sat nearby and watched. She said, "Feels good to be home, doesn't it?"

"Yes," said Henry. "Away."

"Away from that place?"

"Yes."

"Henry, did they hurt you there, at that place?"

He said nothing.

The air was cool but the sun was warm and soothing and Henry began to pan and Iris watched her brother and the smattering of leaves that twirled their way down the river. They'd heard the news that the world had crushed under its own weight and the banks were going under and jobs were scarce and money scarcer and Iris thought about all that and what they might do to survive that didn't include catching wanted thieves and other low-lives. Who knows? Maybe she'd be declared a criminal herself and they'd hang a poster of her in the county courthouse and some bounty hunter would come looking for her.

After an hour or so Henry put his pan down and stood up and held his hand aloft and pinched between his thumb and forefinger was a small nugget.

"It's ready," he said.

"What's that?" asked Iris.

"This is the last one."

"The last one what?"

"The gold."

"The gold is ready?"

For an answer Henry turned and started walking up-river, picking his way with care across the rocky river's edge. This was certainly peculiar behavior for Henry, and Iris jumped to her feet to follow his hunched shoulders as he heaved his way along a rocky trail. In fifty yards he came to a small thicket of young willows, the leafless stems all intertwined. He pulled aside some low-hanging branches and got down on all fours and reached inside and put his nugget under the tangle.

"It's ready," he said again.

Iris stepped close. "What's ready, Henry?"

He backed out and stood but kept the branches held back and then pretended to be interested in the sky. Iris got down on her knees so she could see inside the little cave of branches. There in the rock by the water's edge was a round depression eight inches across filled to the top with bits of gold. There were irregular nuggets the size of a fingernail and smaller round balls that had been tumbled to smooth and glistening by the river and tiny rough bits like a grain of sand. It was unreal, like being inside a fairy tale. Iris reached out and slid her hand into the nuggets and her hand went wrist-deep.

"Henry, Henry, Henry. You panned all this?"

"Yes."

"Boy howdy," said Iris. *All those days panning by the river.* "When did you put these in here, in this hole?" She started to giggle. "How come I didn't never see you do it?"

"You ran."

"You mean when I'd take off into the woods?"

"You're fast."

"But why did you wait until I was gone?"

He shrugged. "It's a surprise."

"Damn, brother, it's a surprise all right." She scooped nuggets, let them run between her fingers. There was some standing water in the hole too and flakes of gold covered her fingers in glittering pixie dust. Iris wiped off as many gold flakes as she could and stood up and Henry let the alder branches spring back into place.

"This is good, isn't it?"

"Yes," said Iris. "Very good. Look." She held her hand in front of his face; her palm sparkling.

"Gold," said Henry.

"Was this here before the big flood?"

Henry looked off, thinking. "Yes."

"How come it didn't all wash away?"

"You know why."

"I do?"

"Yes. It's gold."

Iris grinned. "You mean, it's too heavy?"

Henry scrunched up his whole face, which was one of his ways of registering delight. "Yes!"

"Like how it stays in the pan."

Henry shook his whole body like a wet puppy trying to dry off. "Yes!"

"I'll be damned! You figured that out?"

"Yes. From the books."

"The encyclopedia books?"

Henry bobbed his head up and down. "Gichtel to Harmonium."

"I'll be damned. Gichtel to Harmonium! You remember that?"

"Gichtel to Harmonium. Number twelve."

"Well, damn you're smart! And I do believe you're kinda rich! What should we do with this gold, Henry?"

"A radio," he said. "For Momma."

"Huh! That's right, you said that before. That's a good one. I never would of thought of that. She'll like that."

"Yes."

They walked back along the familiar path. The dog joined them and decided to lead the way, his butt and tail swinging back and forth before them. Iris said, "Brother, you're a gift from God, you know that? Momma's gonna be happy."

"Yes."

"Henry, why did you tell me about the gold today?"

Behind her, where she couldn't see him, Henry smiled. "Because the hole got full," he said. "It was ready."

"It needed that one last bit of gold?"

"Yes."

"And now it's ready?"

"Yes."

And Iris smiled.

They took Emily to the river and Henry showed her the spot and she got on her knees and poked her finger in the little pile of gold and said, "Good Lord, how much do you think is in here?"

"A couple of pounds for sure," said Iris.

"My God."

"It's a surprise," said Henry.

"What are we going to do with all this gold?" wondered Emily, still on her knees with only her butt poking out from the little thicket of branches.

"A radio," said Henry.

"What?"

"He wants to get you a radio. Isn't that right, Henry?"

"Yes."

Emily backed out, stood up, dusted off her knees. "A radio?"

"Yes."

"Well, I wouldn't have put that first on the list myself, but now that I think about it, that'd be a damn fine thing to do. A radio. We could listen to music and maybe one of those detective shows."

"Yes," said Henry. "Damn fine."

"And there'd be plenty left over, wouldn't you think, daughter?"

"Looks like."

"Heck, Henry, you could start another pile of gold."

He shrugged. "I don't want to pan for gold."

Emily looked at Iris. "You don't?"

"No."

"Why not?"

He shook his head. "I'm tired of pan, pan, panning."

"I thought you liked it."

"I like it."

"But you're done for now."

"I want to swim."

The women exchanged another look. Emily said, "Swim? In the river?"

"Yes."

"Well, maybe we can teach you to swim. But I don't want you trying to swim in the river before you learn proper and even then you can't go alone. I lost two husbands and a barn and part of a daughter and I sure as hell ain't gonna lose my only son. You understand me?"

"He threw me in the river," said Henry.

"What?"

"Iris saved me."

"Who threw you in the river?"

"Nobody," said Iris. "It's our little joke."

Emily pursed her lips, looked at Iris, then Henry. "Henry, did somebody throw you in the river?" Iris started to answer but Emily held up a warning finger.

"Yes. The boy."

"What boy?"

"The boy at school."

"What boy?"

"The mean one. Iris saved me."

"Iris?"

"All right, Momma. It was that jackass McClellan boy."

"He threw Henry into the river?"

"He was down here fishing with his brother. They made fun of Henry and then that jackass picked up Henry and heaved him into the river. I had to jump in and pull him out."

"So that's why you creased his skull!"

"Afraid so."

Emily threw up her hands. "I don't believe this! After all this time! How come you never told me?"

Iris looked into the river, the hurrying of it. Felt the rushing past of things. She could feel the hands of the boy on her body as if it was happening, clumsy fingers like scaly bugs. She wanted to tell her momma the whole of it, as if the telling might purge herself of the awful time. Wanted to confess how she hunted Jasper Hibbard in the mountains. But nobody knew any of that. And the telling wouldn't make any of it go away. She said, "Sometimes you just sweep something under a rug and then time goes by and you just can't bring yourself to look under there ever again."

Emily nodded, considering. Then she said, "Let's get this gold weighed up and see where we're at. I got some serious radio shopping to do."

They got the gold out of the hole and dried it off and had it weighed and it came to thirteen pounds three ounces and was worth more than four thousand dollars.

The assayer said the gold was ninety-four percent pure, which was about as good as gold could get. "Where'd you get this gold?" asked the assayer, a small man with an unbuttoned vest and balding head framed by coarse white hair and glasses that he wore toward the end of his nose so he could look over the top of the frames. "Up at your place?"

"Nah. Up Cumby Creek," lied Iris, thinking the assayer was a bit too curious.

They put it all in a leather pouch that John Rink had made for one of his big bench planes and they stashed it out in the smithy shed. Emily wondered about selling the gold because the assayer had said the set price was twenty dollars and twenty-seven cents per ounce but that Miss Jean said if a Democrat got elected President they'd move the price to thirty-two dollars an ounce.

"That's years off, Momma," said Iris.

"I figured it out. That would be a difference of almost twelve dollars an ounce and give us another twenty-five hundred dollars."

"I say we sell it all right now."

"And why's that?"

"For one, the word's out about our gold and there's certain characters I don't entirely trust."

"Amen."

"And further, I've been thinking about it all."

"And?"

"I got some ideas about how this could play out."

Chapter Thirty-Three
February, 1930

EVEN THOUGH THERE WAS a chill in the air they had the top down on Jack's convertible Ford and the sky above was full of slate colored clouds moving under the dark steel of a late winter sky. They'd parked on a gravel turnout just outside the Medford airport, close enough to the landing strip so that planes would pass a scant one hundred feet overhead. They had their heads tilted back and their breaths plumed white into the air. Distant, ephemeral, like it might or might not really be there, was the sound of an approaching machine.

"One's coming," said Jack.

The sound gained in strength. Even at a distance the power of the engines could be felt as well as heard. Iris reached over and took Jack's hand. They both started to laugh.

The engines were full behind them now. Coming on like a tidal wave—voluptuous, inevitable. Iris stared straight overhead. The air and the ground began to shake. There was a fleeting instant of fear—perhaps the pilot has miscalculated and the airship was heading not toward the runway, but was coming in short, directly to the parking spot...

With an intoxicating thunder the belly of a Pacific Air Transport tri-motor blotted out the heavens. Iris whooped as the engines bellowed in her bones and the propeller wash cascaded over her face and rattled the windshield.

Jack faced up also but his eyes were tilted toward Iris. She had on a plain white farm dress and a white wool sweater and she'd taken her shoes off and her bare brown feet rested up on the dashboard and the air stirred her collars and fluttered the hem of her dress around her knees.

"I love you," he said.

Iris smiled and waved her hand, closed her eyes. "I don't blame you. I'm quite something."

"I'm serious."

She opened one eye and squinted. Down the runway the delivery plane screeched onto the pavement and the engines began to throttle back. "I'm not gonna marry you, Jack" she said.

"Why not?"

"Couple of reasons."

"Name one. I know you like me, so it can't be that you don't like me. Right?"

"That's not it. It's hard to explain."

"Try me."

"I think you think I'm somebody I'm not really."

"Well who do you think I think you are?"

"Somebody better than who I am."

"Everybody wishes they were better people sometimes."

Both eyes open now. "I shot men for a living."

"You had a reason."

"I wonder about that."

"That's the past. What you've done. Anyway, it doesn't matter to me."

"It matters to me."

"I'm right here right now and I'm a damn good bet."

"You are, Jack. But I'm not."

"I'm willing to take that risk."

"I'm not."

Pause. "I got a job. You wouldn't have to hunt criminals any more. I'll take care of you."

"I don't want to be taken care of. Maybe I'm just not the wife-ing type."

"What type are you then?"

"I'm still figuring that out."

Jack looked away, nodded to himself. "Can I still see you?"

"Maybe."

"Do you still want to…you know…see me?"

"Like in bed?"

"Well that, and others. Like this. Like sitting here."

"Maybe."

They both stared straight ahead and smiled. In the distance, another approaching airplane could be heard.

Jack said, "What's next for you if you aren't going to shoot folks for a living?"

She laughed. "We're gonna sell the farm. Then buy another piece of ground on the other side of the valley. On the Rogue River."

"You'd do that? Give up your place on the Applegate?"

The roar getting louder, gathering force. Their voices rising to meet the challenge.

"I like our farm all right. I like that river. But it's brought us a considerable amount of heartache, too. We're thinking it's time to move on, start out fresh."

"You're not going to get much for your farm. Times are tough."

"Well that cuts both ways. We'll find a piece of ground that's just as cheap. It'll all even out."

Ever nearer; their voices even louder, almost shouting.

"You going to give up your Medford place? Move out with your family?"

"Yes."

Almost there; the auto shaking around them.

"And do what? Raise chickens?"

The airplane skimmed just above their faces, the motion and the sound so strong it pulled at their innards, like a big moon racking the tides. Iris tilted her head back and yelled, "Pears! We're gonna grow goddam pears!"

Chapter Thirty-Four
1944—Fourteen Years Later

IN DECEMBER OF 1944 in Spokane, Washington, an older man with a gray beard walked into Baxter General Hospital, a facility that was filled with war wounded. The man had a pronounced limp and he walked with a cane. He carried a small box under his arm.

It was open visiting hours. He made his way with his unsure gait and thumping cane along the rows of beds occupied by young men wounded in battles in the Pacific. Some were in terrible shape, burned almost completely, swaddled in bandages, moaning through their morphine. Others chatted incessantly with bed neighbors who may or may not have been listening. Many had various parts shot off—arms and legs were missing. Some had bandages over their eyes.

One man had both legs missing. He was propped up in bed, shirtless, with his dog tags hanging around his neck. He stared hard at the old man hobbling down the infirmary.

The older man stopped. He took in the short stump legs under the sheet. He thought, *He's just a young whip; they're all just boys.* He said, "Would you like to play some chess?"

The boy with no legs stared at the old man with the box. After a long moment he said, "What do you mean, chess?"

"I mean the game." He held up his box and shook it.

Things rattled inside.

The wounded man blinked. "You mean, you and I play a game of chess?"

"That's right. I'll play you chess."

"I don't know."

"Up to you."

"I don't know how to play that."

"I'll teach you," said the old man.

The wounded man took a deep breath. "Who are you?"

"Just a well-wisher old man lookin' to play some chess."

Another deep breath. "Well, seein' as I ain't goin' nowhere. Might as well."

"All right." The old man took a nearby chair, set it by the hospital bed, pulled up a small tray table on wheels. There was a used syringe on the table, a glass half full of water, and a small cloth with dried blood and pus on it. The old man took the hypodermic and the cloth and dropped them into a waste bucket, set the table between them, set the glass of water where the boy could reach it, hooked his cane around the back of the chair, sat down, and opened his box. He took out a folding chess board made of heavy cardboard. He set that on the table. He overturned the box to spill out all the pieces. They were wood and worn and the lacquer was nicked. The white pieces were made of plain pine that had turned amber with age. The black pieces were stained a dark walnut color. "This is where we'll start," said the old man. "I'll teach you the pieces."

So a chess lesson began. After half an hour of talking about rooks and pawns and castling, they set up the lines of pieces and began an experimental game.

The old man played white. He moved out his king's pawn two squares to E4.

The boy stared at the board, at the lines of battle. He said, "I was with the Tenth Corps, Sixth Army. We went into Leyte. We was near the Palo River."

The old man said nothing, pulled gently at his beard, stared at the board.

"Wasn't no hard fighting, really. Duck soup. We rolled on in, as I hear it. Our outfit just got unlucky. We found one of the few machine gun nests the Japs had planted." He took a drink of water. "They had it set up with a big gun. A tank machine gun. Just about cut my legs off. They tell me it killed four of our fellas. I don't remember much."

The older man nodded. He could see the pain on the boy's face, the physical pain and the other kind. He said, "I'm sorry you got shot up."

The boy looked up at the ceiling, closed his eyes until it passed.

"Your move," said the man.

The wounded soldier looked down at the board. "What should I do?"

The old man squinted. "You move your pawn to match up with me. That's a regular start-off way to go."

He moved his dark-stained pawn. He nodded at the old man's leg. "What happened to you? You get shot in the other big war?"

The old man shook his head. "Nothin' near as noble."

"Well?"

The older man shifted in his chair. "I got myself shot up by a girl."

"A girl?"

"Yup."

"What, she tryin' to kill you?"

"She was too good a shot to just try."

The wounded man smiled. It was the first time he's smiled in weeks. "She your wife or something? You mess around on the side?"

"It's a long story."

"Mister, I got nothing but time."

The older man took a long breath. "All right, I'll give you the gist. But here…" and he moved his queen's pawn to D4. "Now you move to D3, right here." He pointed at the square. The boy moved his dark pawn.

"I was a bad seed," said the older man, "let's just say this girl had every right to stick me in the ground. I'll tell you that. Every right. And one day she ambushed me and put a thirty caliber bullet into my knee so I'd never walk the same again. And I'm layin' there in the dirt and bleeding she comes up from wherever she was hiding and she sticks the muzzle of her rifle right in my face and says, *I ain't gonna kill you. I'm letting you off. I don't know why, but I'm giving you a chance. A chance to be somebody better that what you are. So we'll see.* Then she says, *Just know I can hunt down a stinky piece of meat like you any time. And next time I'll just gut-shoot you. And I'll sit around drinkin' whiskey for the hour it takes you to die.*"

The boy shook his head. "That's the damnedest…is that true?"

The older man nodded.

"What'd you do to get her riled up?"

"Like I say, she had every right to put me under. Let's leave it at that."

"Then what?"

"I was in the hospital for six weeks. When I got out, I was as ornery as ever. Skipped out on my doctoring bills. Robbed a bank and ended up in the state pen in Salem. Ten years, armed robbery. That's a long while, I'll say. That's where I learned chess, help pass the days. And I remembered. What she said. That came to me all the time, that rifle barrel pointed at my eyes and those words. I remember them perfect. *Stinky piece of meat.* And after I got released I figured it out, I guess. Why she didn't kill me. And what it takes to mend your ways."

"So, you play chess with busted up boys?"

"I do. That's why I'm here. Maybe teach a few fellas how to play chess. Maybe have a game. Maybe get a little mending myself. If that's all right."

The boy nodded, said, "My name's Lewis."

"That your first or last name?"

The wounded man gave a brief laugh. "First."

"They call you Lew?"

"Yeah."

"Can I call you Lew?"

"Yeah."

He put out a worn and callused hand. "Lew," he said, "my name's Hibbard. Jasper Hibbard."